Midnight
at the
Christmas
Bookshop

Also by Jenny Colgan

The Summer Skies
An Island Wedding
The Christmas Bookshop
Sunrise by the Sea
Christmas at the Island Hotel
500 Miles from You
The Bookshop on the Shore
The Endless Beach
Christmas at Little Beach Street Bakery
The Bookshop on the Corner
Summer at Little Beach Street Bakery
The Loveliest Chocolate Shop in Paris
Sweetshop of Dreams
Meet Me at the Cupcake Café
The Good, the Bad, and the Dumped
Diamonds Are a Girl's Best Friend
West End Girls
Where Have All the Boys Gone?
My Very '90s Romance
Amanda's Wedding
Welcome to the School by the Sea
Rules at the School by the Sea
Lessons at the School by the Sea

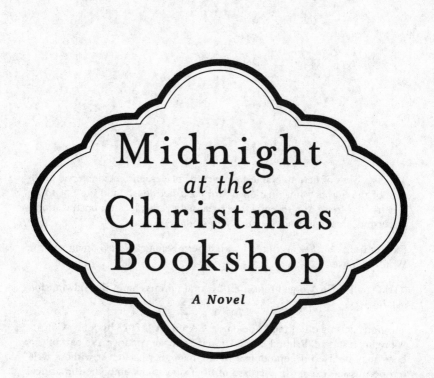

Midnight
at the
Christmas
Bookshop

A Novel

JENNY COLGAN

AVON

An Imprint of HarperCollinsPublishers

Extract from *Coraline* reprinted by kind permission of Neil Gaiman and the Writer's House.

"Trio" by Edwin Morgan reprinted by kind permission of the Edwin Morgan Society.

Originally published in Great Britain in 2023 by Sphere.

FIRST U.S. EDITION

Designed by Diahann Sturge

Christmas wreath © Neirfy/shutterstock

Library of Congress Cataloging-in-Publication Data has been applied for.

ISBN 978-0-06-326045-0 (paperback)
ISBN 978-0-06-334509-6 (hardcover library edition)

23 24 25 26 27 LBC 7 6 5 4 3

For my dearest Mads

Midnight
at the
Christmas
Bookshop

Prologue

Snow was falling gently, piling up on the old-fashioned mullioned windows of the little shops on Edinburgh's Victoria Street; lying calmly on the pavements; covering the world with its softness.

Behind the glass, all was warm and cozy; candles flickered and the fire burned brightly, keeping the icy fingers of winter from creeping in. Dim light danced up and down the decorated bookshelves. Here was a cacophony of books, spilling over, piled high, two deep on every shelf; promising escape: mystery, adventure; treasure maps and tales of old, of cabbages and kings; brave tales, pirates, worlds of frost; worlds that exist above the rooftops. Here was everything you needed for curling up in front of the fire and losing yourself, as snug as a dormouse in the wintertime, nestled in a blanket . . .

"CUT!"

Carmen Hogan stood outside McCredie's bookshop, scowling. The sun blazed down, and the snow machine was making a heck of a noise.

"This is so stupid," she said to her hard-to-impress friend Idra, who had come along to watch and see if she could meet any massive movie stars who might be pivoting to small, local, download-only productions.

"If I put that many Christmas decorations up in the shop, nobody could get to any of the books. And those are stupid, dusty fake books. What are they doing to my shop?"

"They're paying money is what they're doing."

Carmen snorted. "Not *that* much money. And I'll lose it on people not coming in and buying detective novels."

"But you'll make it back at Christmas when you're *that* shop in *that* film."

"Oh yeah," said Carmen, brightening up. "I didn't think of that."

Other shop owners on the street—Bronagh from the magic shop and Bobby from hardware—had come out to watch.

"Why couldn't they do this with hardware?" said Bobby, ruefully. "I could really have done with it."

"Well," explained Carmen, trying to be nice about things because she liked Bobby a lot, "being a bookseller is pretty cool and sexy and romantic, while being a guy who sells brooms is . . . you know, just a guy who sells brooms."

"Being a bookseller is pretty cool and sexy and romantic," sniffed Idra, "as long as you don't mind starving to death and sleeping in your sister's basement."

Carmen ignored this. Bobby just looked a bit sad.

"Well, I sell *magic*," complained Bronagh. "How is that not tremendously sexy?" And she tossed back her long red tresses. Bronagh really was sexy, if a bit spooky.

Carmen had shiny black hair and a sweet round face and eyebrows that made her look cross. Over the years, she and Idra had spent quite some time doing things to those eyebrows, none of which had worked particularly well and some of which (sticking in the extra hairs sprung to mind) actively made Carmen shudder to think of.

"Well, you see, maybe you should have opened a wizard school," explained Carmen regretfully.

The snow machine was doing its best, but it had been the most glorious summer in Scotland. Although Carmen wasn't one hundred percent sure the unexpected heat wave was altogether welcomed by the tourists who wandered up and down Victoria Street, wearing their prescribed summer outfits for visiting Edinburgh—trousers, a fleece, and a waterproof jacket—and carrying increasing amounts of it around in their arms. Everywhere small children were tearing off woolly hats and gloves, except for the film extras, of course, who were sitting unnaturally still, dressed like Victorian urchins. Carmen thought, slightly uncharitably, that she should probably get her eleven-year-old niece, Pippa, down. She was very good at sitting still and looking slightly frightening, like a tiny stern ghost.

She reminded herself that it was hardly Pippa's fault that at the age of thirty Carmen was still living in her sister's basement and had to deal with toy ducks in the bath, due to the number of children—four—who lived there.

The housing crisis was purely theoretical, she reflected a little glumly, until it affected you. Edinburgh wasn't just expensive; it was absurd, solar levels of expensive. She might as well have planned a move to Buckingham Palace. Fortunately, her sister Sofia, currently on maternity leave, didn't seem to mind *too* much.

"Ookay," said the director, who was tiny, with a long ponytail and little round glasses, and was dressed entirely in black, as though he'd walked into a shop called Directors Are Us. Carmen wondered if he spent a lot of money on beard trimming.

Instantly, the onlookers were shooed back from the barriers that were closing off the road, irritating those people who wanted their Instagram pics of the beautiful street that curled upward with its gorgeous colored shops, like Diagon Alley come to life, and exciting those who just wanted to see the slightly faded movie star who was playing the main part.

The slightly faded movie star, Lind Stephens, marched on set. He was wearing tartan trousers and a huge sweater that looked incredibly expensive. Idra stuck out her chest, just in case.

"And *action*!"

Carmen caught herself smiling. She couldn't help it, it was exciting. Come Christmas, this would be on a streaming service, and it would be her shop! Well, Mr. McCredie's shop, strictly speaking. But Carmen was certain that they wouldn't have picked this location if it hadn't been for her hard work turning the shop into a lovely place to visit.

The little shop sat at the foot of the castle, in one of the prettiest areas in an already extraordinarily pretty city. This part of the Old Town curved up and around on two levels—Victoria Street and West Bow—from the great Grassmarket, a huge open space that had always had markets but was now also full of cafés and bars and people partying. The castle loomed above it, towering high and ominous, looking as surprised as anyone to be a huge medieval keep perched on top of a craggy extinct volcano, right in the middle of a modern city.

At night, locking up, Carmen would always glance up at the rows of small windows. She knew that there were still barracks there, working soldiers; their role these days was often ceremonial, but they were soldiers still. She liked to think of them, treading the stones that had been trodden by soldiers since the twelfth century; a battalion, a safe haven under the castle's drawbridge. Also, they were unbelievably sexy in their checked hats and sweeping kilts, especially if you caught them marching. Sometimes they came down to buy Jack Reacher novels or to ask for advice on what to get their wives and sweethearts, far away.

The buildings of Victoria Street connected to the Grassmarket through West Bow and on up to the Royal Mile, so it existed on several different levels. It wasn't always straightforward which level you were on; but Edinburgh was like that, an Escher painting of a city.

The little shops that curved up Victoria Street were all painted in different colors, adding to the charm. Alongside the magic shop and the hardware shop, there was a gloriously tweedy clothes shop run by a man so posh he had Crawford as a first name. And of course there was McCredie's bookshop. McCredie's had been falling into ruin the previous Christmas when Carmen had shown up after her department store had closed down. She'd been reluctant to take it on at first, but somehow she'd managed to make it just about pay its way and cling on, although its future was extremely precarious.

And this was another way to make some money: The film company was paying to rent it out. It wouldn't clear all their debts, but it would certainly help. Even if the film they were making presented exactly the view of Scotland Carmen despised.

The craggy actor entered the bookshop door, which tinged as he opened it. Except someone had decided their normal bell wasn't right—which meant there was someone hiding behind it, actually tinging a different bell. Filmmaking was weird, Carmen decided.

"Hi," said the actor.

"Well, hello there, how's yourself?" said the extremely beautiful actress, Genevieve Burr, who was wearing a full kilt and tartan cap and had a mass of shiny hair that couldn't possibly all have been grown on one person. Carmen frowned. They realized this woman was putting on a strong Irish accent, didn't they?

"And welcome to our mystical, magical land," said Lind. "I'm looking for Robert Burns—the first edition, of course!"

"Of course! I think it still has some plow mud on it!"

Carmen was very glad she'd told Mr. McCredie not to come down to hear any of this.

"Would you like a little wee whiskey while you're waiting?" She indicated a plain bottle full of what was clearly weak tea.

"I would, to be sure, to be sure."

Idra and Carmen exchanged wincing glances, and Carmen wandered off down the road to phone her sister Sofia, who was on vacation.

"You could have come with us!"

"Well, I couldn't have, because the film crew are in."

"Oh yes, how's it going?"

"The bookshop girl just asked the laird if he wants to visit the

Loch Ness Monster with her. Apparently, it's walking distance from Edinburgh."

"Oh good, a documentary," said Sofia. "I think I preferred it when they were making films about how everyone in Edinburgh dies of heroin overdoses."

"Also, I hate Centerlands."

"What do you mean?" said Sofia. "How can anyone hate Centerlands?" She gently shut the door with her foot so that Carmen couldn't overhear the fight Federico was having with Phoebe, their eight-year-old, about going to tennis lessons. Phoebe was of the opinion that they were mean and stupid because she kept getting beaten by Pippa, who was three years older; and Pippa was not making things any better by saying that she was doing it so that Phoebe would play better, just like Andy Murray's brother did, so it was kind actually. Eric, normally the sunniest of babies, surrounded as he was by near-constant attention, was fussing and didn't want to get into his bicycle seat.

"Because it's all, Blah blah blah, here's our lovely family out for a bike ride, aren't we awesome looking at trees?" said Carmen.

"Yeah?" said Sofia slowly. "I'm not sure what's wrong with that."

"Everything's wrong with that! How did you get there?"

"Well, we drove."

"You drove in your gigantic mega car! And so did everyone else! And then you're like, Ooh, look at us, cycling down the lovely woodland path, so lovely. But just for us because we're paying a million jillion pounds. Not for poor people who have to stay on heavy polluted roads."

"It wasn't a million *jillion* pounds," protested Sofia, although, to be fair, taking a family of six, during the summer holidays, it was more or less exactly a million jillion pounds.

"Ugh, I bet it's full of smug families exactly like yours."

"That's not true!"

"How many boys called Hugo have you met? I reckon ninety."

"Carmen, what's this about?"

Carmen couldn't quite answer. As soon as the Christmas decorations had gone up—even fake ones in the middle of the summer—and she could see snow and scarves all around, memories of last Christmas had all come flooding back.

PART ONE

Chapter One

January

Carmen had borked it to begin with.

Because it wasn't exactly Spoons's fault. It wasn't exactly not his fault, either, Carmen would reflect later, during the long, long periods of time she had to be miserable about it.

Oke. Oke Oke Oke, pronounced "Okay," had first shown up at the bookshop before Christmas, hilariously underdressed for the weather, a postgraduate student of limited means and huge green eyes; a dendrologist, or tree specialist, who didn't look entirely unlike a tree himself. From Brazil originally, and a Quaker—which meant he didn't celebrate Christmas—Carmen had fallen madly in love with him. He was like nobody she'd ever met before. They were true mysteries to one another. Once scheduled to return to Brazil, he had decided to stay, just because of her, and she had been over the moon.

Then the trouble started.

THE UNIVERSITY HAD been so delighted that Oke was staying, they'd given him his old room back in beautiful Mylnes Court. Mylnes Court was a six-story building that fronted the top of the Mound, giving huge and extraordinary views over the city. It had been built in 1690; it looked big enough now, but Carmen could hardly imagine what it would have been like back then, with most people in low timbered houses they shared with their animals, if they were lucky. It must have been like going to New York.

Carmen had been excited, having walked through it often—one of the city's many stone staircases went right through the middle of it—from the side of New College. She had, rather pathetically, spent many mornings clambering to work that way, dreaming about Oke, hoping she might accidentally bump into him on the steps. It tended to happen on the mornings when she had just washed her hair and put on makeup—or as much makeup as she could put on without Phoebe turning up at her sink and attempting to draw some on herself before Sofia threw a fit and tried to scrub it off again.

And now they were finally going inside! Oke had squeezed her gloved hand, then taken out a ridiculously oversize key and led her up the steps to the metal-studded main door, then down corridors past the large old-fashioned rectory, with its long wooden benches. It looked incredibly romantic to Carmen, who had never been to university.

They climbed to the second floor: Room 205 was directly ahead—

Carmen worked out it must look out onto the whole of Edinburgh. Lucky Oke.

He knocked lightly before he went in.

"My roommate," he explained to Carmen, who nodded expectantly, ready for his roommate to absolutely love her, and of course make himself scarce at regular intervals.

The door was flung open.

"*Okes!*" came a joyous voice, and a short, wide, bearded man—the exact opposite of Oke, in fact—flung his arms around Oke's narrow waist.

"You told me you were gone forever, man! I thought they were going to send in, like, God, a botanist or something."

"I am a kind of botanist!" said Oke. "You hate everyone."

Spoons shrugged.

"Well, I'll hate them, too," said Carmen. "Hiya. I'm Carmen."

Spoons gave her a look then he looked at Oke.

"She's cool," said Oke.

"What, you have a no-girls rule?" said Carmen.

"It's not a *rule*," said Spoons. "More an . . . understanding."

Carmen peered into the room. It was square and very hot, with a strange odor to it that smelled nothing like Oke at all. There were books and papers all over the floor.

Oke, who was a fastidious man, frowned. "*Spoons.*"

"Yeah, sorry. I'll move that. It's, like, super divided in here," said Spoons. "Normally."

Oke pulled in his small suitcase, which seemed to comprise his only possessions in the world.

"You got any live specimens?" he asked.

"Uh," said Spoons, "no. Almost certainly not."

He couldn't have looked more guilty.

"*Spoons!* We had this conversation! That poor thing could be anywhere!"

"I know," said Spoons.

"Really upset and frightened!"

"I know."

"At Christmas!"

"I don't think she knows it's Christmas."

"Who is 'she,' please?" asked Carmen.

Spoons and Oke exchanged glances.

"I'm a herpetologist," said Spoons. "Snake specialist," he added, seeing Carmen's bemused expression, which rapidly turned to horrified.

SPOONS ALMOST NEVER went out, and Carmen never particularly wanted to return, for obvious, going-to-the-toilet reasons. And of course, Oke couldn't stay over at hers: Sofia was there with the baby twenty-four/seven for starters, and she couldn't bear sneaking him in with the children around. They couldn't afford a hotel, particularly not in Edinburgh; the shop was completely out of the question, and it was –2 degrees Celsius outside.

But it was more than that. Oke didn't seem in the least troubled about it. Not in the slightest.

In a cold and frosty January, normally the darkest, gloomiest month of the year, they spent hours arm in arm, walking the city, clasping hot chocolate in their hands; getting to know each other, laughing and talking without ever running out of things to say. They learned more and more of each other's worlds, so foreign and so strange.

It was a wonderful time. Except for one thing. Oke seemed to be in absolutely no rush to have sex with her. And it was driving Carmen absolutely crazy.

OKE HAD TURNED things over in his head. He had never met anyone like Carmen before; he had dated, of course, but there was something different about this. And that made things complicated. She was Scottish, not a Quaker, and she did not speak a single word of Portuguese; the very idea would drive his mother absolutely crazy (in this Oke was not the first man, nor the last, to underestimate the open-mindedness of mothers).

What's more, he had nothing to offer her: He was essentially a student still, with some teaching on the side. His previous relationships had often been passionate—his tall good looks and gentle nature were deeply attractive to a certain type of woman tired of banter—but they were short-lived and empty, as he rarely gave them a thought for the long term; for academics, the long term—a settled career staying in one place—can often seem unfathomably out of reach.

But Carmen was different. He didn't quite know how to tell her, but she deserved . . . Oke found himself slightly overwhelmed by the direction his feelings were heading. Carmen wasn't at all the kind of person he had expected to fall for—culturally or personality-wise—all of it was completely different from where he had expected to end up. The timing, the geography; none of it was remotely convenient.

He knew one thing, though: He would have to treat her with the utmost respect, like a queen. She would want to wait, he was sure; he could prove how much he respected her; show her that this was real, something they were building together, brick by brick, day by day. He could show her how much he thought of her.

"He thinks I'm a big fat disgusting pig!" heaved Carmen.

Idra was listening patiently.

She had more time now the big Christmas lunches had stopped at the restaurant she managed, although she was considering pretending to Carmen they hadn't, if Carmen didn't stop complaining on and on about her clearly gorgeous boyfriend. The actor had been a bust; he was about sixty-five and being shot through very fuzzy filters. And Carmen was good about Idra's romantic travails, mostly involving lawyers who ate in the restaurant to chat her up, then got notably fat on her very good food, then disappeared to join cycling clubs and do cold-water swimming. Even so, Carmen complaining about Oke was quite irritating; he was patently a tall, clever super-fox. It was like complaining your eyelashes were too long, or you didn't know how to get your tits to stop being so perky.

"Yeah, that's why he didn't go back to *Brazil*—because you disgust him so much," said Idra.

"Well, I don't get it, then," said Carmen. "I just want to climb him like a tree. Is that too much to ask? It's like having a Christmas present you're not allowed to unwrap."

"Didn't you say he was religious?"

"He was born into a religion. So was I. So were you. Not exactly the same thing."

Idra shrugged. "Well, they're not all the same."

"No, I mean. He doesn't practice. Well, that is, he doesn't go to the meeting house." She frowned. "Okay. Well, maybe he does sometimes—to help out with the homeless program."

Idra rolled her eyes. "He's such a dick."

"But he's not *mega* religious."

"Does he lie?"

"No," said Carmen sadly.

"So what does he say when you ask him why he doesn't want to boff you?"

"*Boff* me? What is this, nineteen ninety-six?"

Idra rolled her eyes again. "Yeah, semantics, that's what we have to worry about here."

"Well," said Carmen, "I haven't asked him."

"Why not?"

"Because he can't lie!" said Carmen as they kicked their way through the slush. "What if he says, 'You're too fat!' or 'I'm not really that into you!' or 'I have a strange kink I am revving you up for!' or 'My religion really has messed me up about sex' or 'I'm a child of the internet porn generation and human intimacy is out of the question for me.'"

She and Idra looked at each other in horror.

"Do you think—"

"Don't say it," said Carmen.

"But I mean . . . what if he's a virgin?"

Carmen shut her eyes. "Well, I'll just tell him I'm one, too; he won't be able to tell."

Idra clapped her hand over her eyes. "Oh God, please get this sorted out; your frustration is driving me crazy. Can't you bribe his roommate?"

"Unlikely," said Carmen. "Unless you have a spare boa constrictor kicking about."

But things didn't change. They took long walks, they held hands, they kissed, but nothing more than that, even as they talked about everything under the sun. Carmen felt like an Edwardian lady, walking the ancient streets, glancing around as though she was hiding from a chaperone.

On his part, Oke was reveling in getting to know someone

for once; not constantly being aware he'd be moving on or that it wasn't suitable, or jumping into bed with them. This felt new and he was doing his best to let it take its own time, knowing deep down how important this was; he wouldn't risk one false move.

One day, just as the city was dismantling the Christmas lights and decorations—always a dispiriting day, when you realized how long it's going to be till spring, with only Burns Night to look forward to—they walked past the stage that had been erected outside the National Gallery on the Mound. For a month it had been filled with wonderful carol singers; young choristers doing "Gaudete," or community groups doing jazzy versions of "I Believe in Santa Claus," complete with synchronized hand actions.

Now the Christmas acts were gone and the streets were utterly empty, as people huddled inside in the New Year gloom. Carmen was actually feeling rather sorry about it, when a group of young men carrying drums and guitars got up on the stage, looking around the empty plaza.

"Hey!" said Oke.

Carmen looked at him. "What?"

"They're Brazilians. *Obviously*," he said, smiling and shaking his head at her surprise. He walked up to the group and exchanged a few friendly words.

"Ooh," said Carmen. "What are they going to do?"

The answer was also fairly obvious. As if to banish memories of Christmas songs vanishing on the wind, to blow away the frozen cobwebs of a long winter ahead, one man started hitting the drums in an irresistible rhythm, and a small brass section lifted their instruments to their lips and began to play a dancing samba tune. Oke watched the band, delighted, tapping his foot, and Carmen watched Oke, happy in his delight.

"I didn't think Quakers were allowed to dance," she whispered.

"Well, I am a Quaker second," said Oke, "but a Brazilian first, yes?"

And then this most undemonstrative of men grabbed her and

put her in hold, and suddenly his long limbs loosened and his hips moved, and he was whirling her around at high speed, and making it look absolutely effortless.

"Oh!" said Carmen, gasping in happy surprise. She couldn't dance at all, but she let him take her waist, pulling her thrillingly close, and she felt him move. She could tell the few dog walkers who'd ventured out were watching them, but she found she didn't care. It was joyous and exuberant and she could have danced on the wet gray stones with him forever.

When they finished, red-faced, out of breath, she burst into peals of laughter and refused to separate herself from him, sure that now, of course, it had to happen; that nobody could move you with such confidence, such assured force, hold you so close, and not succumb to the inevitable. She beamed up at him, waiting for him to kiss her, as he squeezed her close, kissed the top of her head—then went to talk politics with the men in the band. She was furious, and he didn't even ask why.

February

It was February when the film company first got in touch and, to everyone's excitement, sent along Genevieve Burr to get "work experience" in the bookshop so that she would look the part.

"I think it must be terribly sad to be a film star," said eleven-year-old Pippa, with authority, at breakfast. Carmen had snorted.

"It's probably easier than working in a shop," she said. "A shop that made forty-one pounds and thirty-nine pence yesterday. Gross."

"It's objectification," Pippa sniffed.

"What's ojjeficatshun?" said Phoebe.

"It means people see you as an object," said Pippa.

"Oh," said Phoebe. "Can I be a chair?"

"Ha ha ha!" said Pippa loudly. "Not like that!"

"That's a great idea," said Carmen quickly. "I'd love to be a soft, squishy chair."

And have Oke lean on me, she thought, but didn't say. It was getting ridiculous. She dreamed about him at night. And then nothing happened by day.

Sofia and Federico exchanged glances.

"It's great that the film is really happening!" said Sofia delicately. "These people are going to pay you actual money!"

In fact, Sofia and Federico had several conversations about quite how long Sofia's sister would be staying with them: She had come for two months for a seasonal job and was still there months later.

"I wouldn't mind," Federico said, "but she eats all the potato chips. And she's going to be here for the rest of our lives."

"I know, I know," Sofia countered, "but she's good with the children."

"When she's not eating all the potato chips. And leaving crumbs everywhere."

"Ssh!" said Sofia.

"And that!" said Federico. "Why do I have to be quiet in my own house? That has seven people in it, and eight when you go back to work and we need a nanny."

Sofia nodded. "I know, I know."

"Do you want me to have a word?" said Federico, who had always got on well with his fiery sister-in-law.

"No," said Sofia. "I'll do it. If it comes from you, she'll think it's a joke."

"It's not a joke," said Federico, muttering to himself. "I just think a man ought to be able to get hold of a few potato chips in his own home, that's all."

WHEN GENEVIEVE BURR arrived, looking impossibly beautiful, she nearly bowled Carmen over with her enthusiasm for playing bookseller.

"I just want to bring real *authenticity* to the part," she told Carmen breathlessly. Carmen was going to suggest she get herself needlessly dirty by trying to dust the shelves in the stacks, then listen to fifteen people telling her they could get books quicker on the internet, then give nine people directions to the castle that was literally right over their heads, then take £4.59 all morning.

She smiled tightly. She couldn't help it, though: Genevieve was utterly breathtaking. Her skin looked airbrushed; her hair shone; the whites of her eyes and teeth were bright and glowing. She was so gorgeous it was almost laughable, ridiculous, as if they were two completely different species. Watching people walk into the bookshop was hilarious. Bob came in to complain he was being undercut by cheap overseas buckets and was halfway through his complaints, staring at his shoes, before he realized that the brunette behind the desk wasn't Carmen, looked up, stuttered, and nearly fell over. Most of the men entering that morning were no better. They swallowed hard, tripped over the shelves, refused to ask questions, and could barely answer Genevieve's cheery "Good morning, y'all!" with more than a weak smile and a frantic blush. Several, however, then pulled themselves together sufficiently to buy something—many of them, Carmen knew, frequent lurkers and browsers who seldom bought anything.

"Glad you made your mind up," she said to Jimmy Fish, who never bought anything, as he handed over a very small, inexpensive book on worms and started agonizingly counting out some change to pay for it.

"She's serving me," grunted Jimmy, ignoring her completely to bathe in Genevieve's huge dark eyes, augmented by Bambi lashes that touched her eyebrows.

"That's lovely," said Genevieve with a smile, handing him back completely the wrong change.

"That's the wrong change!" said Carmen.

"I dinnae mind," said Jimmy. "You're a wonderful saleswoman."

"Why, thank you!" said Genevieve, her eyes wide with sincerity.

"No, she's not!" Carmen almost howled, as the fifth customer stopped by, mooning and asking her to get things down from high shelves.

"Genevieve, don't go up to the top shelf! They just want to watch you climb ladders!"

"I don't!" protested the old army captain who was standing there, bathing in the magnificence of this rare spot of beauty.

"So which book are you after exactly?" said Carmen, folding her arms.

"Uh—that one," said the captain carelessly, pointing at the highest book he could see.

"Excellent!" said Carmen, as Genevieve brought it down, holding it by the jacket, which made Carmen's teeth itch. It was a herbarium, a beautiful Victorian diary of a garden year with full color illustrations, in beautiful condition (if Carmen could stop Genevieve ripping the jacket) and worth rather a lot of money.

"Ring it up, Genevieve!"

"Well, ahem, actually, I'm not sure," said the captain when he saw the price.

"Oh no," said Carmen. "You wouldn't ruin Genevieve's very first day?"

And Genevieve obligingly opened her huge brown eyes even wider, until they were great dark pools, and fixed on the captain sadly.

"I think it's just . . . so beautiful," she said in her soft, honeyed tones.

The captain looked at her.

"Yes," he said quietly, "it is."

And he handed over his card, which Genevieve looked at, baffled, until Carmen swooped in behind her and surreptitiously bleeped it.

Bronagh showed up about eleven.

"There's strange glamours around this building today," she said.

"I know!" said Carmen, half-happy, half-despondent. "We're making a fortune."

"Working in a bookshop is, like, really fun?" said Genevieve, as yet another man bought a completely random book without looking at it. It was shaping up to be their best day since Christmas.

Bronagh looked closely at the actress.

"Yes, the fairy glamour has touched you," she said with her usual spooky manner.

"She means you're wearing makeup," explained Carmen helpfully.

Genevieve touched her face.

"It's just a bit of filler!" she said. "And, you know. Vampire facial, Botox, under-skin threads, laser resurfacing, transfusions, veneers, and a forehead lift. So, nothing invasive? I'm basically natural."

Bronagh nodded as if fully vindicated.

"You would never want to live like that," said Idra. "Think of the pain and expense! Just so you get hit on by seventy-year-olds all day."

"I *know*," said Carmen, who was cashing up. "Thank you, feminist. Incredibly hot feminist."

"Innit," said Idra.

"I'm just saying. She was literally the worst shop assistant of all time. She asked someone to spell 'Dickens.' And then, worse, the guy was slavering so badly he spelled it with an X and we were there half an hour."

"Huh," said Idra.

"Although I got her to sell him the entire matching set," said Carmen. "So actually it worked out all right. Bronagh's right: Beauty is like an enchantment."

"That she went through a lot of pain and agony to get," pointed out Idra. "Like the Little Mermaid."

"If we had her, all our problems would be over," said Carmen. "That's what drives me nuts."

"Can't you hire her? I thought actors were always skint and out of work."

"Not this one," said Carmen ruefully, closing the till. "Also we only get her for one day in case someone puts her on Instagram."

"I totally wouldn't have secretly done that," said Idra. "What?"

"Oh *no!*" said Carmen.

And sure enough, the disappointed men who traipsed through in the next few days didn't buy a damn thing.

CARMEN WAS SPURRED on, though, and started wearing a bit more makeup. Maybe that was the issue. Maybe she did have to do what her mother would call "making more of herself."

The following week a young man came into the shop and shyly asked them for every book on snakes they had. She wasn't sure they had any, until Mr. McCredie's eyes popped open with delight and he vanished through the curtains back into the stacks, returning with pile upon pile of every conceivable tome on the illnesses, symbolism, taxonomy, and medicinal uses of snakes.

"Bloody hell," said Carmen, picking up *How to Taxidermy Your Own Reticulated Python.* "Where did these even come from?"

"The snake room," said Mr. McCredie, without even bothering to explain. The young man's eyes lit up. It turned out he worked at the zoo. Would he, Carmen asked, after Mr. McCredie had gone back for a second pile, be interested in a hefty discount in return for a backstage tour for her friend Spoons? As it turned out, he very much would be.

The stage was set.

NERVOUS BEYOND ENDURANCE, Carmen sent Spoons on his way one icy afternoon. Then, once he was safely gone, she sprayed perfume into the air and got changed, double quick, into a teddy much thought had gone into. Black and silky, but not too sexy and no scary straps on it. And no thongs; she wasn't insane. She had shaved her legs and painted her nails; her hair was freshly washed and her face made up. She hadn't told Sofia what she was up to; in any case, Sofia was busy with the baby and almost certainly wouldn't care if she arrived home or not.

Carmen then tried to pose sexily on the bed, which smelled so gorgeously of Oke she wanted to bury her nose in the pillow. Her heart was beating fast; she was so nervous. But still. Something had to be done. She took out the single rose she'd bought and put it between her teeth, then took it out again as it hurt, and also, it was ridiculous. Every time she heard a tread on the stairs, she stiffened. Her ears were similarly attuned for any sinister rustling noises in the room. It wasn't particularly easy to feel sexy staring at a large picture of a cobra poised to strike.

Finally, when she knew his last lecture would be finished, there came a tread on the stairs she recognized. Oh my God. It was him! She changed her position on the bed, from lying down to sitting up, to splaying her legs, to putting them to the side; checking under her eyes for mascara. The key went in the lock and she sat cross-legged then realized that was ridiculous and sat up on her knees.

"Yo, Spoons," came the sweet, familiar tones, the hint of that beautiful Brazilian accent.

"Aha!" said Carmen, sitting bolt upright.

Oke stopped, surprised.

"What have you done with Spoons?"

"I think something ate him?" said Carmen tentatively. "It's all right, he'll take ages to digest."

She pushed her chin forward. "Plus, I thought we should . . . have some alone time."

His handsome face looked confused. He moved toward her slowly. Carmen raised her arms up and proffered the rose toward him.

"Happy Valentine's Day?" she said, her voice trembling. She knew he didn't celebrate festivals, but it was something.

"I don't . . ."

His face looked puzzled. He sat down beside Carmen, put an arm around her, and kissed her—on the cheek.

"Aren't you cold?" he said.

"No . . . yes," said Carmen, starting to panic. She turned into him, trying to turn the kiss into something more. He kissed her gently, then backed away.

"Carmen . . ." he said. Carmen glanced at his face. It looked kind, but pitying.

Horribly humiliated, she scrabbled back on the bed, pulling up the duvet.

"Yeah, you must be cold," he said.

"What is *wrong* with you?" gasped Carmen. "What . . . ? Why don't . . . ? I mean, what are we even doing? You don't want to have sex with me?"

Oke frowned again. "Here? With you?"

What Oke meant was, *In my horrible student room? With someone as wonderful as you?*

Unfortunately, this very much did not come across to Carmen. Very much not at all.

"*Anywhere!*" burst out Carmen. Temper tears were starting in her eyes "I have given you *every* opportunity, and you don't want to go anywhere near me! Nothing!"

She looked down at the stupid polyester teddy she had thought was so cute.

"For God's sake. I mean, if you don't fancy me, just say it. Or if you're gay or ace or something, that's fine. Or if . . . I don't know. You want someone else. I don't know any of the stupid reasons for it. But I can't go on like this, it's *so* weird."

Oke was completely blindsided. But in the sheer shock of it all, he realized something, something that had been growing inside him; that he already knew.

She was what he wanted more than anything. He was, in fact— and this terrified him—in love with her, with this angry little person in his bed, and he did not know how to tell her, or even what to do about it.

All his life, he had been careful, calm. Trained never to let his emotions get out of control. It was his creed; his core belief. To live carefully, and fully, in the day. To avoid conspicuous displays of emotion.

And now, along had come this girl and hit him like a ton of bricks. It was an emotion nothing in his life had prepared him for, as she sat there, red-faced, breathing heavily, overwhelmingly sexy, and the force of his feelings was suddenly far too much.

Another thing hit him, too: She was furious with him.

"Carmen, I . . . Of course I find you incredibly attractive," he said. Carmen stuck out her bottom lip. He moved closer. Maybe this was just a culture clash and he could fix it easily . . .

Oke was desperately trying to get this right.

"But I think . . . we should have discussed this, maybe. I think . . ."

He took her cold hands in his. She wouldn't look him in the eye.

"I thought you enjoyed our walks and getting to know each other . . ."

"I did," muttered Carmen, her cheeks bright, bright red.

"Carmen, I think sex . . . I think sex is a miraculous thing. A beautiful thing."

"Sent by God?" said Carmen, with heavy sarcasm.

"If there is a God," said Oke seriously, trying to make the enormity of his feelings understood, "then I think absolutely. Even if there isn't, I consider it to be something sacred between people. Something more than two bodies; something you create between you, that is important. Not to be rushed or treated lightly. I think it is holy, yes."

Now Carmen felt even worse. She stared at him, breathless, wounded, as he stared back at her, baffled and terrified.

"So I'm just some kind of desperate slutbag?" she choked out.

"Of course not!" said Oke.

"Who would just let herself into your bed," said Carmen, with some bitterness.

Oke tried to smile. "Well, perhaps that will be funny one day?"

That was exactly the wrong thing to say, as he realized straight-away.

"Oh yeah, really fucking funny," said Carmen, jumping up. "My desperate girlfriend begged me for sex and I said no!"

She started throwing her clothes back on. The tights were an undignified moment and she almost gave up on them.

"Carmen!" said Oke, the danger of the situation terrifying him. But Carmen was too angry to listen.

"Men do this, you know?" said Carmen. "Oh, it's not you, it's me. Oh, I'm just trying to respect you. When what they mean is, 'I'm keeping my options open' or 'I'm trying to see if I get a better offer.'"

"That's not it!" said Oke, stung. "That is not it at all."

She barreled on. "*Yes*, all men. Honestly, if you're not interested in me in sexy underwear with a fricking *rose* up my jacksie, you're not interested in me at all."

"That's not true," protested Oke weakly.

"Well, you go *pray it out*, then," said Carmen as a parting shot, marching out and slamming the door hard, causing a large rustling noise somewhere deep in the pipes.

Is THERE ANY greater rue than knowing you have made a terrible mistake, and being unable to see your way out of it, even as you are in the process of making it?

Even as you know everything you do is making the situation worse and worse and that this is your fault—you've done it to your-self, nobody else? Because that was how Carmen had borked it.

And oh, Oke knew he had borked it, too, and Spoons, it may

not surprise you to know, was not much help in these matters beyond recommending a grass snake as a makeup gift, which Oke, who had never exchanged a gift in his life, briefly considered.

Instead, he called, hoping inspiration would strike. If only he could tell her how he felt about her. If only she would listen.

Alas, Carmen, humiliated beyond endurance, ignored his calls and froze him out, which was completely baffling to Oke, who thought a lot of this girl and was trying to do the right thing by her.

Carmen had planned to freeze him out for five days, until she got over her embarrassment.

By day three, his heart heavy, Oke had accepted as a gentleman that he was bothering her, and stopped calling. He had tried and he had failed; he would never ever pester a woman who did not want his advances.

Carmen took this as proof positive that she had been right all along.

And on March 1, Oke received the invitation.

March

"FINALLY," EXCLAIMED CARMEN. She was in the bookshop, hoping in vain for a few signs of spring. Mrs. O'Reagan was in again, a lovely customer who spent lots of money there and therefore was allowed to come in and discuss at length which Dickens, exactly, she hadn't read. The annoying thing was, Carmen knew—it was *Our Mutual Friend*—but Mrs. O'Reagan refused to believe her and kept insisting that she had read it and it was the one about the ghost stationmaster. At last, Carmen sold her a beautiful, unusual stand-alone edition of *The Signalman* again, feeling slightly guilty but slightly happy, because it was still a beautiful book and a great story. She told Mr. McCredie, but he was looking very distracted. Which wasn't particularly unusual, to be fair.

Then her phone showed Oke's number. She was so overjoyed she almost forgot when she picked it up that she was meant to be hurt and upset, which she was. But also, of course, magnanimous and ready to forgive him. She missed him desperately.

"Hello," she said, as stiffly as she could manage.

"Is this a bad time?"

"It's a Tuesday morning in an independent bookshop."

"Uh?"

"No, it's fine," said Carmen. Then, more softly, "Hey, Oke."

"Hey," he said, feeling hesitant. Hearing her voice, he realized how very much he had missed her. But she had made her feelings quite clear and he was always going to respect that. Still, he owed her this.

"So," he went on awkwardly.

"I'm dressed!" said Carmen quickly, which was meant to come out as a joke, but didn't really sound anything other than odd. One of the browsers turned his head quickly, just checking, in case she was normally naked from the waist down.

"Um, good," said Oke in his slow way. "So I thought I should tell you. I have won a grant to join an expedition."

Carmen felt her heart lurch. She had been full of anticipation, hoping he was going to suggest going to the cinema or something and they would just dial it down and forget everything and . . .

"Where?" she said, a lump in her throat.

"It's the *Coccoloba gigantifolia*," Oke went on. He tried to keep the excitement out of his voice, but this was a big deal. Heart sinking, Carmen recognized this at once. "It's . . . well, it's really rare. And I'm going to be part of an expedition to run some tests on it in situ. It's amazing. The leaves are two and a half meters long!"

"Where is it?"

"It's in the rain forest. In Brazil."

"How long for?"

"Six months."

"Is THIS A rushing-to-the-airport-type scenario?" said Sofia, seeing Carmen's face and deciding, as she had every day for the last two weeks, that today was absolutely not the day to bring up to a sniveling Carmen the whole "New Year New Start New Getting Our Spare Room Back" plan. She had ages left on her maternity leave. She'd get around to it. Although it was very unlike Sofia to leave anything to the last minute. It didn't sit well.

But what was worse was how seriously worried she was about Carmen. She'd known Carmen grumpy, incommunicative, and a bit sulky about things. That was Carmen. She'd never seen her absolutely flat-out miserable, like she'd been squashed by a steamroller. She was lying on the sofa, her skin so pale it made her dark hair look dyed.

Carmen shook her head.

There had been shouting. All of it from Carmen. Possibly some screaming. She had slagged him off as a man. She had dissed his religion. She had called him a coward, running away. It had been awful. So awful. He had remained silent and listened politely to her rantings. Then he had wished her a formal farewell and hung up. Every time Carmen so much as looked at a telephone, she wanted to cut off her own head just to make the screeching agony stop.

Of course she couldn't tell Sofia that. She couldn't tell Sofia she'd behaved like a total lunatic. She was doing her best to make it sound like a mutual decision. Even though she knew in her heart of hearts she was never going to hear from him again, and that this was the worst thing she had ever felt.

"No. No. I mean, he really wants to go. He was delighted, it's incredibly prestigious and hard to get. And he'll see his family. I mean, even if we were still together, it would be hard for him to turn down. It's . . . it's amazing."

"You couldn't go?" said Sofia, clutching at straws.

"Yes, British booksellers are extremely useful in the rain forest on incredibly prestigious research trips," said Carmen. "Also, sleeping in a wet tent for six months watching other people look at trees and being eaten by alligators is very much what I was hoping for this year. And also . . . we're broken up. We definitely are. Even if we weren't . . . we are now."

She burst into floods of tears, desperately trying to swallow her sobs, in real pain, just as Federico arrived home from a party with the children, who yelled and skittered indoors. By the time they'd hung up their jackets they had obviously, Carmen realized, been briefed, because they fell silent when they saw her. Eventually Phoebe stepped forward and sat next to Carmen on the sofa.

"I am sorry about Oke," she said. "But I have a party bag."

Carmen blinked and rubbed her eyes fiercely.

"Sorry, I ate mine before we left the party," Jack admitted, his cheeks stuffed full. "You can have the yo-yo if you like. It's broken."

"It's not broken, Jack, you just don't have the patience to learn to yo-yo," said Federico.

"I am a champion yo-yoer," returned Jack serenely. "I am brilliant at it. But *that* one is broken."

Phoebe, frowning slightly, poked about in her party bag. It had been more a gesture of goodwill than a sincerely meant offer.

"I'll take the Parma Violets," said Carmen, "or even the licorice."

"There's only really good Haribo," whispered Phoebe.

Sofia frowned. "Really? I'd have thought better of the Hills. Oh well."

Pippa stepped forward, holding out her own bag.

"Oh my God, sweets are for babies," she said. "It's never too early to start a good skincare routine, did you know? And sugar is *terrible* for your skin."

October

MANY MONTHS LATER, the thought of Oke no longer made Carmen want to immediately curl up in a ball and scream in anguish. And yet, somehow she was still spending a lot of time, when she wasn't at work, lying wanly on the sofa foraging from party bags. There were a lot of party bags. Pippa was right about sugar being bad for the skin.

The film people had come back and forth but today they were finally gone, which made Carmen feel slightly sad—she had rather hoped that Genevieve Burr might become her new best friend, but it was not to be. Their presence and the Festival had more or less kept the shop afloat through the summer, but now the seasons were turning and the takings grew more meager by the day. Things were getting more expensive for everyone: the cost of living, of heating, of rent . . . Carmen couldn't ever think about rent. She had thought she would get to move out, but the chance of finding a place to stay seemed to be forever diminishing on the horizon. Still, Sofia didn't mind, did she? And those remarks about how much Carmen must look forward to the day she didn't have to deal with Eric's fat little bum crawling around the kitchen, a sight that was one of the few things that cheered Carmen up every day, were only that, weren't they: passing remarks?

Anyway, she had a huge list of things to worry about already. One day last week, for instance, the shop had taken minus £3.99, because somebody had brought back a book they'd found cheaper online. And then she had found a girl on Oke's expedition, Mary, had an Instagram account and kept posting pictures of how amazing the jungle was, or selfies of her stupid pretty face, which sometimes, Carmen thought, had a tiny bit of Oke's shoulder in them. And once, a group shot of the whole expedition. They were young, good-looking, fit people from all over the world, being happy and amazing, like a commercial for being clever and awesome, and it had cut Carmen like a knife. So the fact that Sofia was making noises about interviews and the end of her maternity leave was barely penetrating Carmen's carapace of misery at the moment.

"IT'S MEANT TO take one month per year of going out with someone to get over them. Not six months per six weeks," said Idra.

She had stopped being sympathetic and was now just weary. And absolutely hammering her staff discount on the wine.

"He just left thinking I was such a slutbag."

"You're not a slutbag," said Idra soothingly. "You haven't had sex for absolutely *ages*."

"Well, that's even worse," Carmen pointed out. "Like, I'm a totally virgin slutbag. As if I'm constantly looking for sex but nobody wants to have sex with me."

"I'll have sex with you," said one of the waiters, passing by.

"You will not," said Idra, who kept such a firm grip on her staff that Carmen suspected she might be turning into Mrs. Marsh, their terrifying ex-boss.

"You told me to be helpful to everyone and serve them what they want," said the waiter.

"Yes, but we don't do crabs," Idra warned. The waiter shrugged, then marched over to suggestively ask a table of female diners if they would like a grind from his extra-large pepper mill, which they did.

"Sorry about that," said Idra.

"I didn't mind," said Carmen, looking rather longingly at the handsome waiter. "Oh God, Idra, it's awful. I'm so . . ." She lowered her voice. "I'm so lonely. And Sofia's going back to work soon so I won't even have her around to talk to."

"I'm sure she'll look back on this maternity leave with you as one full barrow load of laughs," said Idra, as comforting as she could manage. Then she blinked.

"Doesn't that mean she'll be getting a new nanny?"

"Yeah," said Carmen, shifting.

"It's very good of her not to mind you staying there," said Idra. "That's a lot of people in the house."

"Yeah," said Carmen uncertainly, pouring more wine. Things were changing for everyone except her, she realized. The shop was staying the same, but the love of her life had gone and they didn't appear to be making any more of them. And now Sofia was interviewing for a new nanny so the house was going to change. There were two basement rooms and one bathroom. So it would be a bit annoying, Carmen figured, but nothing she couldn't handle.

CARMEN'S HEAD WAS certainly feeling the brunt of it on Saturday morning. Mr. McCredie had offered to open up. Carmen knew she should be doing something—anything—to help the shop do better—she could be putting a website together or doing more readings to local children—but heartbreak had sapped her energy, which meant at the moment the shop was so quiet there was absolutely no need for the two of them to be there at the same time. This wasn't encouraging.

The sight of Sofia wearing her work suit and with lots of résumés in front of her, avoiding eye contact, wasn't particularly cheering, either, and nor were the children singing their new song.

"Four children is *too many children*," Carmen said, and not for the first time. The girls were standing at the top of the stairs, shouting a very loud song they had made up that went, "*Man*-ny! *Man*-ny! We want a *man*-ny!" Jack was scuffling about looking for his soccer boots and baby Eric was squalling, happily, in his mother's arms. He was the jolliest of babies, but he was not quiet. He didn't keep anyone awake by crying but rather by making many and varied noises of his own. Phoebe and Pippa alternated between fighting over who loved him the best, trying to put lipstick on him and ignoring him completely. Jack glanced at him warily, feeling on some level that he had been promised another boy to play with in the family and this fat thing was taking its time about it.

On the other hand, Jack was willing to go along with his sisters' request for a man (they had seen one on an American sitcom and decided that if they absolutely had to have someone looking after them, this would be a vast improvement over everyone else's miserable homesick au pair girls) if it meant he might get a kick-about every now and again and a bit of backup on *Star Wars* screening days.

Sofia had hoped to raise her children in a gender-neutral environment; however, when she had bought Jack a doll, he had used it as war fodder, and when she had bought Pippa a racing car, she had caught her tucking it up in bed saying, "Good night, car, sleep well and don't have bad dreams about trucks," so had rather given it up. She had given up a lot of her ideals of what parenting might be like, she thought from time to time. In her head it had involved rather more quiet playing with wooden toys, nice chess games, and lots of reading in front of the fire. Pippa, the eldest and a teacher pleaser of the first order, would do all of the above, but only if she got to hiss secret police-style orders at the others to keep them in line and to tell on people the instant there was any dissent in the ranks. So as far as Sofia was concerned, a bit of mixing up of gender roles might not be an entirely bad thing.

Jack just wanted to play outside with his friends and would like nothing more than to live on a housing estate where you could kick balls over the walls and run about on the communal green. This horrified Sofia, who pretended to her absolute core that she wasn't a snob but was nonetheless thrilled that she had left the council estate on the west coast of Scotland where she and Carmen had grown up, and now owned an immaculately restored town house in Edinburgh's chichi West End.

The town house was made of gray stone, with steps leading up to the front door. There were two windows on the ground floor, each with twelve panes of glass; three on the second, where her and Federico's bedroom ran the entire width of the house; three on the third, where the children had their rooms; and a cupola, which flooded the house with light.

Then there was the basement, originally the servants' quarters, which had the utility room and two tiny cells with barred windows, one of which was still occupied by her slightly annoying younger sister, who had moved in for two months the previous

October, and still appeared to be here; and one where they were keeping all their messy stuff, so the main part of the house still looked like a magazine.

"You don't even need to go back to work," said Carmen, as Sofia was fretting over nannies' résumés. "Do you? Federico earns a fortune. You could become one of those Edinburgh ladies who volunteers for things and is secretly a witch."

Sofia frowned. "What do you mean?"

"Uh, nothing," said Carmen. Bronagh in the magic shop had a theory that immaculately groomed, rich, working Edinburgh women with well-behaved children were all witches, because there was no other way of doing it.

"Well, I have a law degree and if you think I'm going to waste it—"

"What, *being a mom to four children*?"

"I don't mean it like that," said Sofia, conscious that she was making packed lunches and trying to arrange the children's ridiculous vacation camp schedule at the same time as reading résumés, while Carmen was lying on the sofa reading *Heat* magazine, loudly pontificating about whether the Kardashians looked like weird space aliens if you got close up to them or whether they looked even better and what did Sofia think and also, would she be alone forever and was she getting fat?

"I just mean . . ."

Carmen looked over at her. Sofia was looking great: sleek and slim, her long dark hair shiny and swingy, as it had always been. Everything came easy to Sofia, Carmen always thought. Beautiful house, amazing job, four children, nice husband.

Sofia bit her lip. She didn't want to say what she really thought: that if she didn't hurry back to work one of the twenty-five-year-old kids in the office would start making remarks like, "Can you really do fifteen-minute billing if you're waiting for a call from the GP?" and, "How many children do you have again? Don't you find it tiring?" She wanted to make partner, and unfortunately, at the very old-fashioned firm she worked at, this meant coming back to work pretending you'd barely had a baby at all. She hadn't even taken Eric into the office, even though she was convinced he was the loveliest baby she had ever beheld, with his pale hair and dark eyes, and that loud giggle he made for everyone who passed. The reason she was so thin, as Carmen kept pointing out, not entirely flatteringly, was that she was stressed to bits about covering everything while Federico was away, working a lot and traveling for his job in finance.

Anyway, she was interviewing for nannies, and absolutely dreading it. Skylar, her green-juice-and-yoga-obsessed last nanny, hadn't worked out but the housing crisis had driven so many young people to look for live-in jobs, and Sofia couldn't bear turning any of them down, however unsuitable they were. She'd finally narrowed it down to five, all of whom were vastly overqualified for picking Jack up from soccer practice and making spaghetti Bolognese. Four female, one male, hence the girls' excitement.

"What do you think?" she said. She'd emailed the résumés to Carmen, who had glanced at them.

"They all seem like a massive bunch of swots," said Carmen. "'Directional learning' this and 'nutritional awareness' that." She snorted. "All you need is someone to keep them from running out in the road."

"Yes," said Sofia, controlling herself with some difficulty. "That's basically all parenting is."

"Did the man put a picture on his résumé?"

"He did not," said Sofia. "And don't even think about it. Maybe no mannys."

She glanced over. "Are you sure you haven't heard from Oke?"

Carmen bit her lip and looked down.

"I still think you'll make it up, you know. It was just a bit of a shame about the psycho hose beast thing."

"I was not a psycho hose beast! I was a completely normal hose beast."

Sofia would have raised her eyebrows, but she'd booked the Botox specialist as soon as she'd got rid of her nursing bra.

"I'm not sure I want you next to a nubile young man. You need to get back out there, instead of lying on the sofa getting . . ."

"Getting what?"

"Nothing," said Sofia, biting her tongue.

Carmen leapt up in an attempt to be helpful.

"Want me to make supper . . . tea? I'm not calling it 'supper'; that's stupid."

"Yay!" said the children.

"*No*," said Sofia. They both remembered the terrible turkey dinosaur debacle. Sofia was very strict about junk food in the house. Once, she'd come home early and Carmen had forgotten to do what she normally did, i.e., put the cardboard packaging in the log burner. Phoebe had had half a dinosaur hanging out of her mouth and had to be carried out in hysterics. Since then Carmen had very rarely been invited to cook, which suited her just fine.

"Well, get someone who cooks," she suggested.

"They only cook for kids," said Sofia.

"That's all right, I'll eat the leftovers."

"Carmen, stop treating your body like a bin!"

"I'm doing it on purpose. So it will deaden my libido."

"What's *bido*?" said Phoebe, popping her head around the stairs. "Also maybe sometimes we could have just one dinosaur maybe?"

"Well, maybe not," said Sofia. "Because I want you to grow up beautiful and strong."

Phoebe had a grumpy face, always looking slightly suspicious of the world, as if she'd tried it all already and it hadn't pleased her. She had the same grumpy eyebrows as her aunt. Her hair, invariably, was a mess and she was short of leg and round of tum. Carmen pulled her into her arms and tickled her.

"I don't," she said, as Phoebe screamed happily and squirmed. "I want you to grow up to be a *great big dinosaur*."

"RROWWRRR," roared Phoebe.

"Oh my God, a dinosaur!"

"RROOOWWRRR!"

Sofia watched them horse around with regret. She should have been clearer. A live-in nanny—or a manny—was coming. Which meant—she had thought would be obvious (or, if she was more honest with herself: She had tried to explain but had lacked the courage)—that finally, her infuriating, daft sister would have to go.

Chapter Two

"Well, I believe very strictly in holistic rearing? With the latest in early neuro-linguistic programming? And of course, achievement ladders," one intense-looking young woman was saying. Sofia was sitting in the beautiful kitchen, offering water but not tea or coffee—apparently this was important in recruitment for reasons Carmen didn't quite understand. She was looking after Eric, who was doing his usual noisy baby thing of farting, burbling, gurgling, and giggling all at once.

"I think if you just cried it would be more relaxing," Carmen said to him, nuzzling his round cheeky chops. She wouldn't have told Sofia in a million years—and in fact saw it as her job to puncture Sofia's very smug bubble about everything—but she adored her nephew.

Carmen looked over the top of Eric across the open-plan space of the beautiful back of Sofia's beautiful house. There was pure glass across the back extension, which slid open to allow access to the tiny city back garden, where Jack had a lamentably small space to kick a ball into a net; a large dream kitchen with a huge island in the middle, a casual table with eight chairs around it and three perfect glass lamps hanging overhead. Carmen was in the "casual" area; vast velvet sofas. Doors led to a TV/cinema room done out in a gray so dark it was effectively black, lined with bookshelves with expensive arty hardbacks carefully displayed, which drove Carmen bonkers. She was a catholic reader, who would pick up and put down paperbacks anywhere, sometimes with the corners

folded over, which made her boss and Sofia both wince in horror. Carmen loved books but thought they were designed to be
read, not worshipped. Sometimes when Sofia was out she nipped
upstairs to use her huge round luxurious Jacuzzi bath, then dried
the inevitably wet books out afterward. She thought Sofia didn't
know.

She was sitting opposite her sister's line of vision; facing the
back of the hapless interviewee. The poor children had been ban-
ished upstairs, which was driving them crazy. They were to come
down to be inspected at the end. They were whispering furiously
and Pippa had put out a very good plan for why they and not their
mother should be interviewing for new nannies.

Carmen shook her head as the nice girl started outlining her
nutritional policies. The scars Skylar, the very right-on previous
nanny, had left on the household were still pretty deep.

Sofia ignored her. She wanted the best for her children, everybody did. Carmen might not care if they ate chips all day but she
did, and Carmen knew nothing about raising kids, so she could
keep out of it.

"Thanks, Olivia," she said. "That sounds very nice."

Olivia stood up, somewhat uncertainly, as Sofia did, and left,
smiling nervously at Carmen.

"OMG."

The children came tumbling down the stairs.

"She didn't even ask to meet us!"

"Did she not want to meet us?" said Phoebe, who was not on
the whole one of life's optimists.

"Did you do that on purpose?" said Carmen.

"Of course," said Sofia. "If you're not even remotely interested . . .
She didn't even ask their names! Just went on and on about how she
felt she was particularly called to 'follow her own star' with infant
nutrition, positive play, and child-centered accreditation."

"Does 'positive play' mean actually no play or attention at all?"
asked Carmen.

"It means nobody is allowed to win," said Phoebe sadly. "And if you do win they say, 'That doesn't count, Phoebe, it's not that kind of game.'"

"Well, that makes it fairer," said Pippa. "So everyone gets a turn."

"Not everybody gets a turn!" said Phoebe. "All the biggest people take their turns and then say, 'It's positive play and you can't play yet.'" And she folded her little arms and looked mutinous.

"God," said Carmen, "I thought it was bad enough being thirty. At least I don't have to be a child again."

"No," said Pippa, "because you're thirty which is, OMG . . . I mean, really, really, really old. I mean, that's like three times Jack's age. Like, even when I am double the age I am now, I will still have years and years and years and years before I'm thirty."

"Is thirty old?" said Phoebe.

"Yes," said Pippa.

"No!" said Sofia.

"Oh God," said Carmen, lifting up Eric as the doorbell rang.

THE CHILDREN LEAPT upstairs giggling, remembering they weren't supposed to be seen so Sofia's test could be applied to the newbies. Of course, they were incredibly noisy all at once. Sofia went back to looking terrifying and imperious. It was funny to see her in full lawyer mode: immaculate, of course, but also, she had a certain something. Carmen was so used to thinking of her sister as smug and annoying, she sometimes forgot that Sofia had worked hard all her life to get where she was and to have what she had. Now, seeing her sitting with a crisp, slightly distant air, Carmen could imagine what she was like at work, and was quite impressed. She herself had no massive gap between her personal life and her work life, which was probably, she reflected a mite glumly, why she was only hireable by failing retail concerns.

She opened the door, Eric over her shoulder.

"Mrs. d'Angelo?"

Carmen grinned merrily as if the idea of her being married to Federico was hilarious, which indeed it was; Federico spent more on moisturizer per month than Carmen had in her entire life.

"Oh, no, no . . ." she said, looking up at a rather foxy-faced man with a pointed chin, arched eyebrows, a wide grin, and bright red floppy hair. He was wearing a smart blue check shirt with a navy cashmere sweater—very New Town. But the other thing she noticed, simultaneously, was that one sweater and one shirtsleeve were pinned up, revealing them to be empty.

The children, was her first thought. *Please don't let them mention it. Please let Sofia keep them out of the way.*

"I'm Carmen," she managed to finish. "Auntie and . . . lodger."

She said *lodger* quietly in case Sofia overheard, snorted, and started charging her rent.

"I'm Rudi Mulgay—I have an interview with Sofia d'Angelo?"

"Come in," said Carmen, finally. Eric reached his arms out in the air.

"Hello, you," said Rudi. "You seem like a nice baby. Mind you, babies can be very deceptive."

The children weren't visible in the immaculate black-and-white tiled hallway, Carmen was relieved to see, but she could hear telltale whispering coming from upstairs, which ceased as soon as Rudi came into view.

Don't, Carmen mentally begged inside her head. *Don't let them be shocked by the fact that he only has one arm. Please don't let them say anything.*

She put Eric in his bouncy chair as Sofia stood up.

"Welcome," she said. If she was remotely surprised, Carmen thought, she certainly wasn't showing it. Maybe it was in his résumé. Mind you, why would you put that in? Unless it was relevant. Was it?

Sofia put her hand out and shook his right. "Take a seat."

Carmen heard a lot of whispering and shushing coming from upstairs. She shot the children a ferocious look. Unfortunately it was a look they saw often and paid it no mind. Rudi, however, glanced around from where he was facing Sofia, and turned his cheery face up to the stairwell.

"Hello?" he said loudly. There was silence. He gazed up at Carmen and Sofia, still merry.

"Ah, well, I see your children are very quiet. Good, good."

His voice was clearly from the Highlands, with a lilt to every word. Good was "goo-ud."

"Yes, totally silent children with nothing to say, those are my kind of children."

"*We aren't—*" came Phoebe's voice, rapidly shushed by Pippa.

"What's that? Do you, perhaps, have a tiny talking mouse up there? I'm sure I heard a squeak."

Carmen glanced at Sofia. If you hadn't known her very well indeed you wouldn't have seen it: a tiny moue of approval. She raised her eyebrows, and Sofia nodded.

"Guys, come on down," she shouted up. Rudi had passed the first test, at least: mentioning the children.

The children came down slowly. It was almost comical, how much their eyes were fixed rigidly anywhere that wasn't Rudi's stump. They came and stood in a line, staring at the floor or the ceiling.

"Who are you, then?" said Rudi, but not in a try-hard kind of a way, more in a casual kind of a way.

Pippa fixed him with a look. "I'm Pippa and I'm in Primary Seven, so I don't really need a nanny."

"*Neither do I*," said Jack.

"Okay, well, that's useful," said Rudi. "Do you cook?"

"I can make flapjacks," said Pippa.

"Fine," said Rudi.

"Can you play soccer?" said Jack.

"I'm not very good in goal," said Rudi, smiling and holding up his arm.

Jack's eyes went wide and he glanced at his mother, who gave him implicit consent to mention it.

"Where's your hand?"

"Somewhere in a field," said Rudi. Jack's eyes widened.

"Oh, that's *so sad*," said Pippa, tilting her head to one side.

"Not really," said Rudi. "I think having one side of my bum missing would have been worse."

They giggled, except for Pippa, who was still Being Kind and didn't think it was a laughing matter.

"Can't you get a robot hand?" asked Jack.

"Oh, I had one," said Rudi. "But it kept choking the children I was looking after so I got rid of it . . . *or have I?*"

Sofia cleared her throat.

"Oh, sorry, sorry," he said. "I was only joking."

She held up his résumé.

"You were in the military."

"Yes, ma'am."

"You were wounded on active service?"

"Embarrassingly not," said Rudi. "Exercise gone wrong."

"Goodness. I'm so sorry." Her lawyer's head clicked in. "Did you sue them?"

"They made us a good offer. It was an honest mistake."

Sofia shook her head. "Unbelievable."

"Mom, he has a robot hand!" said Phoebe, looking scared.

"He has a *robot hand*!" said Jack, looking delighted.

"Actually, I don't have a prosthesis . . . They don't really agree with me. I manage okay without one for now. Although I should probably tell you, I don't iron."

Sofia indicated for him to sit down. The children stayed, staring at him, fascinated.

"Upstairs, you guys," said Sofia.

"Aww," said Jack.

"Well, surely it's time to get the dinner flapjacks prepared," said Rudi, and Carmen felt her own mouth twitch. She liked him.

SOFIA SCANNED HIS résumé expertly.

"How did you get into this line of work?" she said.

"Well, after the army I wanted something totally different . . ."

"Not sure it's that different," said Carmen, and they both looked at her.

"Plus, I'm from a large family," he began.

"Yes, I know what you mean," said Sofia, and he smiled.

"Oh no, I mean . . ."

She looked up. "What?"

"Proper large."

"I think four does generally qualify as large."

"There's thirteen of us."

"You are kidding me."

He shook his head. "No, ma'am."

"Have they all got your hair?" Carmen couldn't resist it. He turned around.

"I'm not sure you're allowed to talk about hair in a job interview? I think it's hair-ist?"

"Oh well, you're going to have to report me to the Universal Court of Hairy Rights," said Carmen.

"Okay," said Sofia, sounding cross. She didn't like everyone else pretending this was a done deal already.

"So, you grew up helping with the other children . . . Where do you come?"

"Fourth," said Rudi. "While they still had some names in hand. All the little ones are just called by their numbers . . ." He looked a bit cowed by Sofia's sharp glance. "Sorry. I make jokes when I'm nervous."

Sofia looked at Carmen. "Yes, I know other people who do that."

"So, well, I was the fourth, all boys, then we started a big run of girls, and my brothers weren't interested, and after my discharge my parents were very very keen that I didn't let this hold me back." He held up his left arm. "So they made me do more, if anything. I am very good at changing diapers with one hand."

"That is a very useful skill," said Sofia fervently.

"And I cook . . . I love cooking, actually."

"What kind of food?" asked Carmen quickly.

"Oh, nothing fancy," he said. "I think for kids, good plain wholesome food works best. I make a mean shepherd's pie . . . a good lasagna . . . that kind of thing."

"Do you soak anything overnight to make it sprout?" said Carmen, who had strong views on the last occupant of the role.

"God, no. I mean, is that the kind of thing you'd be wanting?"

"Actually, Carmen, I don't think we really need you?" said Sofia.

"Well, I think you do," said Carmen. "Seeing as the free room is right next to mine and we'll be sharing a bathroom."

Sofia looked up.

"Ah," she said.

"Ah what?" said Carmen.

"Well, it's just . . . We'll talk about this later?"

Carmen gave Sofia a look that they both knew meant, *We will talk about this now, otherwise I am going to make a massive fuss.*

Rudi looked away politely as Sofia lowered her voice.

"I mean . . . I kind of figured . . . you know . . . you've been here nearly a year. I mean, we really used that room for skis and whatnot. You're hardly going to want to share a bathroom with a man . . . and I won't really need as much help once we've hired someone."

"I do want to share my bathroom with a man," said Carmen, slightly bitterly. "Just one I actually know."

So now it was clear to both of them . . . Sofia's hints hadn't worked at all.

"Okay, let's talk about this later," said Sofia, in a warning tone, and Carmen marched out of the room as Sofia started cross-questioning Rudi about his qualifications.

"We have had a meeting," said Pippa officiously as Carmen neared the nursery floor, where the girls shared the large front room with the beautiful wrought-iron beds, covered with pretty White Company duvets and pink spotted blankets. A large doll's house covered one wall, and the sash windows had pink spotted blinds you could pull down. Fairy lights sparkled above Pippa's bed. Phoebe's somehow didn't work anymore. Nevertheless, it was a dream of a room; like all the top rooms, warm from heat traveling up through the house, the sloping roof insulated within an inch of its life. Even though the girls were getting big now, it still carried that whiff of baby powder and Sudocrem.

"Okay," said Carmen. Jack's room was smaller so they normally met in the girls' room.

"We like him," said Jack. "Even if he doesn't have a robot hand."

"I don't think I would like the robot hand and nobody is listening," said Phoebe. Pippa eyed Carmen suspiciously. She always took Phoebe's side.

"Forget about the robot hand!" said Carmen. "I heard him explaining to your mom: It was just a joke. But he does have twelve brothers and sisters."

"Whoa," said Jack. "How many sisters?" He shook his head. "Whatever the number is, it'll be too many."

"That's like a story," said Phoebe, breathing through her mouth. "Maybe they are twelve dancing princesses."

Carmen privately thought it was probably a little more hard-scrabble than that, but didn't mention it. By the time she got back downstairs, Sofia and Rudi were making jokes about who was the most Catholic and he was asking about Pippa's plans for her First Communion (Pippa's plans for her First Communion were extremely thorough and well thought out, even though it wasn't for another eight months), and Carmen realized, heart sinking, that this was really happening. She had not been honest with herself—and Sofia had not been honest with her, either. She had lost Oke. And soon, she was going to lose her home.

PART TWO

Chapter Three

At first, Oke had enjoyed the novelty of being home, in his family's small, neat apartment in Brasilia, away from the bad memories in every gray flagstone.

"Here, have more," said Patience, looking worriedly at her youngest child, and only son. Obedience—Oke—had always been thin, but it seemed to have gotten even worse since he'd been on the other side of the world. She ladled some extra farofa onto his plate.

She tried her absolute best not to look too desperate to have him home. It was exactly the kind of thing, she knew, that made children clam up, if you got too clingy. Particularly her beloved, but frustratingly elusive, son; so academic, so clever and dreamy; who had spent so long as a child climbing trees and heading into any forests he could find.

They had hoped he would follow Obidiah, his father, into carpentry—a respectable, solid trade—and indeed he had spent long days learning the grain of wood, breathing in the scent in his father's workshop. Wood, he loved.

But a non-brethren biology teacher at school had spotted Oke's deeper gifts early on—his intense thirst for knowledge; his love for plant life of all kinds, wood in particular—and had recommended him for the scholarship to São Paulo university, where he had flown through his courses and won a prestigious fellowship award, which had taken him right across the world.

She had been terrified he would never come back; that he

would meet a stranger, settle, vanish forever, her beautiful baby with his long limbs and high hair and slow smile and inquisitive green eyes, so like her own mother's.

And now here he was back, large as life, thank goodness, but looking thin and pale and sad.

"You were freezing?" she said.

He laughed. "I can't . . ." Patience had never left Brazil. "It is hard to describe. Like living in a fridge, if the fridge was also full of wind, and also full of rain. But mostly the wind. It goes through you like a knife."

"You hated it," said Patience, nodding happily and refreshing his glass of milk.

He tilted his head to one side. "But somehow," he said, "somehow it is still beautiful. And glorious. The darkness settles and the windows everywhere glow warm, and there are lights everywhere, and it is cozy and lovely to come in from the freezing cold, into a warm glow of a fire . . ." His face looked wistful. "And the children run around, pink-cheeked and laughing . . . and the great old buildings stand firm against the wind, and the squares are full of history of hundreds of years, tiptoeing over old stones. It is such a beautiful city, turning in on itself to keep the wind away."

"I don't like noisy children," said Patience.

"No," said Oke. "I understand."

"You are happy to be home?"

"I . . ."

Oke loved his family very much, but it wasn't like Carmen's. Her family talked about anything and everything; they were freewheeling and traded insults and stupid inside jokes, and fought and made up as if it were perfectly normal. His family lived good, decent, quiet lives and did not overexcite themselves or approve of anyone else being overexcited. What his mother would think of quicksilver Carmen, with her sudden laughs and terrible moods, was anyone's guess. He flashed back to her lying on his bed. Even though he had done what he thought was right, he couldn't get the memory of her out of his mind. Couldn't stop thinking about her, and how she had looked: red in the face; angry, twisted; very, very sexy. He couldn't blame her, in retrospect, for breaking up with him. He wished she hadn't. Life would probably be calmer. But not as much fun. And he missed her more than he had thought possible.

"You know," said Patience, "Mary Clemens is going on your trip, too. Her mother and I are such friends."

"Okay," said Oke. He had thought, once, that he and Carmen would spend the summer learning together, growing together. Unbeknownst to his loving, trusting mother—and, indeed, to Carmen—he had sown his wild oats at university, and found it unsatisfying and contrary to his beliefs about what he wanted: a strong love, a meaningful life.

"I've invited them over for dinner," said Patience, apropos of nothing.

Oke narrowed his eyes.

"She's a nurse."

"They were advertising for a nurse," said Patience serenely. "I sent it over to her mother."

Oke rolled his eyes.

"Okay, Mom."

The door banged open and suddenly the small apartment was overwhelmed with noise, as his sisters arrived, beaming, carrying food, with his nephews and nieces. He scooped up as many of them as he could in his long arms and squeezed them tight.

AND MARY HAD indeed come to dinner that evening, and been very sweet and enthusiastic, and even though Oke was terribly sad, it was hard not to be a little bit excited, as the team came together, equipped and ready for some difficult exploration in the jungle, and the great prize: time he could spend learning about this wonderful, ancient, mysterious tree, a deep-rooted part of the world that had been there long before Oke had been thought of and would be there, hopefully, long after he was gone. The heat and damp of the jungle, and his new companions, Oke faithfully hoped, would cover up his memories; possibly even heal him completely.

As he set off in the expedition Land Rover, his entire family having bid him a quiet farewell that morning, he sat on the open back, bumping along roads that grew less and less flat the further from the city they got, watching the world he was familiar with fade behind him. He was looking forward to the job ahead.

"Amazing, isn't it?" said Mary, pouring him a cup of sweet tea from her flask and coming to sit next to him as they bounced along. The birdsong was cacophonous in the trees; fluttering color flashed past the thick foliage. Water gurgled, the river they were following brown and thick with mud and movement. The air was heavy and scented. It was like being on a different planet. Surely this was far enough.

"It is," he said, accepting the tea with a smile.

Chapter Four

The late autumn light hung gold in the air, as if trapped in the heavy stone of the northern city.

Carmen had chosen a meandering route that morning, along Princes Street, dodging trams and crossing into the large Princes Street Gardens, wandering past the huge blue fountain, around the gardener's cottage, which looked like a beautiful little house from a fairy tale, skirls of brown and orange leaves drifting cross the immaculately cut grass. Few people were about at this time of the morning: There were some dog walkers and a couple of people feeding the pigeons—which you really weren't supposed to do, partly because it meant too many pigeons crapping everywhere and partly because the seagulls would barge in and elbow the pigeons out of the way. Seagulls were the lager louts of the bird world, loud and annoying and shouty and pushy and generally ruining everything they came into contact with. *Like me*, thought Carmen.

She was having a very self-pitying morning. She and Sofia had had a hissed fight, which they'd tried not to escalate in front of the children, about insane rental prices in Edinburgh, and about useful work (e.g., being a shop assistant) and stupid work (e.g., being a lawyer), and the terms *showing off* and *wallowing* may both have been used, and afterward, their mother may have had to turn off her phone for the entire afternoon and watch old episodes of *Call the Midwife* and reflect on how much easier her life had been when they were tiny.

Not even the rare sun's rays on the back of her neck could cheer her as Carmen climbed slowly up the Mound, the city swelling behind her at her feet, between the twin tops of the two great hotels—The Caledonian and The Balmoral—which framed the main street. Perhaps she could move in to one of them, she thought; find a little room on the top floor, scurry in and out all day past the doormen in tartan trousers and the smart black-and-white-clad maids; a tiny corner of the city to perch.

Then she sighed and remembered that rooms there cost per night more or less what she made in a week, and carried on her way.

The bright morning sunshine had inspired more than a few of her neighbors on Victoria Street to wash the smears from their windows or sweep up the litter. Street cleaners sometimes had trouble keeping up with just how many people wanted to come and visit the beautiful little row of pastel shops that curved gracefully upward from the busy, noisy open space of the Grassmarket—where they had burned witches once, and which now played host to hen parties galore, as if in happy, gleeful revenge for the crimes of long ago—up toward the austere, formal splendor of the George IV Bridge, which held national libraries and museums, vast flat-fronted seats of learning.

The shops on the street burrowed back into the very rock the castle stood on; the original volcano. Sometimes it looked like they had grown out of Edinburgh hill itself.

Carmen had taken the long way around, walking up from the gardens and around Ramsay Mews, the exquisitely odd country cottages perched next to the castle, and down to the Grassmarket where, this early, she could normally spot one or two people doing the walk of shame and feel a little better about things. Also if she started from the bottom of Victoria Street she could pop into the gorgeous coffee shop. It was staffed by Dahlia, who hated her for getting off with Oke, whom Dahlia had very much had her eye on, but the coffees and pistachio-filled croissants were so very good, Carmen steeled the stink eye anyway.

Carmen went on past the dark green of Crawford's clothing shop—the most formidably posh emporium she had ever encountered—and the hardware shop, just as Bobby was cheerfully putting out his mops and buckets. His Aladdin's cave of a shop contained just about everything you could ever need and lots of things you didn't realize you did. Then came Bronagh's magic shop, which she took very seriously, and even if you thought it might be funny to start with, you certainly wouldn't after a ten-minute grilling once you set foot over the threshold.

"Well met, Bookmistress," said Bronagh, who was outside, dusting off some of her taxidermy. Carmen eyed her suspiciously.

"Hi, Bronagh," she said, doing her best not to look sad or in fact betray any emotion at all, as Bronagh wasn't past going in to find a remedy to fix it.

"Hard times ahead," observed Bronagh. Today her ravishing hair was glinting all the colors of autumn, from lightest auburn to a deep true scarlet.

Carmen tried to wonder what about her body language had suggested any of this; was she slouching? Probably; her mom and Sofia always told her that she slouched. Had Bronagh heard something on the grapevine? Maybe. Carmen always chose to ignore the Occam's razor option: that Bronagh actually was a witch.

She carried on up, and opened the door of McCredie's bookshop.

A year ago it had been a fading, falling-apart, dusty old mess of a business, ignored by the man—Mr. McCredie—who had inherited it and ran it. Mr. McCredie adored books; that wasn't the problem. The problem was he had absolutely no idea how to turn that passion into a going concern that wouldn't bankrupt anyone who came into contact with it. Born to money, it was as if he felt the mere mention of it was indecent—vulgar, even. Carmen, born to absolutely no money, felt quite the opposite and had worked in shops since she left school at seventeen. She had no compunction about talking about money. Together, they made a good team.

But today, Carmen's mood was weighing her down. Because whichever way she tried to do the sums, she couldn't make it work. She could go home and live at her mom and dad's, but they had sent her to Edinburgh precisely to get her out of that rut.

She could move, with Sofia's help, but the thought of Sofia having to give her financial help was yucky. Okay, she was five years older, but even so. It felt like Sofia pointing out, yet again, how much better she was than Carmen, with her posh house and her four kids and her handsome husband and literally so much money to spare she could shower her kid sister with a full apartment deposit and *not even notice.*

Carmen's eyes closed when she remembered her dream last Christmas: that she and Oke would find something nice and small somewhere, cozy, the pair of them. Perhaps in one of the high aeries over the Royal Mile, where little rooms at the top of the ancient buildings had no elevator, and were five stories off the ground, but snug and warm under the ancient rafters. She could imagine the pair of them, laughing and doing the stupid things they did in ads for building societies, like painting but getting a fleck of paint on somebody's nose, and giggling, or curled up under a blanket watching TV. Actually, Oke didn't watch TV, having been raised without one, but she could overlook that maybe.

Anyway. None of that was happening and she was, incredibly, in a worse situation this year than she had been last. And her mood seemed to be rubbing off on Mr. McCredie, who appeared sadder and more taciturn than ever.

She looked at the beautiful orange-and-brown wreath she'd placed on the old door of the shop—now the front of the shop was painted a beautiful petrol blue, a color that had only taken several thousand letters to Edinburgh City Council and Historic Scotland to get approved. The wreath on the door seemed in keeping with the season. Bronagh had not approved, having plenty of actual pumpkins and gourds outside her shop, which she lit with real candles, giving the slight aroma of burning soup to the entire street. Bronagh also shut on October 31 because "it was too dangerous."

Well. At least there was still the children's reading hour to arrange.

Chapter Five

They had shot a children's reading hour for the film. Carmen had watched. All the children, each of them startlingly beautiful and from a variety of ethnicities and ages, had sat around in a lovely circle, nodding and smiling along with Genevieve Burr's slightly halting rendition of "Tam O'Shanter," much of which she mispronounced.

> *Now Tam, O Tam! had thae been queans,*
> *A' plump and strapping in their teens!*
> *Their sarks, instead o' creeshie flannen,*
> *Been snaw-white seventeen hunder linen!—*
> *Thir breeks o' mine, my only pair,*
> *That ance were plush, o' gude blue hair,*
> *I wad hae gien them aff y hurdies,*
> *For ae blink o' the bonie burdies!*

Carmen wasn't sure this verse was particularly deserving of the cheers and smiles the children gave it, but she was hardly going to step in; she'd already been thrown out of the shop because the phone went off, with someone asking for the original Roald Dahls—the ones before they had made the giant average-size, and Augustus Gloop suffering from a glandular disorder—and it had completely ruined the take.

Now Carmen was wondering why the children who had shown up to her event couldn't behave themselves the way the stage children could. She carried on: "*And then came the mother . . . she looked like Coraline's mother in every way. Except for one. Her eyes were stitched-on black buttons.*"

One of the children screeched slightly and someone else looked to be crying.

"Oh, for *goodness'* sake!" said Carmen, looking up. "It's just a book! You are all just going to have to *toughen up.*"

"Buttons for eyes?" said Phoebe. "I think this is *very much* too scary. *Again.*"

Carmen rolled her eyes, which is hard to do when you are wearing fake witch eyebrows, one of which had fallen off. You would think this would be funny, but apparently it was even more frightening.

Sofia, who was obviously feeling guilty because she'd shown up so early, tried to take out the sugar-free lollipops she'd brought without Carmen noticing, who got annoyed when she did this, thinking there was nothing wrong with a real lollipop every once in a while.

"It's *Halloween*; it's *meant* to be scary," said Carmen, throwing her hands up. "You're all dressed as witches!"

"Iz a *ghost*," corrected a small ghost.

"And ghosts and stuff."

"I thought we were just coming to get sweets," grumbled one girl, clutching an orange plastic tub shaped like a grinning pumpkin. It was full of empty wrappers.

"A story is nice to have on Halloween," said her mom, her cheek bulging slightly.

"Not that one."

"It's a masterpiece!" said Carmen. Then she shook her head in despair.

"Honestly, you're all scaredy-cats. You'd better just have your Milky Ways. Give me your party pieces."

She stood, patiently, in the Scottish tradition, while every small witch either told her a gruesome joke or recited a little poem, or, in the case of one highly energetic threesome, performed the "Three Craws" song, complete with actions, as the other mothers rolled their eyes.

"You have all earned your sweeties," Carmen said.

"Why can't we just do Trick or Treat like in America?" complained the Alpha Witch.

"Because I don't want egg on my window?" said Carmen, passing out the treats. "Now, who's going to see Bronagh?"

"Nooooo!" chorused the children.

"She'll turn our legs into the legs of a frog!" said one.

"She almost certainly won't!" said Carmen.

"It's shut," said one kid.

"That's because she's out flying on her real broomstick," said Alpha Witch.

"Oooh!" said the children.

"Come on," said the moms, ushering them out. "There's bobbing for apples at the hardware shop."

"You should do that," said the Alpha Witch to Carmen. "That *isn't scary.*"

There was a new line of tiny ghouls outside the bookshop awaiting admittance.

"Now," said Carmen, opening the door, "I'm going to tell you a story but it's a *very scary story.* Are you ready for that?"

"YAYYYYY!" the children yelled. But that's what the last lot had said.

"Okay," said Carmen, unraveling the autumnal wreath from the door the next morning, and talking to Mr. McCredie, even though he wasn't there yet, so she was really talking to herself. She was trying not to think about moving. "You know what comes next . . ."

She glanced into the depths of the stacks behind the curtains. She would start bringing out the Christmas stock. She couldn't help feeling a little flare of excitement. Edinburgh at Christmas-time, earth frozen solid; darkness and lights and anticipation on every icy breath. Despite everything, it was her favorite time of year.

Further back there were more bookshelves: behind the children's fiction, poetry and beautiful editions of classics that Carmen liked; behind the cash desk, nonfiction, bigger formats, full of esoterica and unexpected items. Here could be found old cartography, shipping architecture, dendrology, and anything else that caught Mr. McCredie's magpie-like attention. This was where his real interests lay: in esoteric areas of knowledge, captured like butterflies on a pin, held safe in books.

There was a closed arched door at the back of the shop that led to the stacks, or the storeroom. The stacks were far, far deeper than the shop itself: a lifetime of book collecting and book obsession that held much more than the small percentage they had on display. Mr. McCredie could find everything in the stacks due to some weird filing system of his own that Carmen was often trying to pin down before he died and it was lost forever; but it was in the stacks he was happiest. At the back of the stacks was a cozy fireplace, with armchairs and soft lighting, where he was usually to be found reading. A staircase led up to his large and untouched house, which confusingly was at ground level on the street that ran above the street the shop was on. Edinburgh was like this: layer upon layer of houses and buildings on many levels, that felt not so much built as grown.

Mr. McCredie was currently nowhere to be found, although there were Christmas plans to be made. Carmen clomped around the desk, trailing leaves as she went, and cursing having to use a broom instead of a vacuum cleaner.

"Mr. McCredie?"

But there was no answer. She liked to get in a good twenty minutes or so before they opened for the day; dusting and straightening and getting everything ready, whether the people who came in when the door opened were a flood or a trickle. It helped to feel on top of everything. Carmen sighed and checked the answering machine. It was the old kind—the kind you had to press to play—and often had messages from quite old people, mentioning books they kind of remembered but weren't quite sure about, perhaps they'd know it, it had a red cover and they thought it was by somebody called David and everyone in it died.

Nope, nothing.

She cranked up the ancient computer she had come across on Freecycle. It still ran Windows 98, which meant it was very hard to start a proper inventory of any of the stuff they really needed and Carmen couldn't get rid of the Clippy paperclip she remembered from trying to write school essays as a child. It had been annoying then and it was annoying now.

She looked at the spreadsheet, then looked at it again.

IT LOOKS LIKE YOU'RE TYPING A SPREADSHEET, wrote Clippy.

"Go away," muttered Carmen, trying to get rid of it by clicking too hard on the old, not entirely accurate mouse. Every so often one of their nerdier customers would get a nostalgic look in their eye when they saw what they were running and would come over to have a look. She would have to shoo them away, otherwise they'd play Minesweeper for four hours and not buy a damn thing.

It didn't matter how much she looked at the figures. The film shoot had helped, of course it had, but it had disguised their deeper issues. Maybe her Halloween stories had been too scary (or not scary enough, as one small boy in a *Scream* mask had informed her, but she wasn't quite sure what to do about that). They had sold lots of perfect Halloween fare—*Marianne Dreams, Meg and Mog at Halloween, The Weirdstone of Brisingamen*, and *Gobbolino, the Witch's Cat*, and *Coraline* itself, but even though they had done well, they were barely treading water. She certainly couldn't ask for the sort of pay raise that might get her a deposit on an apartment. She sighed. Oh God. It was so hard to keep things running evenly. The only thing that worked in their favor was that they were heated by a small fireplace, with a seemingly inexhaustible supply of peat Mr. McCredie had found in a cellar (which was, infuriatingly, slightly higher up than the shop level). This meant they could have a cozy fire burning in the little grate, with a large fireguard and several warning signs around for small people who walked in and cooed when they saw it. It wasn't, Carmen knew, ideal to have an open fire in a shop made entirely of paper run by a forgetful old man, but the alternative was paying heating bills that made her want to cry, so lighting the fire it was.

But everything else was so expensive. Keeping the lights on, stock, taxes, delivery charges; everything was going through the roof, and people had less spare money to spend on books—she could see it on their regretful faces, as they lovingly handled a hardback edition of *Middlemarch* with William Morris endpapers, or asked for all the children's schoolbook editions secondhand. She frowned at the computer and decided to reuse the tea bag she had put in the little sink. Christmas was coming. It had to be good. It would be good. It was a lovely, busy time of year, wasn't it?

THE BELL TO the shop rang. It was Bobby, who ran the hardware shop. His face looked as grim as Carmen felt.

"Hey!" said Carmen. "Did you bring coffee?"

"Naw," he said.

"Okay," said Carmen. "But I'm warning you, I'm down to one tea bag."

"Naw, we should get coffee."

Carmen winced. Spending that extra money—coffee had gone up, too—when she was soon going to need a deposit and have to pay for some grim bedsit miles away on the outskirts of Edinburgh—if she could afford Edinburgh at all, which wasn't likely. Fife and the Lothians—the regions surrounding the city—were beautiful, but they were far away, particularly when you couldn't drive into the city, protected as it was by the traffic warden zombie army.

Bobby saw her face.

"Water is fine," he growled.

"What's up?" said Carmen.

IT LOOKS LIKE YOU'RE SAVING A FILE! typed Clippy. Bobby looked at it and frowned.

"Well," he said heavily, "I've had an offer from the landlord."

"What do you mean?"

"For the shop."

Carmen instantly felt worried. The tight infrastructure meant everything: They weren't just a street; they were a community.

"Uh-huh?" she said carefully. "I mean, it's really useful to have you there."

"There's been a hardware shop on that site for two hundred years," said Bobby sadly. "I don't think I could look my family in the eye if I was the one who let it go."

Carmen looked at him. Already they had seen the steady encroachment of horrible gift shops running up and down the main shopping streets like wildfire, turning so much of their beautiful city into some kind of cheesy historical theme park, a city under glass. This wasn't what they wanted at all. The city had to live, Carmen felt, fervently. Not just for tourists; for the people who made their homes here. They weren't curators or caretakers. They were lucky, of course, to live in one of the most beautiful cities in the world. But it had to be a living city.

"Who is it?" she said.

He shrugged. "Just . . ."

He almost couldn't say the name out loud. Carmen looked at him.

"Jackson McClockerty," he said finally, as if Carmen should have heard of him. She shook her head. "Jackson? McClockerty? Aw. Well. I thought you'd know who he was. Everyone does."

Carmen shook her head again and sipped her now disgusting dishwater tea.

"Is he, like, a very famous hardware shop owner who can supply you with hugely discounted buckets and mops and make your fortune?" she said, with only a faint hope in her voice.

"He is not," said Bobby.

The door flew open.

"We're closed," said Carmen weakly, but she glanced up regardless. Standing in the doorframe was Bronagh, her hair gleaming in the cold morning sun.

"My thumbs are pricking," she said. "Who are you talking about?"

Carmen gave her a side-eye. "Well, obviously Bobby doesn't come here very often so there has to be news; stop trying to be spooky."

Bronagh fixed her with those green eyes.

"Crossing a witch on All Souls Day doesn't seem very wise to me."

As she said so, a dark shape passed the window behind, casting a shadow. They all glanced up, but it was only a traffic warden, plying their sinister trade.

"I don't have any tea," said Carmen.

"Don't you?" said Bronagh, heading back to where the sink was and reappearing with three steaming mugs of something that wasn't herbal tea or plain tea or anything recognizable, but was strong and delicious.

"Continue, Brother Smith."

Bobby sighed.

"I was just telling her . . . I got an offer from Jackson McClockerty."

Bronagh hissed.

"Do you know who that is?" said Carmen.

"Everybody does," said Bronagh. "Owns half the shops on the Royal Mile. He deals in cheap nonsense. Rubbish and broken dreams."

Carmen looked at Bobby for a translation.

"It'll just be a gift shop," he said, still looking ashamed. "Just, gifts, you know. Little keepsakes for people to take home."

"Plastic Nessies?" said Carmen, horrified. "And tea towels with wee dogs on them?"

"Lots of people like tea towels with wee dogs on them," said Bobby in what sounded like a pleading voice. Bronagh was making unimpressed noises.

"Oh my God," said Carmen suddenly, "he's not going to play loud bagpipe music outside all day, is he?"

"He . . . uh. He might do that," said Bobby, his head held low. "He does in his other shops."

Carmen covered her face in her hands. "Bobby! We're trying to build something lovely here, a street people can come to for lots of different things! For clothes, for cake, for coffee, for their home needs, for books, for . . . uh, you know, wind chimes and things."

"*Wind chimes and things?*" said Bronagh in quite a scary voice.

"If we turn into a tartany kind of stupid heritage place, local people won't come anymore and we need both sorts of people! Tourists and locals! It's not always August!"

"I know," said Bobby. "But I don't . . . Carmen, people don't want to buy tins of paint and varnish at the bottom of the city and lug it up to the top. It doesn't make any sense. They want to take their cars out of town."

Carmen screwed up her face. "You can't sell smaller pots?"

Bobby shook his head. "That doesn't really solve the problem." And Carmen had to admit that it didn't.

"But everything else . . . all your nails and screws!"

"Yeah," said Bobby. "The screws retail at fifteen pence each and the nails are about six pence each."

"What about buckets?"

"The thing is," said Bobby, "when people buy a book they read it and then they buy another one. But when people buy a bucket, that . . . I mean, quite often that's them for buckets, they're fine."

"But there're so many businesses around that need you . . ."

He nodded. "I know. But fewer and fewer because of the gift shops . . . and then, the rent goes up and up so only gift shops can afford it, and everyone has less money and I'm trying to keep the lights on . . ."

"Yeah," said Carmen, acutely aware of her own issues. She understood.

"Oh, Bobby, what will you do?"

"He's offered me a job in the shop," said Bobby.

"Oh, so you're not leaving?"

He shook his head. "I'll be an employee."

Carmen gave him a sympathetic look. From the sounds of him, Jackson McClockerty wouldn't be as easygoing an employer as Mr. McCredie.

Mr. McCredie, in fact, now pottered in, wearing pajamas and a large and ancient red smoking jacket. He seemed to make very little distinction between what was his house and what was the shop and he seemed equally unsurprised to see lots of people in there. Under his arm was a book titled *Scaling the Antarctic Wastes for Beginners*.

"Ooh," he said. "Bronagh, could you possibly . . . ?"

Bronagh quickly produced another steaming cup of the strange tea and he accepted it gratefully.

"Bobby is going to work for Jackson McClockerty," said Carmen. Mr. McCredie frowned.

"Och no," he said. "As if things aren't bad enough."

"Seriously. Everyone's heard of him?" said Carmen.

"There were people dressed up as him last night," said Bobby.

"It's all right," said Bronagh. "I'll curse the entire enterprise."

"Don't do that!" said Carmen. "Then someone else will take it and turn it into Edinburgh's grisliest disgustingest escape room or something!"

"Aye, don't do that," said Bobby. "If you don't mind, like. I'll be inside and I'll be the one ending up with the legs of a frog."

"I am going to do that," muttered Bronagh.

"I'm not sure that man is a good fit for this street," said Mr. McCredie.

"I can't believe you've heard of him when you haven't heard of . . . I don't know, Chanel Number Five."

"Of course I have," said Mr. McCredie mildly. "He seems to be on an imperial mission to take over every vacant or failing shop in Edinburgh and bring it down to the lowest possible level. I don't know what his end goal is. Neither does he, I suspect."

"I want to meet him," said Carmen.

"Oh, you will," said all three together, as Clippy bounced ominously in the corner of the screen.

THE OTHERS LEFT, but Mr. McCredie was still in his pajamas, looking around distractedly.

"Has the mailman come?"

"Mr. McCredie," said Carmen, worried now, "are you feeling all right?"

"Uh. I think so. I was. I was thinking . . ."

This wasn't the first time, Carmen realized, that he'd been a bit odd recently. He was so eccentric most of the time that she barely noticed a little extra strangeness; but the pajamas, this was new.

"I was thinking the mail might have come."

"I don't think so," said Carmen. The bell tinged and two older ladies came in looking for Josephine Tey novels. Their thin eyebrows arched in shock at the pajamas.

"Mr. McCredie, can you *please* go and get dressed?" said Carmen, packing him off and turning toward her customers with a broad smile.

"Uh, morning!"

MR. MCCREDIE REEMERGED in his more customary tweed jacket and striped shirt a short while later, but he still appeared distracted and confused. Carmen glanced at him repeatedly.

"Are you all right?" she said finally, after cheerfully dealing with someone asking where her Christmas decorations were, one day after Halloween, and searching for a Christmas cookbook, which she had had to dive deep into the stacks to find, receiving precious little thanks when she did so.

"Got to get on," said the customer, who was wearing a red-and-green sweater with a bell on it. "Turkey to buy!"

Carmen watched them go, bustling down the road.

Mr. McCredie turned to face her and Carmen looked at him—really looked at him, rather than, as she usually did, skirting around him to reach something else, or dusting over the tops of his feet, or yelling his name whenever someone professorial-looking came in with the satisfied expression of a dedicated book lover who was going to be very happy to get lost in a conversation about the shortfalls of the Dewey Decimal System or a book of a set of blueprints for a Sopwith Camel, or discussions about what Roman music might have sounded like, for the next ninety minutes or so.

His normally pink cheeks were looking more agitated than normal, his blue eyes distant and unfocused.

Carmen started to worry. He wasn't getting any younger; he'd been born just after the Second World War, the result of an ill-fated liaison between his beautiful, very young mother and a teenage German POW. Surely he was okay? Her dad had had a stent put in last year, and he was only in his sixties. On the other hand, Mr. McCredie didn't put away nearly as much bread, wine, and ice cream as her dad.

"Is everything okay?" she asked him.

"I'm . . . I'm not sure," he said, looking at her; he seemed puzzled rather than upset.

"I mean, how are you feeling in yourself?" she said.

"Well, that is a little confusing."

"Are you getting confused? I think you should see a doctor."

He smiled. "Oh no, I don't think . . . I'd see Bronagh if anyone."

"Don't be *ridiculous*," said Carmen.

"But I'm not confused, my dear," he went on, as if he hadn't heard her at all. "No. I have rarely been more certain of anything in my life. Now, where's that mailman?"

He looked up hopefully as, indeed, Beto the mailman pushed open the door, his arms full of special orders as usual.

"Thank you," said Carmen, smiling.

"I thought people bought books off the internet and got them delivered to their houses," said Beto. "I'm not complaining, I'm just saying."

"Sometimes people need to get a feel for a thing before they know they want it," said Carmen. "Sometimes people need to know something feels and smells and looks right."

She held up a box from a publisher and opened it quickly. Inside was *A Layman's Guide to Borders*, an exquisite hardback book of maps. It weighed about a ton. Inside was layer upon layer of maps, from earliest times, setting out the layout of the world people knew as it expanded. The paper was ridged, three-dimensional tiny mountains rising from the pages. You could crouch down and feel you were going to walk straight down a silk road. It was beautiful.

Beto gazed at it. "Well, isn't that something?"

"Isn't it?" said Carmen, who was smugly enjoying the fact that her hunch to order it had proved right, even at an eye-watering price. "You wouldn't ever get this from a computer screen; you'd never realize how beautiful it was."

Beto carefully ran his fingers over the ridges and dips.

"Oh," he said, "it's weird. I want to have it but I'm not sure why."

"That's books for you," said Carmen. "Done right, they become a little piece of your heart. Want me to keep it for you?"

He looked at it longingly. "Let me put it on my Christmas list." He patted his bag. "I do have a direct line to the North Pole."

Beto turned to go, then felt in his bag again.

"Oh, sorry, there's one more thing. Probably a bill, man."

Carmen nodded. Usually was. Beto pulled it out. "Strange stamp."

Mr. McCredie moved surprisingly nimbly for a man his age.

"I believe . . . that is for me."

It was.

"What is it?" said Carmen suspiciously, as Mr. McCredie handled the envelope with some reverence. His eyes were shining, his cheeks pinker than ever. For a moment, Carmen worried it might be from the hospital.

Hands shaking, he opened it, read it, and gave out a long sigh.

"*What?*" said Carmen, bouncing with impatience. "What is it? Is it the doctor?"

He looked at her. "Not at all," he said. "No. In fact . . . I . . ." His eyes went distant and slightly moist. "I have decided I must make a voyage."

"What do you mean?"

For just a second Carmen thought he was being flowery and meant the ultimate voyage.

"Are you sick?" she said, more loudly this time. "You have to tell me, it's not fair."

He turned his mild blue eyes back to her.

"No, no. At least I don't think so. Nothing more than can be attributed to my age, at any rate. No. I mean, I feel called. I must make a journey."

"Where?" said Carmen. Maybe he wanted to visit the British Library in London. Or Shakespeare and Company in Paris; or the Tromsø Bokhandel, to see one of the great bookshops in the world. That would make sense.

Mr. McCredie focused once more on the road outside, leading down and far away.

"*Antarctica*," he said finally. "To the utter south."

Carmen looked at him. "You are kidding?"

Mr. McCredie looked at her. "I thought perhaps you might have learned," he said in his usual mild way, "that I never kid about anything."

That was true.

"But how . . . how are you going to get to Antarctica?" she said.

"There is a supply boat leaving just after Christmas," he said. "It's summer down there. You can get down before the ice closes over. I shall pay it my proper respects. It's leaving from Leith Docks."

Mr. McCredie's ancestors had been Antarctic explorers, and the blood ran in him, or so he thought. He had a fine collection of ancient finnesko and snowshoes up in the attic.

"Hang on," said Carmen. "They'll take you? You've asked them?"

"I wrote them a letter," said Mr. McCredie.

He held the reply. On the top was printed "British Antarctic Survey."

"And they're taking *you*?" said Carmen, not realizing quite how rude she sounded.

"They will," said Mr. McCredie. "If I can pay."

And Carmen took the letter from him, read it, and whistled.

Chapter Six

The Amazon

Oke had been there for months now—the survey had extended itself, as these things do—and everything that had once seemed extraordinary to him to begin with—living in a tent, working in the largest, wildest jungle left in the world—had almost become quotidian. The heat, the dense moisture in the air that slowed down your limbs, and the incredible birds and wildlife that they had started to see as they had advanced deeper into the rain forest, all increased Oke's desperate need to protect as much of this world as they had left. The startling cries of the wild parrots and the exquisite translucent shimmering hummingbirds left him breathless. He stopped dreaming, quite so much, of cool dark passageways, fresh bright mornings, crackling ice, friendly welcoming bars, and roaring fires that were a pleasure, rather than something they huddled around to try to bat back the oppressive darkness and many insects of the nights. He had almost stopped dreaming of a girl of impetuous moods and wicked laughs, who couldn't dance the samba but so wanted to learn. But sometimes, just sometimes, the sense of longing, the loneliness for what he had left behind, was almost overwhelming.

Yet here, in the heart of the jungle—constantly attuned to its dangers; respectfully either approaching or circling its communities, depending on what they knew was expected; taking his turn paddling the raft up the great tributaries of the Amazon—here, he felt better. Not so sad, not all the time. When he was engrossed in examining the great trees—testing the sap, counting them and marking their positions on maps, feeding as much good data back to the university as he could—it all felt good and useful.

And Mary was always there, of course, bouncing around, suggesting songs to sing around the campfire, none of which he knew; always helpful and jolly, even though many of the team were serious experts who would be happier discussing nothing more than sap levels.

She was on catering duty as well as nursing, and was always the one to bring him a cup of coffee when he woke up; to ask him about his mom or to let him know when it was his turn on the satellite phone. They were now very far out of mobile range and his phone hadn't been charged for weeks.

It was easy, he found, to fall into step with her; to remember funny stories from growing up in the same town and going to the same meeting house; the childhood games and of course their respective mothers, best of friends; his sisters, again.

She knew exactly what she wanted to do after the expedition: finish her degree, then work in their hometown, settle near her parents, live happily . . . And looking at her young, clear-eyed, enthusiastic face, Oke found he envied her certainty.

All his life, although he was not the best Quaker, Oke had staunchly believed in the tenets of his creed: a quiet acceptance and a strong commitment to truth and community.

He wasn't blind. His mother had been fairly upfront about it all. He should accept Mary, or someone very like her, and live in the same strong, quiet community that he had been born into. It was what he had always, more or less, expected. It would make the families very happy. Love that was steady and nurtured and grew. Mary was a good person, there was no doubt about that. And there was also his sense of self-reproach: He had tried it another way, and only succeeded in making two people extremely unhappy. Perhaps there was something in the older wisdom after all.

One night, nearing the end of the tour, Mary appeared late at night, almost out of the blue. They had had a tough day: a move upriver; a long, exhausting hike in search of a mapped tree that turned out not to be there after all; followed by a battery failure on the flashlights; and, well, overall, it had just been a fairly gnarly waste of a day.

Oke's tentmate, Juan-Castillo, was a funny, skinny, loud-mouthed guy from Rio that Oke hadn't taken to initially, until the endless jokes had ceased to be an irritant and became rather comforting. When you were listening out in the night to see if a crocodile was going to run up the banks and bite you on the leg, or you wanted a proper bath in a house with a roof on it, not a plastic bag shower, or you just longed to walk into a coffee shop and order a decent cup of coffee, it made sense to have someone relentlessly upbeat on the team.

Juan-Castillo was out for the count and snoring his head off, but Oke had stayed up later, lying on the hood of the Land Rover, staring at the Southern Cross, which never lost its magic. There wasn't a television series they would ever make as compelling as the brightness of the stars in a clearing, far far away from cities and pollution and the noise of the world. A world he sometimes longed for, more than anything he could imagine, and sometimes was happy he had left behind, as he felt himself, misshapen and awk-ward, a paradox of desires, as the loose threads of the world pulled and stretched him every which way. His family wanted one thing; the university needed other things; a cool, strange corner of the world still awaited him, even if he couldn't imagine it now. Ed-inburgh: an eighteenth-century city, while he had been raised in a seventeenth-century religion, trying to live in a twenty-first-century world.

But here, so far from human concerns, surrounded by a rain forest so old, dinosaurs would have known its ways, his ears filled with the noise of the jungle at night: wild cries, screeches, chat-tering birds, and the occasional growl from, hopefully, a long long way away. Oke looked up at the bright diamonds above him in the bath-warm air and felt comfortable, happier about his deep and settled belief that the world was all connected and that there was something—something—out there, in deep space, or at the edge of time, the end or the beginning of creation. And your place within it was barely anything at all. And there was comfort in that, too: Make all your choices as well as you can; that is all you can do. The universe is bigger and stranger than anything he or anyone else could comprehend. Even in this tiny corner of it—the glory of one of the greatest, oldest living things on earth—there was still so much they didn't know. Never would. And that was all right.

He was half in a trance, half-asleep, when Mary, coming back from the field toilet, came across him.

"Hey," she whispered. "What's up?"

"Not much," said Oke, gesturing emptily at the sky. "Everything."

She made to join him and he obligingly scrunched over.

"There's Cassiopeia," she said softly. "And Pegasus."

He nodded. Humans putting names on constellations was a shallow business as far as Oke was concerned; not much different to the children's stories Carmen sold. Although he wasn't thinking about Carmen.

"I love it out here, don't you?" she whispered. "What an amazing country we live in. You must miss it so much when you're away."

Oke grunted noncommittally. Mary looked at him sideways.

She'd known Oke since she was little. She had always, always adored the tall, clever, studious boy who rode his bike with a book in one hand; who stayed silent in meetings and didn't boast or brag outside of them; who listened carefully to the elders telling him exactly what he should do with his life, but then did exactly what he wanted. And now he was a man of the world; traveled, educated; a doctor. Not rich, but that didn't matter. Both the families wanted it to happen. Mary had been quiet, holding back. But she felt the time had come to accelerate matters. The field trip would finish soon and it would be nice to have everything . . . settled. Because she had been in love with him half her life.

She turned so she was looking at his fine profile, and it was an act of considerable restraint for her not to run her fingers down it.

"It's been amazing, this trip, don't you think?"

"Oh yeah."

"I can't believe it's nearly finished. Wouldn't it be wonderful to . . . get research jobs? Spend our lives exploring? You know, I can be a nurse anywhere."

He looked at her, noticing as he did so that while she was wearing shorts and a vest, she had put on mascara.

"Hmm," he said. She crept her arm out toward his.

"I think . . . I mean . . . We get on well, don't you think?"

Is this what the universe wants? wondered Oke, staring at the sky. He thought of his mother's face, his family's joy. He thought of Carmen: upset, red-faced, furious. He thought of cold mornings and a world that seemed so far away; an expensive, freezing world. His brain seemed to disassociate itself; his thoughts swirling. The stars above looked as if they were moving. The sky felt as if it were leaning down on him, oppressive, heavy with the weight of the heat: every day, he thought; every day, waking drenched; swimming in the muddy river to get clean—clean water was for drinking, not for washing, and the solar shower was so much fuss to get working they normally didn't bother. By the time you got out again, it was so humid you were wet through, your shirt sticking to your back in ten minutes.

He had never felt it before; had barely noticed the weather at all. But now, here, even at nighttime, it seemed incredibly difficult to live in such a hot climate. It felt oppressive. He missed, suddenly, the sharp clearness of a frosty morning. He wanted to wear a hat that wasn't just to block the blinding light. The world felt too hot; as if you couldn't escape. He felt his blood getting more syrupy; his already slow heartbeat slowing more and more with the torpor of the warmth; his mind adrift, in heavy hot seas.

"Oke?" said Mary, looking into his face as his eyes widened, slid to the side. Then, with some urgency, "OKE?"

Chapter Seven

November

"Run that past me again," said Carmen, shaking her head. It didn't make any sense.

"So I need to get down to South America by the end of January, and the boat will pick me up, stop at the Falklands, and then set sail for McMurdo Sound. We're leaving on Boxing Day."

Mr. McCredie's eyes looked misty and faraway once again.

"*This* December?" said Carmen. "That's not possible! It's only weeks away."

"Oh well, it is, you see, because their summer is—"

"No, I don't mean that. I mean, how are you going to get down there? It's November already."

"Ah, yes," said Mr. McCredie. They both looked at the now very creased letter from the British Antarctic Survey. There was a fair bit about how they were taking him as a proud descendant of the Bruce expedition. At the bottom was how much they were going to charge him. It was an eye-watering amount.

"You don't have this money," said Carmen, who knew how much less than zero money they had. "The paperclip will tell you."

IT LOOKS LIKE YOU'RE TRYING TO BRING UP A FILE, said Clippy, not bringing up a file.

"Yes, well," Mr. McCredie said again, his eyes looking round and eager, not even glancing at the computer. "That's what you're for, isn't it? Cleverly coming up with ways to make money?"

"Well, I've kind of thought of them all," said Carmen. "Did you not hear my bloodcurdling Halloween tales?"

"I find that story remarkably frightening," said Mr. McCredie.

"It was for Halloween! And what about the film?"

"That was vulgar," said Mr. McCredie.

Carmen blew out her cheeks.

"I do have *one* idea," said Mr. McCredie.

"Oh yeah?" said Carmen excitedly. Nobody knew the shop better than Mr. McCredie; what might lurk, somewhere, buried.

"Well, it's a little unusual."

"Even better," said Carmen. "Quirky is good!"

Mr. McCredie pursed his lips.

"Well," he said. "There's a man . . ."

"Uh-huh?"

"He's called Jackson McClockerty, and he has some *very* interesting ideas about what we could do with this place . . ."

"What do you mean?" said Carmen hotly.

"Oh, Jackson McClockerty's been asking about this place for years."

"HE'S CRAZY," SAID Carmen that night, pacing the floor, Eric bouncing up and down in her arms. "He's gone completely mad."

"Jackson McClockerty," said Sofia, shaking her head. They were in truce mode, because the alternative was too grim to consider. Rudi moved in in a week.

"You know him?"

"Everyone knows him! He's the Tartan Tat King of Corstorphine! Except I imagine he doesn't live in Corstorphine anymore."

"Oh God," said Carmen. "I just . . . I can't bear it. I just want to sell books."

Sofia frowned. This seemed such an obvious solution she didn't know why Carmen was so resistant.

"Mr. McCredie needs money," said Sofia. "Quickly."

"Uh-huh."

"And he has all those empty rooms upstairs . . ."

Carmen's face fell again. She kept forgetting, or trying to forget, and Sofia kept reminding her. Every time it hit her like a ton of bricks. She hated her sister sometimes.

"Sofia, it's uninhabitable! You know it has no central heating?" she said. "I don't think he can climb the stairs. It's basically an abandoned shell."

"I know it's in an amazing area and very handy for work," said Sofia.

A silence almost as icy as Mr. McCredie's upstairs rooms settled over them.

Sofia busied herself.

"You know," she said, finally, as an olive branch, "you should excavate the back of the shop. It's ridiculous how tiny the front is and how far back the back goes. If you opened it up there'd be more to look at and people could buy more stuff."

"How am I going to knock down the wall and light the back rooms?" said Carmen. "With magic invisible money? That's a completely stupid idea."

It wasn't, actually, a completely stupid idea, which was even more annoying, and the pair went back to sullenly ignoring each other, until finally the door opened and Pippa burst in.

"Hello, darling," said Sofia, delighted to break the atmosphere.

"Ohhhh," said Pippa, uncharacteristically. She slumped down at the kitchen table. Normally Pippa arrived trumpeting her latest day's successes: questions answered, spelling tests aced, compliments received. Today she looked downcast and was staring fixedly at the kitchen table.

"What's up?" said Carmen. Pippa shot her a look. She considered Carmen to be a terrible taker of Phoebe's side in all disputes (to be fair there was a modicum of truth in this; Phoebe and Carmen had a lot in common).

Pippa let out a long sigh.

"Would hot chocolate help?" said Carmen.

"*Carmen!*" said Sofia in exasperation. Carmen shot her a look in response.

"Sorry," said Carmen. "I just thought it might help."

"Sugar is not the answer!" said Sofia.

"*Kind* of depends on the question?" said Carmen.

"Well," said Pippa, unwilling to give an inch in the secret endless war that waged between her and Carmen. "Maybe."

Carmen got up and went to the stovetop, sticking Eric into his bouncy chair where he would happily yell "BA BA BA BA" for hours as long as everyone gave it a kick as they passed. She poured milk into a pot and reached on the high shelf for Sofia's very expensive secret cookies while Sofia glared at her.

The front door flew open again. It was Phoebe this time. Even though the school was close by and the two girls could technically have walked home at the same time, they never did. Pippa walked with her best friends, any two of whom were on nonspeaking terms at any one time. They all had identical long ponytails, sleek and high on their heads. Phoebe either cavorted along on the outskirts of large groups of girls and boys in the school walking in neat lines, for all her might looking as if she was by herself, bag open, trailing lost socks and dirty pieces of paper, like a Quentin Blake character.

On Mondays, when the shop was closed, Carmen often wandered down with Eric to meet her, and her heart went out to her little buddy if she was struggling up the hill toward the West End alone, hockey stick clattering around her ankles while Pippa marched ahead. Sofia had been similar, Carmen recalled, but she didn't remember feeling annoyed about it; sisters simply didn't mix at school and that was the rule. And not very often at home if they could possibly help it.

"Hey, Phoebs," said Carmen, smiling warmly. One of Phoebe's tight plaits had somehow unraveled itself and was tumbling down her sweater, which was untucked at the side and had holes in the sleeve from where Phoebe pulled it down with her thumbs however often she was told not to. She got hand-me-downs from Pippa, in perfect condition, and somehow managed to destroy or lose everything in weeks. "How was your day?"

Phoebe slumped. "Well, Mr. Lochin said I was going to have to do more concentrating."

Sofia glanced up. Mr. Lochin was exactly the kind of teacher she liked: traditional, old school, with high standards expected from all the children in terms of manners, behavior, and work. It was proving a total disaster for Phoebe.

"What kind of concentrating?"

Carmen stirred up the hot chocolate.

"Actually, Phoebs," said Pippa loudly, "I need to have a *grown-up conversation* at the moment, please?"

Phoebe looked doleful.

"I'll keep you some hot chocolate," said Carmen.

"I don't get hot chocolate," said Phoebe, "when I have problems."

"Because you have problems *every day*," said Pippa. "Hot chocolate would just add to your problems."

"Pippa! Don't be mean!" pleaded Sofia.

"I'm being kind and telling the truth! I thought we were supposed to tell the truth!" protested Pippa.

Carmen poured out four cups of steaming hot chocolate, diplomatically not giving one to Sofia, who would have said no, without making a big deal about it. Jack would be crashing through in a minute or, more likely, would text and say he'd gone to Olly's house. Olly lived in what Jack thought was paradise: a huge new-build in a gated community complete with a den in the basement with a snooker table and a huge backyard. They also had a steam room and a lot of identical houses around a green they could all kick a ball on. Sofia thought it was vulgar, with the cars lined up out front and the cinema rooms and the gumball machines and huge subzero fridges and immaculate plastic lawns. Jack thought it was actual heaven.

Phoebe eyed her hot chocolate carefully. "Can I take it upstairs?"

"You cannot."

"Can I take it down to Carmen's room?"

"Sure."

"What?"

Carmen loved Phoebe but there was no doubt that kid spilled stuff wherever she went.

"Oh come on, you don't care."

And you're moving out soon, was the unspoken line.

"Ahem," said Pippa.

"Maybe I'll stay?" tried Phoebe one more time.

Pippa gave her an imperious glance. "But this is grown-up stuff for grown-up people. You can't interfere."

"I won't say anything."

"Not a *thing*."

"Okay."

"And also it is a secret—you can't tell anyone or I will find out."

"Okay," said Phoebe in the quietest, meekest voice imaginable.

"What is it?" said Sofia.

"Well . . ." said Pippa and left a dramatic pause. "Alfie Broderson wants me to be his girlfriend."

The room went quiet.

"But you're a tiny child," said Carmen.

"I'm nearly twelve!"

"Literally the definition of a child."

Sofia sat down.

"Is that Alfie Broderson the rugby kid?"

"Yeah, he's awful; I don't like him," said Pippa quickly.

"Well good, because you are a child," said Carmen.

"Everyone says he likes you," said Phoebe shyly.

"The Primary *Fours* are talking about it?" said Pippa, trying not to look delighted. "That's terrible."

"Everyone's talking about it," said Phoebe. Pippa appeared to have forgotten her strict "no talking" rule. "He's the handsomest boy in the school. Some people say," she continued, muttering, "I think he looks like an idiot."

"So I just don't know what to do," said Pippa.

"Well, do you like him?" said Sofia, sitting down with her head at Pippa's level.

"*Sofia!*" said Carmen. "Stop it!"

"No!" said Sofia. "This is an important part of development. Anyway, I remember you at this age, don't forget."

"Not in *Primary Seven*!"

"Not long after," said Sofia.

But Sofia knew she had to take this seriously. Pippa's shape had already started to change. Lots of girls in her year, Sofia had noticed, had got breasts and some had started their periods. It used to be unheard of for that to happen in primary school; things were changing, she supposed. And she was absolutely here to support her daughters. That was very much the kind of mother she aspired to be, like all the handbooks said.

"But you don't want to go out with him?"

"I'm far too young. And he's a stupid boy."

"That's very sensible."

Pippa was nothing if not sensible. She beamed.

"The problem is," said Pippa, "when I say 'no thank you,' that just makes him ask more."

"Yes, that's true, darling," said Sofia. "I did explain that's what happens."

Carmen stared at her suddenly.

"What?"

"Oh, you know," said Sofia. "If you want a guy to really like you, treat them tough. You know that. It's hardly new science."

"It's Victorian nonsense is what it is!" said Carmen. "Don't fill her head with that rubbish!"

"Actually, I'm having a personal chat with my daughter right now?" said Sofia crossly.

Carmen swallowed. She couldn't help taking it as a dig. All that time she had been so over-the-top crazy about Oke, had pushed herself at him. For nothing.

"Did you think that about me?" she said, her voice low. "When Oke was here?"

"Carmen, you're a big girl who can run her own life," said Sofia. "And you wouldn't want my advice."

"But did you, though? Did you think I was throwing myself at him?"

"I don't think it's appropriate to talk about this in front of the girls."

"That means yes," said Pippa.

"Oh Lord," said Carmen, tears pricking her eyelids. Sofia turned to her.

"Oh, darling, you were so happy about Oke! You were so nuts about him! I thought I'd better leave you to it. What would you have done if I'd said he was looking a bit hunted? You'd have torn my head off."

Carmen blinked away tears.

"Where is Oke?" said Phoebe, out of the blue. "Is he still in the jungle? I thought he was going to be my new uncle. I liked him. Except for no birthdays," she said. "But you would still have got me a birthday present so that would have been okay. Well, maybe you could have bought me two. You know. To make up for Oke not believing in birthdays. But otherwise, I liked him a lot. Is he still in the jungle?"

Carmen swallowed hard. "I don't know," she said. "According to your mother, I threw myself at him and I should have behaved more like Pippa."

"Everyone should behave more like Pippa," said Phoebe sadly. "But it's very difficult."

"It isn't!" said Pippa. "Just be kind!"

Carmen looked at Sofia, who wasn't looking at her.

"Forget it," said Carmen. "You know, you're right. I think I should move out."

There was a gasp.

"You're doing *what*?" said Phoebe.

PHOEBE HURLED HERSELF at Carmen.

"You can't go!" she said. "You live here, with us?"

"Actually, she just came for a visit," said Pippa. "Then stayed for a *really long time*. Mommy said. I heard her on the phone."

"PIPPA!" said Sofia, and it was the first time Carmen had ever really heard her speak harshly to the child.

Sofia turned to Carmen. "I wish you'd let me know you were organized, so I had a chance to tell the children myself," she said icily. She was clearly furious. *Good*, thought Carmen.

"I thought you were going to stay here for*ever*," said Phoebe, looking tearful. Carmen pulled her into her lap, even though she was getting a little big for it.

"I'll come back and visit," she said. "And Rudi's coming! You'll like him!"

"Where are you going?" said Pippa.

"Ah. I don't know quite yet. But there are a lot of people in this house, aren't there?"

"Yes," sniffed Phoebe. "Daddy is for Jack, Mommy is for Pippa, and you're for me."

Despite the warm stove from heating chocolate, the underfloor heating, all the lovely comforts of Sofia's lovely house, the temperature plummeted.

"Don't be silly, darling," said Sofia, but there was a hiccup in her voice. Inside, she couldn't help feeling mutinous. It wasn't her fault that Pippa was her little shadow, always behaving herself, making friends, never in trouble, whereas Phoebe seemed so determined to make life difficult for herself. She loved the child—of course she did, to the ends of the earth. But sometimes she was just so *tricky*.

But she never thought she'd betrayed how she felt.

She moved over but Phoebe was still sitting on Carmen's lap

and Carmen studiously wasn't looking at her. *Bloody Carmen*, Sofia thought suddenly, teaching Phoebe it was okay just to lie around all day and not care about looking a total mess and eat sweets and drink hot chocolate, as if ending up in a minimum-wage retail job and sponging off your family at thirty was something to be proud of.

Bloody Sofia, thought Carmen. As soon as anyone messes up, they're out on their ear. Hopefully Phoebe won't take that lesson from this.

Chapter Eight

"Do you think I'm being evil?" said Sofia to Federico. She kept her voice low, even though the children were fast asleep a level above them, Eric was snuffling on his baby monitor, and Carmen was a full two stories below in the basement. "I mean, she's great with Eric, she really is."

Federico nodded. "Of course she has been," he said. "I'm just saying. She's staying here basically rent-free; I haven't seen any evidence of her saving any money for a deposit, which she absolutely should have been doing."

"Oh no, I have it," said Sofia, who had taken the peppercorn rent Carmen gave her for board and put it in a fast-growing investment account—a fact that would make Carmen absolutely furious when she found out about it. "But it's still not very much."

"Well, regardless . . ." said Federico. "I mean, you know I don't mind, really. But my mom really wants to come over and spend some time here, and she'd be happier down there, and when that guy moves in . . ."

Sofia looked at him. "You don't mind that he's a guy?"

"No, why would I?" said Federico. "I think it's what we need. Unless you're desperately hankering for an affair with a one-armed, ginger, religious maniac."

"That is *not funny*," said Sofia. "And if you say it any louder the kids will repeat it the second he arrives and he'll sue us for discrimination. And he'd be right to! I'd take that case."

"Uh-huh," said Federico. "Anyway, I like it. Time we got some God into those little heathens."

Sofia gave him a look.

"Do you want to take them to Mass?"

"Nooo," said Federico.

"Okay then."

"And what about Carmen?"

"SSSH!"

"This is what I mean," said Federico. "I know we have to have someone, but do we have to have *everyone*? I'd kind of like to be able to speak above a whisper *in my own house*. That's all. And eight people, even in our lovely big house . . . it's a lot. Most thirty-year-olds wouldn't even want to stay here."

"I know," said Sofia. "I know. You're right. It's time." She looked up at him. "I hope Phoebs doesn't mind too much."

"Don't worry so much about Phoebe, okay? Getting great grades isn't everything; we've said that before. As long as she tries her best."

"I know, I had a talk with her."

"There you go, it'll be fine. Stop worrying so much. The kids are lovely, the baby is lovely, Carmen will get over herself, you'll like being back at work. We are very lucky people."

She kissed him. "We are."

UPSTAIRS THE GIRLS were whispering.

"Mommy gave me the 'You Are Fine as You Are' talk again," said Phoebe.

"Oh no," said Pippa. "That is never good."

"Noooo. I didn't even do anything bad."

There was a long pause.

"Do you think Carmen is leaving because of me?" said Phoebe quietly, into the dark.

"Phoebe, I am going to be kind," said Pippa.

"Good," said Phoebe.

"So I will say nothing."

Chapter Nine

"*Oke?*" said Mary again, worried.

But Oke was hardly there; he had turned his head back up, face to the stars. His breathing was thick in his throat.

Mary shook him.

"Wake up . . . wake up . . . *Juan-Castillo!*"

The next few hours were a blur. A blur of helicopters, insurance papers, drips. Mary was, thankfully, an exceptionally good nurse. She accompanied Oke, delirious with malaria, back to the nearest town with a hospital. Oke, completely stupefied, was aware on some deep level that something was terribly, terribly wrong and yet he seemed quite unable to do anything about it.

The pain was intense, a burning ice, and Oke found he was dreaming of snow. Of white stars falling down on him while he lay down—on a car? Where was he? On the car? No, now he was on the ground. It was freezing; icy stars tumbling. Or snow. Or ice. Or he was boiling; the ice turning into hot shards that bored into his skin. He was burning up; he was too hot. He pulled at his clothes. People kept shouting at him. He couldn't hear what they were saying. It came and went; and now the sun was burning into him once again.

He was on the hood of a car staring at the sky. He was in a snow storm. Or was it? He was bumping along the ground, turned this way and that way. A woman was looking at him. He didn't under-stand. It wasn't his mother. It wasn't Carmen. Where was Carmen? Carmen was his . . . Was she in the snow? Why did it burn so?

Why wouldn't it stop snowing? How could he get cool? He tried to make a snow angel, but everything burned underneath him. He tried calling Carmen's name but nobody would answer, or if they did they had someone else's face, or he just couldn't get straight at all. And where had all the trees gone? Were they covered in snow? But these were jungle trees. It didn't snow here. It shouldn't snow here. It wasn't . . . it wasn't.

He heard a clanking noise from somewhere, like a hammering, but couldn't figure out what it was. He fell asleep—did he?—and awoke to a world white as snow, or was it not snow? Had it never been snow? Was it just a room? A white room? Had there been no snow all along?

He slept again. He did not know for how long. He woke up. He was no longer warm and no longer cold. He had no idea where he was; no idea what direction he was from home.

Chapter Ten

It was a freezing Sunday morning. Sofia had invited Rudi around for a getting-to-know-you session before she went back to work in a couple of days. Therefore Carmen had very huffily been looking through the Extra Room website and reading out the particularly sticky ones. "'Sharing with five men. Fondness for Computer Games and admiration for Vikings preferred' . . . Gosh, what does that mean?"

"Nazis," said Federico over the top of the *Financial Times*. "Incel Nazis."

"Okay," said Carmen. "But bills are included, right?"

The children ran about the tiny windy yard, collecting orange and yellow leaves that Sofia had some vague plan of turning into a collage. She was taking lots of pictures as it was supposed to be a lovely heartwarming family activity she could show off about on Instagram. However, Jack was already sneaking off to knock his ball against the wall, while Phoebe and Pippa had got into a fight about who was being most careful with the snail they had found. They had decided they wanted to keep it for the winter, the terrible result being they had dropped the snail and the shell had cracked. Sofia had wondered, not for the first time, how on earth that "no shouting" parenting technique worked out. Did they just call the dead snails collateral damage?

Eric was trying to crawl among the leaves, making loud noises of satisfaction and surprise and gummily eating quite a lot of leaves in the process, as the girls sniveled and blamed one another.

"What about this one?" said Carmen, totally ignoring the commotion. "'Drum specialist seeks similar. Must enjoy late nights' . . . twelve hundred pounds."

"Whereabouts?" said Federico.

"Mars . . . oh, hang on. Open-minded individual . . ."

"NOOOOOOOO."

The doorbell rang and a notification appeared on Sofia's phone.

"Oh yes," she said. "That's Rudi. For his acclimatization session. Before he moves in."

Carmen went quiet.

"On Tuesday," Sofia continued, her face pale as she scooped Eric up under one arm and went to answer the door.

Carmen glanced at Federico, who shrugged, unwilling to look like the bad guy. Carmen could tell, though, that there was no dividing Federico and Sofia on anything, ever; nothing they wouldn't have talked through. It might be bloody Sofia's idea, but he certainly wasn't going to disagree.

She sighed. Phoebe came up and put her sticky face next to Carmen's.

"Are you sad about the snail?" she said.

"I'm sad about leaving you, pumpkin," said Carmen, which immediately made Phoebe's face turn even sadder, and Carmen felt awful for employing emotional blackmail. "But you'll see me lots," she added hastily.

"Yes, but who's going to do Midnight Cookie Meeting?"

Carmen made a scandalized face. "We *never* talk about Midnight Cookie Meeting!"

"Oh no, I forgot!"

Sofia appeared at the sliding back doors with Rudi in tow, his freckly face cheerful.

"Hello, yon De Angeolo," he said jovially, holding up a bag. "I brought tiny bananas!"

Phoebe looked up at him, her face tearstained and mucky.

"You're not going to have Midnight Cookie Meeting!" she said, snottering and wiping it on the sleeve of her expensive Boden sweater. "And the snail is *dead*."

All credit to Rudi, he didn't show the slightest surprise at this incomprehensible statement, but moved forward to where Phoebe was now crouching on the ground.

"Aha," he said, seeing the snail. "Okay, well, can someone tell me where the nail polish is kept? I'll probably need to know that anyhow."

Pippa leapt up and got him some that Carmen had bought her for her birthday, much to Sofia's disgust. She was eyeing him suspiciously.

"What are you going to do?"

"You think I don't know how to fix a snail?"

"Do they teach you that in the army?" asked Jack. "Will you teach me what you learned in the army? Apart from the snail stuff."

"Okay. Get me a Band-Aid, too."

Rudi looked impressed by the entire first-aid armory Sofia had assembled in the drawer. "You could run a decent field hospital from here," he said over his shoulder, picking out a roll of bandage tape.

"That," said Sofia, with some surprise, "is the nicest thing anyone has said to me in ages."

"Oi," said Federico, grinning at her.

The children followed Rudi carefully as he knelt down by the snail. Carmen glanced over. His shoulders were broader than she'd realized.

"Okay, little fella," he said, opening the nail polish bottle with his teeth. "No sudden moves."

He grinned quickly and the late autumn sun struck his red hair, Carmen noticed, and turned it a sudden shocking gold.

He painted over the crack with nail polish, carefully taped up the slit in the snail's shell with the bandage tape, holding the tape neatly with his stump and pulling it off with his teeth.

"Can you hold the snail steady?" he said to Phoebe. "It's a big job."

"I can do it!" said Pippa. Rudi blinked.

"I need you to make him a field bed, though," he said, thinking quickly. "We're going to put him in a cozy leaf bed and leave him a treat. Of . . ."

"MINI BANANAS!" shouted Jack, pleased.

"You got it," said Rudi. "I see our youngest member already has the banana situation sussed."

Indeed, in all the commotion Eric had crawled through the leaves, beaming gummily, toward the bag of dwarf bananas, and was already grabbing merrily at them.

Carmen watched them all together. Phoebe's tears were drying, and Sofia and Federico were exchanging very excited looks that said, *Surely, finally, after years of unsuitable nannies ranging from the merely awful to actual burglary, do you think we've cracked it this time?*

Pippa was carefully building the most immaculate snail house there had ever been, and Jack was looking at this new man-around-the-house in an awestruck daze. Carmen realized for the first time, sadly and properly, that . . . she needed to move. She shouldn't be here. Sure, they loved her, but they were trying to build a family. They *were* a family. They didn't need her hanging around, eating all their food, getting in the way. Sofia was already so worried about going back to work, and she didn't need a little sister to stress over on top of everything else.

She went into the kitchen to make a pot of tea for everyone, which in itself was a bit unusual. Normally Sofia asked her to make tea when she was nursing and Carmen, who was usually in the middle of complaining about how she hadn't heard from Oke, would pout and say, "I'm not your slave." Then she'd remember she was living practically rent-free in her basement and get up to make it with terrible grace and quite badly.

But this time she did it of her own accord. Sofia came in and stood beside her.

"Look," she said, "Phoebe really doesn't want you to leave. There's not a ton of space down there but . . . please, stay if you like."

"No," said Carmen, forcing it out. "No. It's the right thing. I see it."

Sofia patted her arm, and didn't offer again.

"Rudi seems nice," said Carmen.

"I am *very* nice," said Rudi, reappearing. "Can I have tea?"

He twinkled at Carmen, who at first didn't notice, until she did and handed him the cup of tea with a grin and Sofia thought, *Thank God she's going.* And thank God she was going back to work. She might deal with family law, wills and divorces all day, but it was still a lot less bother than her own family.

Chapter Eleven

Carmen was decorating the shop and sizing up the house, ferreting among the contents of dusty attic and walking through the frigidly cold rooms of Mr. McCredie's living quarters. He had a very fancy drawing room that hadn't been touched since 1952; a very old kitchen, likewise; then the stairs went on up, curling to places she'd never even been. The house was completely unsuitable for living in: freezing, dusty, and with scary Bakelite-style plug fittings. Carmen thought of Sofia's delicious underfloor heating and sighed. Maybe if she'd been a better housemate, or a better girlfriend, maybe maybe maybe . . .

Carmen looked around the old rooms, full of regret. Of course, Mr. McCredie might not even say yes.

Well, she gave herself a talking-to. Buck up! Things to do! So that, at least, she'd still have a job.

She went up to the attic and fetched down the Christmas doll's house, populated by toy mice, and put it into the window on a bed of cotton wool, then turned on the little fairy lights. Their warm glow lit up the front of the shop, cozy and pretty. The other window was for the train set. All around the two displays were as many popular Christmas books as she could find: beautiful editions of lovely old stories, and new adventures; ghost stories set in snowy wastes; love stories that hinged on whether or not someone was Santa Claus.

At least the shop looked gorgeous, even if everything else was a mess. Despite her worries over what she was going to say to Mr.

McCredie, there was something calming and wholesome about decorating for Christmas. It was hard not to feel a little cheered by the shop turning twinkly and adorable. She was just admiring her handiwork when she heard a loud, grating. skirling noise coming from outside.

Carmen was from the west coast; she'd grown up with the sound of the pipes (and excellent ice cream). She liked them, and occasionally found the music extremely moving. In appropriate amounts.

This skirling, coming from the open door of Bobby's hardware shop, was absolutely relentless. And the grating piped versions of pop songs, once they started, carried on all day.

Everyone up and down the street had complained about it. Not only that, but Bobby's beloved buckets and pails that used to line the opening of his shop were now filled with cheap tam-o'-shanters, horrible plasticky tartan-wearing dolls—made overseas, of course—and other cheap and nasty tat. Worst of all—for Carmen and Mr. McCredie, at least—were the big signs above it all, advertising "DOLL'S £6.99" and "T-SHIRT'S £9.99" on luminous orange flash cards, the apostrophes black and vivid. It was unbelievably hideous.

Bobby knew it. He still wore his draper's apron, but he looked embarrassed and awkward and kept pretending he hadn't seen anyone. Crawford in the clothes shop was writing long, elaborately worded letters to the local council, who were underfunded, understaffed, and didn't have this high up their list of priorities as long as someone was paying the rent. Bronagh had muttered about it—she obviously had plans afoot and Carmen didn't know exactly what they were, but she hoped it involved some kind of silencio curse.

Cheap plastic flags fluttered in the wind and Carmen, who needed a box of staples to make the mice stand up in her window display, hoped Bobby had some in stock. She had to get the staples quite quickly before a child came past and caught her stapling a mouse—she didn't need the trauma again. She headed down the street.

The once-beautiful, useful little store had become a blot on the landscape. You could already see, when people came to take pictures of the street, they were cropping it out, and moving their loved ones out of the way; whereas for a long time, the picturesque mops, buckets, old-fashioned brooms and broomsticks in the quaint little shop had turned up regularly on Instagram. Of course, not many people had then bought a mop to take home as a keepsake.

Carmen stared at it in horror. Bobby was trudging about inside. He'd been made to wear a tartan cap and a kilt, except the kilt was cheap, with no real pleats, in a bright red synthetic Royal Stewart, and Bobby was just wearing it with normal socks and slip-on shoes. It looked absolutely horrendous.

He caught her staring through the window and blushed. Carmen was about to walk back up the hill but she remembered the staples.

"Hey, Bobby," she said, going through the open door. "How's it going?"

She had to raise her voice to be heard above a frankly horrible bagpipe version of "Silent Night."

"I always liked the pipes," she said, a bit mournfully.

"So did I," said Bobby. His normal, round-faced yeoman appearance had gone. There were dark shadows underneath his eyes. A large pair of noise-canceling headphones was sitting on the desk. He followed her gaze.

"Aye, sorry. I'm not allowed to wear them when there's customers."

"Oh God," said Carmen. "I'm so sorry. Can't you tell him to just buzz off?"

Bobby shook his head. "I signed a thing. But also, Carmen, I'm making money."

"Oh God, really?"

He nodded sadly. "Yeah. People want this . . . stuff."

Carmen picked up a Velcro Nessie that gave her a static burn. As she did so one of its spikes fell off.

"I don't mind people having stuff," she said. "But does it have to be such very awful stuff?"

"I don't get to choose what I have in stock," said Bobby sadly. "It's all centrally ordered."

"I bet," said Carmen, looking around at the mass-produced tat. It even smelled horrible: like a fire in a nylon factory. "Oh, Bobby."

"Aye."

"Was there nothing else?"

"Nothing else that would make the money that doesn't require a food license for coffee."

"And you wouldn't want to fight the coffee people anyway."

He shook his head. "Naw."

The door opened, and Carmen realized, to her horror, that Bobby's original bell had gone. Now the door made a harsh electronic beeping sound.

"New security system," muttered Bobby sadly.

"That is bloody *awful*," said Carmen. "I mean, it's all shit, but that's *desecration*."

"Glad to hear your opinion," said a voice. "Who the hell are you?"

THE VOICE BELONGED to a tall, overweight man dressed in a very loud purple-and-blue tartan suit that Carmen recognized immediately as coming from Crawford's clothes shop and, thus, must have cost a fortune.

There are some people you can just tell are so irritatingly confident that anything you might want to say to them would simply bounce off, like titanium. Jackson McClockerty was undeniably one of them. He was the kind of guy, Carmen thought, that if you disagreed with him in any way would, depending on how much he wanted to sleep with you, either call you "feisty" or ask if you were on your period. It seemed unlikely there was a middle ground. His eyes flicked her up and down in a way she couldn't bear and made her want to kick him and run away, the way the children weren't allowed to.

"Carmen," she said, unwilling to give any more away. Bobby, meanwhile, was surreptitiously hiding his noise-canceling headphones under the cash desk.

Jackson's eyes narrowed. He had a large face with big features, a lot of overlong curly sandy hair cut in a mullet, and thick eyebrows.

"I recognize you," he said. "Don't you work with that crazy old man up at the bookshop?"

"I *beg* your pardon?" said Carmen, appalled, before she realized she'd fallen for it.

"Ooh, a feisty one!" said Jackson. "Come on, you know who I mean. He's hardly a spring chicken."

"If you're referring to my boss, his name is Mr. McCredie."

"I like snotty girls," said Jackson. "You'd almost think she was posh, wouldn't you, Bobby? Except she obviously isn't."

He laughed, satisfied with himself. Bobby stared straight at the floor. Carmen decided she hated this man so much she would kill him with one of his own crappy cheap "heritage" swords, if they wouldn't immediately bend on impact.

Jackson propped his ample backside up on a beautiful old wood chest, not unlike an apothecary table, which used to hold every type of screw and nail imaginable. Now, it was stuffed with crappy bagpipe fridge magnets, their plastic sides over-spilling the drawers, lending the entire thing an untidy fly-by-night look. It went against all of Carmen's shopkeeping instincts.

"Actually, I'm coming up there today," he said, waiting to see her reaction.

Carmen knew he was doing it on purpose, and it drove her crazy. When someone is trying to wind you up and succeeds in winding you up it is one of the worst feelings on earth. You feel irritated and cheated all at once. Carmen, whose temper could get the better of her, felt herself bristling all over.

"Oh yeah?" she said.

"Oh *yeah*," he said, mimicking her west-coast vowels. "Yeah, he asked me to drop in. See if I could help his business out. Hear he needs cash."

He watched Carmen's swallowed-down fury with amusement.

"We're doing fine, actually," said Carmen, annoyed that she was finding herself showing off in front of this horrible man.

"Oh well, I'm so *delighted* for you," he said. "I mean, we all want the same thing, don't we? We all want Edinburgh to prosper. We don't want our beautiful shops taken away and turned into chain fast-food shops with plastic frontage."

His face was smiling but his pale eyes were as cold as a reptile's. Carmen knew full well he was trying to get a rise out of her and she was desperately struggling against the urge to give him the satisfaction.

"I have to go," she said. "Bye, Bobby. Oh, wait. I need some staples!"

"Um," said Bobby, and she could see this was the cruelest cut of all. "We don't stock them anymore. Sorry."

Chapter Twelve

"Mr. McCredie?"

She had to get to him first, and she felt pink and a bit shaky. Sofia, of course, would have dealt with him with elegance and condescension. Only stupid Carmen, she thought, would let a guy like that wind her up.

"Mr. McCredie!"

He came lumbering through from the stacks. In his hand was a beautiful first edition of *The Modern Prometheus*, which absolutely should not be handled like that, so obviously she'd startled him.

"That is a lot of noise for this early in the morning, Carmen," he said, somewhat reprovingly.

"It's nearly eleven o'clock! Also, I met Jackson McClockerty. And he's evil!"

Mr. McCredie frowned. "I believe . . . he's coming to see me with several interesting ideas about how we could maximize income from the shop to do with . . . uh . . . Scottie dog tea towels, as I recall. And obviously I need money. Rather soon, too!"

Carmen took a breath. The time had come. She swallowed hard. She was ready.

"No," she said. "No. You can say no to Jackson. We'll make the money. Listen. You need to rent out one of your bedrooms."

"I *beg* your pardon?"

"To me. You need to rent a bedroom to me. I need somewhere to live. And I—well, Sofia—well, anyway. We will pay you money for it."

Mr. McCredie looked puzzled. "And you want to live . . . here?"

"God no," said Carmen. "But I need a place to live, you have extra rooms, and I have cash. Well, Sofia has cash and she said she'll pay a deposit."

"Goodness," said Mr. McCredie. "I hadn't thought of that. It's not really in a fit condition."

"Nothing is," said Carmen glumly. "Oh, but also, we need to find a way to open up the stacks. I don't know how, but we have to do it. So people can properly look for books, not just ask you in case you've heard of them."

"But I always have heard of them."

"You so haven't! Someone asked for the new Floriana Grawford mystery the other day"—Carmen was referring to the zillion-selling series about a clearly once-beautiful lady GP who ran a beautifully appointed, inexpensive rest home for people and their adorable dogs and also solved murders in her spare time—"and you looked confused."

"I mean real books, books that matter."

"All books matter!" said Carmen. "I should get that on a T-shirt. No, hang on, I absolutely shouldn't. Anyway. In our case, it's true. You should know what people want and what's just out."

"But why wouldn't people rather read great works of import?" said Mr. McCredie, polishing his glasses.

"Well, for the same reason that sometimes you want boeuf bourguignon for dinner and sometimes you want a cheeseburger."

He looked at her in consternation. "A *what* burger?"

Carmen rolled her eyes. "All right, sometimes you want . . . a lemon posset."

"Well quite," said Mr. McCredie. "What's your point?"

"I'm saying you put values on types of books that other people don't have. I think if you really love books you love all sorts of books, not just dusty books."

Mr. McCredie frowned. "You want me to love books where

someone is married to a psychopath for twenty years but hasn't realized?"

"Yes! If they're good."

"Aha," said Mr. McCredie, looking around. "But how . . . how are you going to sort out the stacks?"

"I don't know that yet," said Carmen. "But you'll get your money without shilling tea towels for that . . . rogue. And I can move in, like, tomorrow. And pay you rent straightaway." She tried to keep the desperation out of her voice.

She could hear heavy footsteps approaching.

"Well, let me do it! We could make more money if we increased the square footage, put more out on display?"

Mr. McCredie sighed.

"I'll even dust it all!"

"Am I going to lose my reading nook?"

"Well," said Carmen, "I'm sure we can move it. And anyway, you'll be in the *Antarctic*; you won't miss it."

"Hey! Hello!" came a loud, aggressive voice from the other side of the door.

"You'll be sitting, all wrapped up in wet-weather gear, at the very front of the prow like Reepicheep, looking out, always out . . ."

"To the ever further south," said Mr. McCredie, his voice sounding dazed.

"Great vistas of white sidle into view," improvised Carmen. "The great snowy deserts of the tip of the world. Untouched. Pristine. So many places where no human has ever set foot. And. Uh. Penguins. Absolutely everywhere. You can probably have one as a pet."

"You very much cannot," said Mr. McCredie, but his voice was far away.

"You can make your pet penguin wear a little hat and scarf and set foot on your . . . foot skis."

Carmen's knowledge of what actually went on in the Antarctic was hazy at best.

"And you'll set off toward the horizon of a sun that never sets, of a great white light, gleaming off the ice fields like diamonds. Mountains towering higher than anyone could imagine. A great crystal hall of palaces . . ."

Carmen realized she was about to recite bits of "Let It Go" from *Frozen*, but Mr. McCredie didn't seem to have noticed, his eyes still fixed on a point far away. He didn't seem to hear Jackson McClockerty, either, who was now chuntering about having his checkbook open and ready.

"Yes," he said, and his pale cheeks glowed pink.

"So you'll let me?"

"Yes."

Carmen sagged with relief.

"Okay. You go and sit down; I'll bring you your tea."

She marched back into the shop, looking smug.

"Hi there, hen. I think I've got a meeting with your boss?"

"I'm afraid he's unavailable."

"Really?" said Jackson, folding his arms.

"Really," said Carmen.

Jackson looked around. "What even is this place?"

"It's the tax office," said Carmen sullenly. "No wonder it looks unfamiliar."

"Books," went on Jackson dismissively.

"Yes," said Carmen. "It's a bookshop. It's where people come to step into other lives, other places, for a while."

"Why do they want to do that, then? I love being me."

"Good for you," said Carmen.

He snorted. "Well, good luck surviving Christmas."

"Thank you," said Carmen.

Jackson reached into an expensive man bag and pulled out a flimsy, folded-over book covered in tartan.

"You could just put up a stand of these," he said defiantly.

Carmen took it. It was a tiny book titled *History of Your Clan*, in this case Lindsay, made up of the most cheaply printed and photocopied bits of information Wikipedia had to offer.

"Oh God, no thanks," she said.

"Twelve ninety-nine retail," said Jackson.

Carmen's mouth dropped open. "You are kidding me! They look like they're worth about twenty-five pence!"

"You've got a lot to learn, darling."

"Well, we'll try it our way," she said, going pink again.

"You do that," said Jackson. "I'll see you after Christmas, when the desperate trade has gone and you're all about to starve to death."

"Oh my God, you're *horrible*," burst out Carmen.

"I'm not horrible!" said Jackson, taken by surprise. "I'm saving these shops from being turned into apartments or closed down and left empty! I'm a philanthropist! I've got awards."

"For selling people flammable Nessies."

"For selling people reasonably priced novelties to remember their happy trip to this lovely city."

"That you are making very much *unlovely*," said Carmen.

Jackson opened the door. The horrible sound of "A Spaceman Came Travelling," performed on the bagpipes, filtered through, and Jackson marched off up the street.

Chapter Thirteen

It was actually happening. On a freezing, freezing day in late November she was moving. Everywhere was the sound of cars skidding off icy roads. It was a day for the full thermals. And a spare pair of gloves, for when you inevitably left yours on the bus.

Carmen looked around the tiny basement room and sighed. There was only one more thing to pack: the card Phoebe had made her for her thirty-first birthday, a slightly awkward affair as Carmen had gone out with Idra and some other friends the night before and had far too many Negronis, i.e., more than one, seeing as she was in no way a professional Negroni drinker, and it is not a drink for lightweights. She had stumbled in extremely late and attempted to call Oke, leaving several very long messages on his voice mail, the contents of which she was subsequently not exactly sure of. As Oke hadn't responded in any way, she couldn't tell what she'd left and it made her want to curl up and die every single time she thought about it. She did not know what Oke was doing that day.

"MEA AMOR!"

At least he recognized it was his mother by his bedside, in the white room. So many faces came and went. None were the one he wanted to see, but his mother was something.

"You have been *so* ill!"

His mother bustled around the room, folding up the clothes

she'd brought for him—after months in the jungle, his were effectively a bunch of rags.

"I know," he said weakly, happy to see her again.

"You're so thin! Here!" She proffered a huge box of pastries. He looked at them, unable to think of anything he'd like less.

He blinked. "It was malaria, yes?"

"Bad one, too," said his mother. She did not emote—it was not in her nature—or tell him how horribly worried she had been; but there was a quiet moment between them.

"I don't understand," he said. "I had my injections. I took my tablets."

His mother shook her head.

"You were so deep in the jungle," she said, with some pride in her voice. "It was an unusual strain. The doctors were very worried. Trust my son to get a very rare and special disease."

He half smiled at this. "It's nothing to be proud of," he said. "It's awful. I can't believe we ended the expedition like that."

"Pff," said his mother. "I am sure you did wonderfully."

He looked around. "I can't . . . I can't find my phone."

"It didn't make it to the hospital," said his mother. "I think Mary said it was lost at the helicopter."

"Can I . . . ? Can you get me a new phone?"

"No," said his mother. "Rest and peace and quiet. That's what you need."

PHOEBE AND JACK had bounced *very* noisily into Carmen's room at 7 a.m. on her birthday morning, Pippa following behind at a safe distance to show she was too grown-up and cool to bother with the fuss, just as Carmen was beginning to stir. She had a horrible sensation that something had gone terribly wrong, somewhere, and everything was a total disaster and also she hurt all over and wanted to be sick.

As Phoebe and Jack showered her with kisses (Phoebe) and gifts (Jack) and Pippa made several pointed remarks that it smelled weird in the room, like Christmas trifle, and had somebody been *smoking*, Carmen gradually came around. Her head was thumping like the nightclub she'd inadvisably ended up in, and it was dawning on her that she had left Oke at least one message and, checking her phone, saw in fact that it was three, and one was seven minutes long.

"OPEN THE PRESENT!" Phoebe shouted in an agony of waiting, unable to believe someone didn't appear to be as uncomplicatedly excited about a birthday as you did when you were eight.

What had it been about? Oh God. Carmen remembered now. She had begged him—*begged* him—to call her. And there had been a brief fight with Idra over the phone. Oh God.

She checked her phone again.

Of course he hadn't replied. There was just a message from Idra that said, I forgive you. Drink some water.

"Maybe I will just open a window," said Pippa, ostentatiously waving her hand in front of her face.

Carefully, every crinkle of the paper hurting her head, Carmen unwrapped the gift. It was a bottle of perfumed bath oil the children had obviously chosen themselves. Sofia wouldn't have had something like it in the house, as the lid was a huge synthetic rose, scattered with glitter, and the oil itself smelled like melted ice cream that had fallen on hot pavement.

"Wow, that's . . . that's very strong," said Carmen, her eyes watering.

"We chose it!" said Phoebe.

"I let the girls choose it," said Jack. "Perfume is stupid."

"Jack, stop being so *sexist*."

"I'm not *sexist*!" complained Jack, who rarely rose to the bait of being surrounded by females at all times. "I hate aftershave as well! That's stupid, too!"

"I think something that smells nice was a Very Good Present today," said Pippa.

"All right, Pippa," said Carmen. "I get it. Can I possibly have a shower?"

"*No!*" said Phoebe. "It's your birthday breakfast! Come on!"

"It's seven o'clock!" said Carmen. "And I've got the day off just so I don't have to get up this morning! Don't I get breakfast in bed?"

Phoebe shook her head.

"Mommy said you can't because you'd make a mess."

Carmen would have laughed if she hadn't been so miserable and in so much pain. She got up. Her skin felt sticky and unpleasant.

"Please can I have a shower?" she said.

Pippa shook her head. "We have to get to school," she said.

"Oh well, as long as it's convenient for you," said Carmen, dragging herself upstairs.

Sofia raised a perfectly curved eyebrow. She had joined Carmen and her mates for two drinks early on in Tiger Tiger then excused herself to go back to the baby, which she didn't mind doing, seeing as it looked as if it were going to start getting messy, which, predictably, it did. She hadn't wanted to be there for the inevitable "Evil Sofia is chucking me out" conversation, which had indeed taken place, but only as a brief interlude between the "Why doesn't Oke love me?" tears and the "I think I'll just phone him" all-in wrestling match.

Upstairs the kitchen was immaculate and Federico was turning out pancakes on the stovetop. He smiled at her sympathetically. "The kids really wanted to see you," he said.

Carmen nodded. It was nice, it really was. Phoebe had made her a card. It was a picture of a unicorn with stars coming out of its bum and she had written, *You are 31 which is a bit old but not as old as Mommy.* Carmen had thanked her for her frankness. Jack's said *Happy Birthday Carmen*, which was the bare minimum but Carmen was okay with that. Pippa cleared her throat and drew out a piece of paper meaningfully. Carmen glanced at Federico, who immediately handed her a vast freshly made latte which she gulped at gratefully. Sofia was feeding Eric on the sofa and waved a hand vaguely.

"C is for *caring* she is our great aunt," announced Pippa solemnly, declaiming from the piece of paper.

"I'm not your great-aunt, I'm just your aunt," said Carmen, rubbing at the mascara gloop in the corner of her eye.

"You're a great one," Phoebe said. Carmen smiled.

"Well, it's just to make the poyum fit," explained Pippa.

"A is for *amazing*, you try to help even when you can't."

"Oh," said Carmen.

"R is for *red wine*, Carmen likes it a lot."

"Yeah, all right."

"M is for the *man* that Carmen has not got."

Everyone laughed, but Carmen definitely thought she caught a slightly gloating expression from Pippa.

"E is for *every day* you go to work in a shop.

"N is for *nice things* we hope you have got.

"For your birthday," she added quickly.

Federico started the clapping, and Carmen joined in wearily.

"Thanks, Pippa, that was lovely," she said.

"You can keep it forever," said Pippa, handing over the paper.

"I will," said Carmen sincerely.

"Pancakes?" said Federico, and all the children shouted "Yayyyy!" for the object of their early wake-up and birthday-card distribution.

Carmen sat down—she couldn't face the pancakes and the smell of the maple syrup made her want to hurl, but she had to look willing as she opened Sofia's typically thoughtful gifts: a classy evening bag, for all the amazing social events Carmen never went to; a lovely bottle of Pickering's Gin; and a delicate bracelet that was nicer than anything Carmen would have chosen for herself. She was lucky, Carmen knew, despite everything; despite the disappointments and the awfulness of the situation. She was lucky to be in a world where she had a family who loved her.

Now, PICKING UP Pippa's card to pack it away—she would keep it—her heart sank further. That had been the last time she'd tried to contact Oke. That had been the final nail in the coffin. She had handled the whole thing so badly.

She knew on one level Sofia had been more than good to her and needed the room. But she couldn't help how she felt on this freezing morning.

She threw her stuff carelessly into her suitcase, sighing mightily all the while. Under her bed she found a wooden ornament for a Christmas tree. Goodness knows how it had landed down there. Oh, now she remembered: Phoebe had adopted it and started taking it to bed like a soft teddy bear, even though that had proved extremely uncomfortable every time she tried to roll over. It was a wooden circle quartered by a cross. She remembered the night she and Oke had shopped at the Christmas market for it; remembered explaining to Oke what they did at Christmas. Oh dear. This was not helping, not at all.

There was a rap at the basement door. Carmen officially had her own entrance, which Sofia preferred she used so as to keep her muddy boots, coat, bags, and books out of the pristine upper house. So Carmen always used the upstairs front door, partly to be annoying and partly because she didn't like feeling like the hired help who had to use a separate entrance. Even though that is exactly what the basement door had been used for since the house was built, two hundred years before.

Carmen frowned. She knew, of course, who it was; she just hadn't expected him quite this early.

Standing there, tugging a large bag with his good arm, was a beaming Rudi.

"Hello!" he said, shaking raindrops off his red flopping hair like a dog. "Well, I'm here!"

Carmen stared at him.

"You're expecting me today, right? One arm, good with small people?"

"Yes, of course," said Carmen. "I just haven't gone yet, that's all."

"Oh," said Rudi. "I thought they were going to empty out another room . . ."

"Well, they're not," said Carmen. This came out so much more bitter than she'd expected. She was cross with herself.

"Where are you going?"

Rudi peered into Carmen's room, which was at the front of the building; it was small and below ground level, with bars on the windows to discourage thieves, but it was neat, warm, and clean. Sofia, to Carmen's annoyance, had just had a cozy new beige carpet fitted.

"Wow," Rudi said.

"Uh, is it okay?" said Carmen, who had herself slagged it off almost nonstop to Idra.

"Oh yeah, it's just . . . well, I'm not used to having a room to myself, that's all. Between barracks and home," he added.

Carmen felt guilty for complaining about it.

"The trucks come past early morning and bang all over the cobbles."

"That's still quieter than reveille, believe me."

"Okay," she said, heaving out her bag. "I'll leave you to unpack."

She turned around.

"I'm really sorry," said Rudi. "I genuinely didn't mean to kick you out."

"You're not," said Carmen, her guilt getting the better of her. "Sofia's going back to work, she needs someone full-time, not just occasional babysitting. It's nothing to do with you, honestly."

"Well," said Rudi, with a twinkle in his eye, "you'll be in and out, won't you? This isn't the start of a blood feud that will cascade down the generations?"

"No," said Carmen. "We'll be okay. I suppose."

"Good," said Rudi. "And maybe I can take you out for a drink sometime, make it up to you."

Carmen looked at him to see if he meant it, but he was neutrally putting his suitcase down, as if completely unconcerned.

She thought little of it, but the idea, at a very very low point, warmed her cold heart.

"Thanks for that," she said, and meant it.

THEY WERE PUTTING up the Christmas market as she rattled her case across Princes Street Gardens: acres of little wooden huts, glühwein sellers, rides and balloons and grottos for children, and a huge Ferris wheel that went all the way up over the top of the city, while a disembodied voice sternly and repeatedly told you to keep your fingers away from the doors.

Lights were strung from every lamppost and glistened in every shop window, so that even if it got dark at 3 p.m.—which it did—there was still glittering magic to be found in the heart of the city; vistas that would lift the spirits regardless of the weather. There was the scent of coffee and gingerbread in the air, a touch of frost on the garden, a happy anticipation, even as the mornings grew darker and frostier.

Carmen took the long way around, trying to walk herself out of her bad mood. She found herself retracing the steps she'd taken when she'd first arrived in the city, when Sofia was worried she would get lost. Through the beautiful gardens, up the Mound, the great winding road past the art galleries—well, one art gallery, that she'd been dragged around with the children several times to see the skating minister—and one mysterious building that didn't seem to do anything, which Jack was convinced was the entrance to a top-secret organization.

Then the great row of buildings at the top of the Mound that led up to the castle itself, including Mylnes Court, which Carmen refused to look at.

On up; Carmen tried to count the memories of chilled nights on these ancient stairs, stairs that felt carved out of the rock of the volcano on which the city stood; stairs that had been worn smooth by many years of scampering feet, up and down. Even shop girls' feet, sad and disappointed in life, thought Carmen, feeling slightly comforted. How many had scampered up here, to beg forgiveness for their sins and lustful hearts, at the Tolbooth Kirk, or at the great cathedral of St. Giles itself, with the ancient heart of Lothian stonework outside, where, even now, locals would spit as they passed, to show their contempt for the hangings that once took place there.

It was hard, as she climbed, inside and through the ancient courtyards, not to feel a part of it somehow. In a city like Edinburgh— where the trams didn't go anywhere; where the hills were too steep to cycle easily; where everybody walked, knowing the many shortcuts to avoid the hordes of tourists and the back routes you could thread your way through—it all made you feel more connected. On these ancient streets, with the living, breathing city that went back for centuries, you were only ever one step, really, one quiet ancient back staircase, from stumbling across an actual market full of hay and cattle at the Grassmarket, with people touting their wares; the noise of squealing pigs and charging chickens everywhere; soldiers marching in bright red jackets; horses tied up at the many water troughs that remained for them; people on their knees in the kirk in every manner of fashions. Edinburgh didn't change; the ancient stairs grew more worn; the cars had come, but now they were being driven out again. The witch burning had stopped but there was, according to Bronagh, still more than one way to burn an Edinburgh witch, and they never stopped trying.

The solidity of the city, it's never-changing nature, soothed Carmen somewhat. It always did. It might be street-cleaning wheels on those cobbles, not cartwheels, but it was a reminder that things happened and changed and the walls of the houses still stood; the castle remained, stern and proud, with every citizen assured of its protection.

It was hard for Carmen to make out Mr. McCredie's house from the Royal Mile side. The shop was at the bottom of the building, but it was about one and a half floors below the part of the Royal Mile she had just come up to from Princes Street. She had lived here for a year and still found it utterly bamboozling.

There were a couple of gift shops, some notably tackier than others, which Carmen immediately blamed Jackson McClockerty for, and the buildings of the Lawnmarket were alternately high gray and white, with little gilded moldings that mentioned the year of construction, 1639 in this case, although the shop was later. Mr. McCredie's had a tiny narrow entry with a large black gate, surrounded on either side by knitwear shops. She didn't expect an answer as she pulled the old clanging bell.

But to her surprise, there was a sound from behind the gate.

"Carmen?" came Mr. McCredie's voice. "Is that you?"

There followed a cracking noise as someone attempted to rattle the bolt. Then again. Then a horrible screech.

"Ah," said Mr. McCredie. "You see, I don't . . ."

"You never use your own front door?" said Carmen, incredulous.

"Well, I . . ."

He never had any visitors, thought Carmen. Of course. Oh God. Well. Here she went. Armed with the new electric indoor throw Sofia had bought her as a guilty leaving present. Suddenly, she felt nervous.

"Okay, if you turn the handle at the same time . . ." came Mr. McCredie's voice. They went for it and gradually, and with a horrible creak, the old metal gate slowly pulled open. Carmen took a deep breath and prepared to step into her new home.

Chapter Fourteen

Carmen found herself standing in a long, half-paneled hallway. She was on the ground floor from the Royal Mile side, which made it the top of the stairwell from the Victoria Street side. Underfoot were black-and-white diamond tiles; on the walls were large portraits, and at the end of the passageway stood a grandfather clock that ticked sonorously. The hall was freezing. The clock, however, was beautiful: dark polished wood, with a gold-painted angel figure inside of it, pointing at words in a book. Carmen would have liked to linger. There were several doors leading off the passageway.

"So . . ." she said. Then she handed over a large box of chocolate cookies which Sofia had also pressed on her as a present for her new landlord.

"Good, good," said Mr. McCredie. "These should travel well. We can perhaps break them out on voyage as a special treat on New Year's Day."

Carmen frowned. "I think it's just a normal ship," she said. "I don't think it's going to be a terrible hardship voyage."

"Oh, but only on a hardship voyage," said Mr. McCredie, "does a man discover his mettle! His very forged-iron heart!"

"Okay," said Carmen, but couldn't help thinking of Oke, deep in the lost jungle. Was he finding himself? Or finding that really good-looking girl with the excellent braids?

"So, which is my room?"

Mr. McCredie immediately raised his hands to his head.

"I knew I meant to do something," he said. "Sorry, sorry, sorry. I'm afraid you'll have to choose one."

He gestured around the corner from the grandfather clock. This was another narrower, darker passage, lined, inevitably, with bookshelves. And off to the left, a winding staircase, quite different to the staircase that led down to the shop.

"Head up there," he said. "Pick one. I hardly ever go up there myself."

Carmen squeezed her eyes shut. Oh God. How bad was it going to be? Edinburgh was wet year-round; there was absolutely no chance he'd done repair works on the roof. When he'd said yes, that it would be fine for her to move in, she'd assumed he had a room for her, something laid out.

Instead . . .

"First, let me show you around here," said Mr. McCredie. And Carmen obediently followed him. "Now, here's the kitchen."

The kitchen did actually look like it could be stuck in a museum of some kind. It appeared completely untouched since about 1955. There was an old black range that looked utterly impossible to use, a sideboard full of china all on show, wooden shelves which held bowls and ancient cooking tools, a fireplace, and a scrubbed wooden table. There was slightly curled-up linoleum on the floor and no extractor fan. There was a window that looked out onto two opposing walls and gave Carmen absolutely no further insight into the layout of the property.

There were old products on the shelves, too: Brasso and Omo and an ancient-looking twin tub with a hose protruding from it. Carmen was frankly surprised not to see a mangle. On the plus side, it was clean. That was definitely something.

"What do you eat?" said Carmen.

"Well, I like sardines," said McCredie. "And cookies, of course!" He thrust a hearty tin toward her.

"You eat *ship's cookies*?"

"And many limes."

Carmen's face fell. She followed him through to the large drawing room she had seen already, with its slippery armchairs, ancient photographs, and cheerless air.

Up the front stairs was another floor filled with doors. Carmen attempted to open one. Behind it was a space entirely filled with books. And another.

"Oh yes. I must get those sorted," said Mr. McCredie.

"Mr. McCredie, if you cleared these books out and Airbnb'd it, you'd be a millionaire by now," said Carmen.

"Yes," said Mr. McCredie. "Well, there are many things in my life I've been told to do to be a millionaire. Also, I was a millionaire, I think. Once."

Carmen looked at him, but you couldn't be cross with Mr. McCredie for long, especially with the rent he was charging her.

"I spend most evenings downstairs in the shop," Mr. McCredie was saying, and Carmen didn't blame him. Oh, how she missed the Wells Street house already, with its lovely big kitchen, something always cooking in the AGA or the slow cooker, someone always around to chat to. She might even miss Pippa's bassoon practice, and she never thought she'd feel that. She'd even managed to get Sofia addicted to *Married at First Sight* after the children had gone to bed—a guilty pleasure Sofia would never have entertained before—and they would sit together on the sofa in the TV room with tea or, depending on how close they were to the weekend, wine and a packet of potato chips. Sofia would fret that she should be doing more yoga and she hadn't been to her book group in months, and Carmen would cheerily say, screw it, it was maternity leave, and someone was about to have a big bust-up at the couples' dinner party and anyway she was recovering from a terrible heartbreak and needed the company.

Those had been good nights. Better than she'd realized at the time.

Now . . . now she would be going downstairs to work then coming back up here to do what? Perch on the divan? Of course there was no internet; she'd have to sort that out, too. The plugs in the walls didn't even look like they took modern devices; they were round and brass and frankly dangerous-looking.

Well. If she'd looked properly before . . . if she hadn't been so pigheaded and given herself more options. It wasn't a huge deal, it was completely normal to go and find an apartment, to meet some strangers you didn't know and hand them all your money. She sighed. This place was a steal, that much was true, and in the very heart of the city. She supposed it didn't matter that spider's webs stretched over every doorframe. Carmen did not like being mean to spiders, which included breaking their homes, but there was going to be absolutely no help for it. They spanned the kitchen like it was still Halloween. The drawing room, despite its four windows, front and aft, was static and dust-filled and cheerless. It was like a curated museum of pieces that must have been old even when Mr. McCredie was young. Carmen half expected to find little exploratory notes on the walls, or creepy faceless models wearing old-fashioned clothes picking up a coal scuttle. It looked like a doll's house. It was frightening and she hated it and she wanted to go home.

Carmen swallowed hard and told herself she was a grown-up, and she had to be brave.

"So, I can choose any room?" she managed finally.

Mr. McCredie shrugged. "Oh, go on up; choose one on the top floor," he said. "I never go up there except to water the plants." His face brightened. "Mind you, you can do that now. And anyway, I keep forgetting."

"Why do you keep plants upstairs if you never go upstairs?" she grumbled, huffing her large bag to the top floor. Mr. McCredie looked puzzled.

"I'm not quite sure," he said. "They were my mother's."

On the plus side, Carmen thought, she didn't have to bring her books: She had ultimate access. She tried to encourage her gloomy self to think that when she was small, the idea of living in a bookshop would have been a dream come true; a little bed over rows and rows of books on every subject her little heart could desire.

On the other hand, it was currently Phoebe's dearest wish to go to bed on a cloud and she almost certainly wouldn't like that, either.

Somewhere very deep in the heart of the house a bell rang, and Carmen realized it was connected with the bell on the other side of the bookshop door, which Mr. McCredie was not at all good at locking. Presumably this was why: He could hear people come in all the way up here.

"Do you want to see who that is?" she said. "We're expecting a delivery of Broons annuals."

Mr. McCredie's forehead furrowed.

"I am not interested in you pretending you don't know who the Broons are," said Carmen. "I'll dump my stuff and be down in a minute."

MR. MCCREDIE'S FOOTSTEPS faded away as Carmen made her way to the attic staircase. Well, before she'd been in a very damp basement, so presumably this was a step up, she tried thinking to herself. Attic servants' quarters rather than basement, but still more or less . . .

She sighed. She couldn't keep being so miserable. It wasn't helping anything. She had done the right thing not making more of a fuss about Sofia's—she knew in her heart of hearts her sister would have given in if she'd insisted and made a big deal and got their mom onside. The comfort of having done the right thing was not, she surmised, quite as comfortable as staying put in her sister's luxurious home.

She had to open a heavy door to reach the bottom of the stairs to the attic. Immediately she could hear a little trickle of water. Oh God. The pipes must be terrible. It was going to be so damp and cold up there.

It was so weird having different sets of stairs all over the place.

This house certainly hadn't been designed; it felt, more or less, as if it had grown limbs of its own accord. A floor plan would look like a pretzel.

There was some light coming in; perhaps Mr. McCredie left a bulb in. The steps were old wood, very creaky, and the curving staircase was precipitously steep. She left her bag at the bottom to get the lie of the land.

As she emerged at the top, she frowned, not quite sure what she was seeing.

At first, she thought that the impossible had happened: that Mr. McCredie had let the roof deteriorate to such an extent that there was now no roof at all; that everything had been left to sprout through the top of the building and she was now standing outside.

Gradually, as her eyes adjusted to the light, she realized what she was looking at.

Completely invisible from ground level, the top floor of the house was not, in fact, an attic, but instead, a glazed conservatory. The floor tiles were black and white; there was a carved cherub at one end and the noise she had taken to be bad pipes turned out to be, of all things, a little rustling fountain from a stone cherub's head.

"Oh my God," said Carmen, moving forward. Plants towered over her head; they were dusty and ancient and barely clinging to life, stumbling under their own weight. She didn't know the names of any of them, but they were very beautiful.

"Mr. McCredie?" she called over her shoulder, but no doubt he couldn't hear anything behind that thick door; it was practically a self-contained apartment up here.

There was a little stool next to the tinkling fountain, and Carmen sat down, staring around in wonderment. A wall opposite the plants was covered in mirrors, to reflect the abundant greenery; and a shaft of winter sunshine broke through the slanted panes of the roof, washed clean by the rain.

"Oh my God," said Carmen again, looking around, pulling her jacket tighter because it was freezing. "This is *nuts*."

She looked at the plants. There was a musty smell, and they hung in the air, and she wondered if, beyond occasionally remembering to water them, Mr. McCredie gave them any care or attention at all. They were half-dead, in fact, and brown leaves were scattered on the floor, which added to the inside/outside effect.

There was a pair of French windows at the end leading to a flat section of the roof, and Carmen tried the handle. The door wasn't locked but it was rusted and sticky and she had to shake it a few times to get it open. But she finally did, and there it was, right in the middle of the top of the building: a little stone patio with more plants out on it, which also looked damp and uncared for. She was peering down into a cobbled courtyard, hugged closely by other stone houses with inward-facing windows, but higher than any of them, and out of their view; facing south, where she could see the top of the vast College of Art and, beyond, the rolling Pentland Hills.

There was a polite cough right behind her.

"I'd quite forgotten this was here," said Mr. McCredie.

"*How?*" said Carmen, utterly astounded. It was a surprise beyond anything she could have imagined. "Hang on . . . you forgot *an entire balcony* on your house?"

He shrugged. "I don't really . . . I occasionally water the plants, but I don't really come up here. It was my mother's pride and joy."

"I bet it was," said Carmen. "It's spectacular. It's like something out of *Up on the Rooftops*."

"Oh, do you think?" he said, pleased. "What a wonderful book that is. Of course, you never see it nowadays. Yes, we used to keep birds up here. My mother would sit here for hours when she wasn't too . . . sad. Well. Yes. It's rather past its best these days."

"Aren't we all?" said Carmen, looking around. "Well, I don't know anything about gardening . . ."

"No, neither do I," said Mr. McCredie. "I've always rather preferred slightly cleaner landscapes."

". . . but I could certainly check out a book or two."

"Well, quite!"

They smiled at one another.

"Oh, bedrooms!" said Carmen suddenly. There were three doors on the other side of the landing; the conservatory took up half the roof, glazed, and the entire long side of the house itself. It sat, Carmen figured, two stories above the street on the north side; five stories from the shop on the south side. It was baffling.

To her incredulous delight, on the other side of the stairwell were two identical bedrooms: clean, plain rooms facing across the Lawnmarket—to Mylnes Court, she noticed, and above the Quaker Meeting House at the top of West Bow. They had two windows apiece and were high enough up so there was no noise from the street, and the vista they looked out on hadn't changed in hundreds of years. One had twin beds. This, Mr. McCredie said, had been his as a child, when they had been in the city, rather than the grand country estate that had been sold decades ago to pay taxes.

The other had a small double, so she took that, and the third room was a bracingly cold bathroom, with a vast claw-foot tub. Carmen couldn't believe they ever got enough hot water to fill it, but was happy to see it nonetheless.

The bed was old, but comfortable, and Mr. McCredie fetched her ancient sheets from the press; they were darned and very old but softened by use and time. Carmen had never made up a bed with blankets and sheets before, so she decided to wait until she didn't have an audience.

"So, this will be . . . satisfactory?"

"I think," said Carmen, looking around. She looked out of the little glazed windows and across the great city spread out at her feet, and then back into the astonishing sky garden in the middle of the city. She thought she probably deserved a break for moving out so uncomplainingly (eventually) and, heating or not, this was it. She took out the envelope full of cash Sofia had given her and handed it over.

"I think this is going to be fine."

Chapter Fifteen

Sofia had started back at work, and it had hit her like a ton of bricks. She'd done it before, she told herself. Starting back a month or so before Christmas was a good way to ease herself in, meet her old clients, remember what lawyering was like.

She'd thought she'd enjoy it more, being back in her business self, back in the world she knew so well, helping and advising. But Eric was such an enchanting baby, and she knew absolutely and definitively that he would be the last. So his babyhood was less a gradual unfurling of a new person, and more the losing of the last baby she could ever call her own. She found herself, uncharacteristically, wanting to hold on to every second of it, to smell his powdery head, kiss his button nose, watch his gummy grin for hours. Every day, it seemed, she lost something. She hadn't felt like this with the others; she'd always been excited to see them move on to the next stage: walking, talking, exploring. But if she could have a vampire bite Eric she would have.

No, she wouldn't, she told herself. That's ridiculous. And horrible. Anyway. It was time. But she was snappish and cross. The other children were being irritating, too. Like many children, they were incredibly small "c" conservative and hated change of any kind. Mommy and Carmen both not being there when they got home from school, again, however much they had taken to Rudi, felt tough and they were each playing up the only way they knew how. Jack was bouncing off walls and breaking anything his hands came anywhere near; Pippa was insisting her mother sit through essays and music and long recitations of how everyone else was misbehaving but she had got another gold star, and Phoebe was huffing long sighs and was completely unable somehow to do the simplest task asked of her, whether it was washing her hands before dinner or moving her schoolbag away from the dark corner of the stairwell where it was tripped over repeatedly by every single human being in the house.

It would be okay, Sofia told herself on her first day back. It was cold and gray; the kind of day when it almost certainly wasn't going to get light at all. Sofia's black suit still fit, just about, apart from around her breasts. It was ridiculous, she knew. With the others she'd happily given up breastfeeding on the stroke of the WHO-sanctioned six months. With Eric, she couldn't bear the thought, as she fed him, his little face blissed out, his cheek taking long draws, everything working as it should, his body utterly relaxed, tucked in, tummy to mommy, against hers. She couldn't bear that it would be the last time. She'd kind of stopped—Eric didn't mind the bottle at all, and was already eating any solids he could get his hands on, including plasticine and sand—then found herself weakening and going back to him. It was entirely selfish. And as a result she still had ridiculous jumbo tits that looked like porn and were going to leak all over everything, which was not at all the impression she wanted to bring to the partners meeting. Well.

Rudi had appeared early, smiling, and offered her a coffee, which was a good start. Federico was in Tokyo, and she was missing him.

"The porridge oats are there—full-cream milk, even though Phoebe says she doesn't like it . . . likewise with raisins . . ."

"It's fine," said Rudi. "So, let me get that straight again: Frosties and chocolate milk whenever they feel like it."

"Rudi!" said Sofia, but she smiled. She liked him already. He possessed that most underrated of virtues: amiability.

"I'll whack them in strict age order to get them in the shower."

"Yes please," said Sofia, then, in a low voice, added, "Someone is peeing in the shower. I assume Jack but don't want to let on, so any . . ."

"Being a private detective is extra," said Rudi. "But of course I'd be delighted."

"Speaking of being a private detective," said Sofia, who was still entirely suspicious of how her sister had gone down without a fight. "Feel free to take the children into McCredie's bookshop whenever they want to go."

"Will do," said Rudi. "Come on, my boy."

He expertly tucked Eric under his right arm.

"Does he want a last feed, do you think?"

"He's learned how to work the toaster," said Rudi. "On you go."

THE FIRST MORNING, the sky was cloudy and gray. Carmen woke up in the high bedroom to a church bell sounding, not knowing for a moment where on earth she was. It was very early. The heavy old blankets felt comforting on her; cozy, like a nest. She liked the weight, she realized, surprised.

She hopped through the chilly conservatory, filled the old sink with tepid water, and grimaced; it really was freezing up here. There were strange drafts from the thin-paned windows. The French windows in the winter garden were beautiful, but one thing they did not do was shut particularly tightly. No wonder the poor plants were suffering. She frowned. Mr. McCredie was obviously doing the bare minimum to keep them alive. There were moss and weeds everywhere. She took the tepid water from the sink in a tooth mug and poured it into all the pots.

There weren't even radiators, just another empty fireplace in her room, without even dried flowers in it. Carmen thought longingly of Sofia's underfloor heating and she sighed.

Just get on with it, she told herself, pulling on a sweater then adding her dressing gown on top of that. She'd never owned slippers. This told her something about just how spoiled she'd been, she thought, because in this house, she was going to need every-thing. Pulling her dressing gown close to her and touching the end of her nose to see how cold and red it was (very), she crept downstairs.

There was no sign of her landlord, which wasn't surprising, as he rose late. Now she understood why: He was probably waiting for some sun to creep in and warm his bones a little. But to her ab-solute surprise, in the kitchen, there was a merry coal fire cracking in the little black woodburning stove. Oh my goodness! The room was warm, and there was a heavy kettle there, all ready for setting on the iron peg. She crept closer to it, adoring its heat.

"Thanks!" said Carmen out loud, in case Mr. McCredie was around somewhere, but she didn't hear anything. It was most pe-culiar, but very very welcome. She peeled off a layer and, with some difficulty, heaved the heavy kettle on its peg and found the tea bags. There was a larder off the kitchen in a room that jutted out over the courtyard—it was a most peculiar house—and was about the same temperature as a fridge. There she found a jug of heavy cream, a large knob of butter, and some rough-hewn bread. Back in the kitchen, Carmen saw no sign of a toaster but did, to slightly less surprise, see two toasting forks. Shaking her head, she made a mental note to get some more bread and went at it with a will.

What she saw when she opened the little burner was shocking. Inside, burning merrily, were books.

Carmen was distraught beyond belief. It was sacrilege, terrible. Also, was this how bad things had got for Mr. McCredie?

"What . . ."

The old man shuffled in.

"Ach, Carmen," he said, as he saw her face. "It's not real."

"It *looks* real."

"No, no. Look."

And he put the poker inside the stove and showed the title. It was the autobiography of one of the more corrupt of the recent politicians.

"All political autobiographies," he said. "All awful. All venal. All a complete waste of paper and only worth their weight as fuel."

Carmen swallowed hard. "Well," she said, half-mollified. "No, seriously, this is crazy!"

"I have some 'influencer' memoirs if you'd rather? I'm not sure what an influencer is, but they burn well. Carmen, don't look so shocked. They were only going to be incinerated anyway. This way we all benefit."

"It doesn't sit right," said Carmen, but the heat was so luxurious on her nose and fingers.

Mr. McCredie put two slices of bread expertly on the toasting fork.

"I need money," he said simply. "You've been a great help, thank you. But we're not there yet."

Carmen stared at the bread browning, then Mr. McCredie took out something which she realized was dripping, and while being about to refuse, found it was actually delicious on toast. There was more toast with marmalade for dessert, and plenty of strong tea; in fact, they breakfasted rather well. Carmen went back up the attic stairs and changed as hastily as she could, swearing blind she would find a way, somehow, of solving Mr. McCredie's problem. There had to be a solution.

CARMEN WAS STARING at the stacks at the back of the shop—if only there was a way to open them up that didn't cost them money they simply didn't have.

But the front of the shop was cozy with the fire, and the mice, and the tiny train set toot-tooting its way around the wintry track. Anyone visiting would think they didn't have a problem in the world.

A fresh delivery arrived. She perked up—Christmas books!

Next came a customer, and she recognized the shock of red hair immediately.

"The usurper!" he said as he jingled in.

"I only left yesterday!" said Carmen. "Don't tell me, Sofia's got you spying on me to make sure I didn't steal anything when I left."

"Did you steal anything when you left?"

"Never you mind," said Carmen, who might have helped herself to Sofia's new tights drawer—who even *had* a new tights drawer, honestly?—and perhaps one or two cashmere items that, come on, she was obviously going to need more. And a foxy dress, on impulse.

"What are you doing, anyway?" said Carmen, after she'd lifted Eric out of the front sling where he was gurgling merrily at the world.

"I've dropped the kids at school and I'm going to the farmers' market after to get organic food for dinner, nosy parker," said Rudi, who had a large empty rucksack on his back. "So I thought I'd come and be polite."

"You just called me a nosy parker!" pointed out Carmen. "Plus, you could just buy them turkey dinosaurs and save the spare cash. Sofia won't be back for hours and the kids will lie for you."

"Stop trying to get me fired so you can move back in," said Rudi. "You may or may not recall that Sofia has an informer in the ranks: I wouldn't get anything past Pippa in a million years."

"You won't," said Carmen. "It's like looking after Hillary Clinton."

"Good to know," said Rudi. "Any more tips?"

"You ever upset Phoebe the way the last nanny upset her . . ." Carmen looked at him, meaning it furiously.

"You'll chop off my other hand?" said Rudi.

"I didn't say that! Oh my God!"

"You were clearly thinking it."

"I was not!" lied Carmen.

"While holding a Stanley knife and a baby at the same time."

Carmen was in fact holding a box cutter, and she handed Eric back and sliced the tape open on the cardboard.

"How are your digs?" asked Rudi.

"Bracing," said Carmen, who was wearing fingerless gloves and fully intended to keep them on until April.

"Yikes," said Rudi.

Carmen softened slightly. "But there are plants."

"What sort of plants?"

"I don't know? Really big ones."

Rudi stuck out his bottom lip and nodded. "Okay."

"I'm not quite sure what to do with them, but they look nice."

"I grow a few things," said Rudi. "Maybe I could bring the children over and—"

"Yes," said Carmen, trying not to betray the desperation in her voice. "Please. Please bring the children over. Whenever. Whenever they like."

The binding on the box gave way and it popped open.

"What's that?" said Rudi.

"Christmas books!" said Carmen with a smile. "It's just . . . it's a huge time for buying books as gifts, and we like to get as many out as possible. They're such wonderful gifts for children, too, so lovely to have in the home, to read year after year, cuddled up in bed, waiting for Santa." She pulled one out with a flourish.

"Oh."

Rudi picked one out of the box, frowning. "What, *The Farting Christmas Bear*?"

Carmen was also staring at it.

"Oh God," she said.

"What?"

"No matter," said Carmen. "It's just a stupid guy who used to hang around the shop."

"Blair Pfenning! He's, like, some huge celebrity doctor or something, isn't he?"

"He's a nob-end. And he's not a real doctor; he bought his degree from the University of Shiny Teeth and Saying Obvious Things in a Serious Way. I think it's in America somewhere. He already wrote one book about a bear."

She leafed through the new one.

"Oh, now he just does the same stuff, except also while farting."

She sighed. "And now I have to sell twenty-four of them. Oh man, he's such a nob-end."

"Did you sleep with him?"

Carmen gave Rudi a look. "What makes you think that?"

"Most people don't get quite so annoyed about farting bear books written by daytime TV celebrities."

"Well, maybe they should!"

She opened a page at random.

"'*Be kind, Mr. Penguin!' said Mr. Bear. 'Farting is something we all do! Like remembering to clean our teeth!' 'Quite right!' said Mr. Penguin.*"

"Penguins don't have teeth," said Rudi.

Carmen gave him a look. "I doubt that's the worst thing about this. And no, I really didn't sleep with him. But listen to this: '*Would you like this gigantic Brussels sprout, Mr. Bear?' 'Yes I would. Vegetables are delicious and everyone knows that. We all love Brussels sprouts! With all our hearts! Even though! They make you . . .*' This whole thing is just a *web of lies*," Carmen burst out.

"Goodness," said Rudi, turning the book over. "That's a very large author photo. Are his teeth really that shiny?"

"Yup," said Carmen.

"And his hair, wow. Hot."

Carmen looked at him. "Oh yeah?"

"Oh yeah. Would not kick him out of bed."

I did, thought Carmen, feeling lonely all of a sudden.

"So, you like boys . . . ?"

Rudi shrugged. "Sure," he said, "and . . ."

The doorbell tinged. An incredibly beautiful woman walked in, midforties, with a dark geometric bob and bright red lips.

"Oh my God, Rudi!" she said, beaming, and pressing her hand into his upper arm. "I thought that was you."

She looked around the bookshelves. "What a lovely shop." She was instantly the kind of person Carmen would have liked as a friend. "What lovely stock . . ."

She picked up a copy of *The Farting Christmas Bear*.

"Oh," she said, looking disappointed, and Carmen resolved to hide them at the back.

"Anyway, darling," she said to Rudi. "I heard you're back in town, and this is *excellent* news! You must come over."

She wandered over to examine more stock, then gave Rudi a very obvious side glance. "Tonight, if you're free."

"Sure," said Rudi. To Carmen's surprise the woman moved very close to Rudi and put a red-tipped fingernail on his cheek.

"I've missed you," she said in a husky voice, her meaning unmistakable.

Carmen looked at Rudi, wondering if he'd be embarrassed, but he wasn't at all. She also wondered if she should cover Eric's ears. But mostly she just felt a bit jealous. If you had really shiny hair you could flirt all you liked.

"I finish work late," he said. "After eight."

"Even better."

"I thought," he said to Carmen, who had her eyebrows arched, "I'd keep my personal life out of your sister's house."

"I'm sure she'll appreciate it," said Carmen, rather reassessing the freckly young man in the light of the incredibly sophisticated woman who appeared to be all over him.

"Oh, look at this," said the beautiful woman, turning around. She had a copy of—Carmen felt a small stab—*White Boots* in a beautiful hardback edition, immaculately preserved, even though it was old. Ramsay, their antiquarian supplier, had turned one up.

Carmen couldn't fault the woman's taste, but it was so gorgeous she'd be sad to sell it.

"I'll take it," she said. "It'll be something to do while I'm waiting."

She smiled flirtatiously at Rudi, who smiled back.

"Well, you can come to the farmers' market with us if you like."

"I might have to squeeze a few vegetables."

"Not in front of the baby, please," said Rudi.

And they laughed, looking happy and attractive, and departed together. Carmen remembered Rudi asking her out for a drink, and her thinking, ridiculously, that he might have meant it, and had felt flattered. Of course not. A huge pile of farting bears fell off the counter, and Carmen growled at them.

Chapter Sixteen

Carmen decided, freezing, the next day that she would act as if the money to fix the stacks was going to happen, in case it would manifest or something. Plus, she needed something to sublimate her gloomy mood.

At the moment the shop had two large picture windows, dressed for Christmas. There was a curtain that went back into the stacks, but nothing more than that; she wouldn't have to knock down any walls. On the other hand, it was dusty and grubby back there, and the floors were very different. Also it was a maze, and reorganizing the stacks would be the work of a lifetime. Mr. McCredie had accumulated books from all corners of the world, going back decades, and had filed them according to his own prejudices the best he could. There was only horrible strip lighting back there, too, which hardly worked in a shop.

Well. There was nothing for it, Carmen thought, but to roll up her sleeves and get started. After all, it wasn't as if she had to commute anymore.

She pulled the curtain first, but it was a cold gray day and there wasn't much light coming through the windows. Half the strip lighting was flickering and buzzing unpleasantly. It didn't just look unpleasant. Carmen wasn't one hundred percent sure it wouldn't fall on her. Even with the lighting, it was hard to see how far back the shelving went; all the way, effectively, through the rock that made up the castle cliff, all the way to the other side of the road above, where the house more or less began. It was more of a series of caves full of books than a sensible merchandising system.

She knelt, making out as best she could what was in the first stack. Maps again; Mr. McCredie loved them. Carmen grimaced. She pulled out one large hardback book.

It was glorious, a Mappa Mundi early edition going back to the start of the nineteenth century. Full-color plates were covered in soft tissue paper, and a beautiful bold placeholder of silk was connected to mark the page of wherever the reader wanted to look, or go. Unsurprisingly she saw, as she blew the dust off the top, it was open at the Antarctic page, which had no place-names inscribed whatsoever; it was terra incognita. Carmen smiled. This book had existed before anyone had landed, before anyone knew there was anything down there. Now you could hop on a cruise ship. Humans were extraordinary.

As she turned the pages, though, she became slightly more wary. Almost every country in the world, it seemed, was indicated as British. It was beautiful but it was formidably, dangerously out of date. By the time she was examining beautiful woodcuts made by, apparently, the people of "Siam," she wasn't sure the book should be in the shop at all.

A woman came in, the door pinging, and smiled pleasantly as Carmen emerged from the stacks.

"Hello!" she said. She was a longtime regular, a professor at the university with hair that changed color once a month, on a schedule. Today it was pink and purple braids, and her glasses matched. "Erich is keeping a Codex bib for me?"

"Sure," said Carmen, dropping under the desk.

"What's this?"

"Well, it's geography, but it's kind of racist geography. I'm opening up the stacks a bit, giving us more selling space for Christmas. We need the money, to be honest. But I'm not sure how much of this I can actually sell."

The woman was engrossed, flipping through the beautiful pages.

"Nonsense," she said finally. "This isn't geography, Carmen."

"Umm, what is it, then?" said Carmen, who was still very chippy about never going to college and was always intimidated by the many members of the nearby university faculty who regularly dropped in.

"It's history, of course. And art. Look how we change the way we talk about the world. Look how something can be dangerous and beautiful at the same time."

Carmen watched the woman's tracing finger, which followed the silk routes, and the routes of the trade winds, shivering slightly to see them set down so carefully.

"Look at this," said the woman. "Cotton, sugar, slaves. Plain as day. Not a quiver of conscience about it. Published by learned people, too. Who almost certainly thought themselves *incredibly* progressive."

She shook her head. "I'm going to take this," she said. "As good a teaching aid as I can imagine."

"I'm not sure how to charge you for it," said Carmen awkwardly.

"Well, you must," said the woman. "We learn from bad things, too. Perhaps it won't be too expensive? But there will be more treasure in the stacks, I think. I hope. Better things?"

Carmen nodded.

"It's a huge job."

"Are you going back the entire way?" She squinted into the dark recesses. "Goodness, how exciting! Who knows what you're going to find back there! It will be like treasure hunting! People will lose themselves for days."

She stared at the horrible lighting and dusty stacks as if it really did lead to a magical land. Carmen felt a flicker of excitement. "I know. It will take a bit of cash to do it."

The professor nodded. "I think it will be worth it, though. A dragon's lair!"

And she left, leaving Carmen feeling rather more optimistic, even though it was the only book they sold that morning and there wasn't enough in petty cash for a sandwich. She was reduced to eating the hideous Blair Pfenning–branded "nutrition ball" that had been included with the children's books as a promotional item and tasted absolutely revolting. Things were really bad.

BRONAGH CAME IN after lunch to see what was up.

"This is an absolute bazaar," she said. "And I don't mean that in the amazing way."

"I know," said Carmen. "It's a huge job. And we absolutely don't have the money for it."

"Hmm," said Bronagh. "I thought as much."

And she brought out a small bottle filled with viscous yellow liquid.

"What's that?" said Carmen.

"Call it an early Christmas present. It's a good turn. Seems like you need it."

"What do you mean?" said Carmen, putting on her best skeptical face and managing to forget that she herself had been attempting to "manifest" two hours ago.

"Drink it, and someone will do you a good turn. Then you will have to give a good turn, too, or it won't hold."

"Are you *sure* this isn't made up?" said Carmen. Bronagh looked mortally offended.

"That's correct, Carmen; you and you alone have ascertained the divine mysteries of the universe. Congratulations on understanding how absolutely everything works."

Carmen kept on looking at it. Bronagh folded her arms, refusing to move.

"Oh, for goodness' sake," said Carmen.

"Or, thank you," said Bronagh.

Cornered, Carmen opened the bottle and took a tentative sniff. "What is it, dragon's phlegm or something?"

"Just drink it."

Carmen knocked it back and gasped.

"Oh my God. Oh my God, that's horrible. That's vile. OMG."

"It's advocaat," said Bronagh.

"I know! It's so hideous!"

"Charmed advocaat."

"Couldn't you charm it not to taste of congealed custard?"

"I'm a witch, not a God."

"*Bleargh.*"

"And now a good turn will come your way," said Bronagh. "But don't forget you owe the universe. Good day!"

CARMEN ALMOST FORGOT about Bronagh as she carried on trying to figure out the stacks: The floor needed fixing up; the lighting needed redoing; the bookcases needed painting; there was just so much work to be done. And absolutely no money with which to do it. She sighed, remembering Jackson suggesting she take just one of those little silly stands that sold clan info and how much money they could make . . . No, she told herself sternly. They were a bookshop that sold good books that people loved. That was what they were doing. It was a slippery slope.

As if she'd been imagining it, the bell rang, and Jackson was standing there again, his florid, self-satisfied face beaming as widely as ever.

Carmen looked at him. He wasn't Bronagh's good turn, that was for sure.

"What?"

"Is that how you treat your customers, darling? Look! Come on, would you?"

He opened a briefcase and showed her a selection of rubber Nessies wearing Santa hats.

"Big line of these. You'd have your holiday cash in a minute."

"No thank you."

"Come on! Little Santa hats! Irresistible!"

"We're fine, thank you."

He glanced over to where the curtain was pulled back.

"You can't expand without cash, can you?"

"We'll be *fine*," said Carmen.

"Oh yeah? Got a ton of spare cash, then? Doesn't show," he said, looking pointedly at Carmen's cheap shoes.

"You're a very rude man."

"And you're a very stupid woman. Look. I'm sick of being nice."

"I hadn't noticed."

"*You* are going to lose this shop. You're going to lose it and everything in it and it doesn't matter how many boring old dusty books you drag out. Who even reads books anymore? Have you heard of . . ."

He held up a stupid oversize folding phone. Even his phone, Carmen thought, was utterly obnoxious.

"A bleepy, depressing distraction device?" said Carmen. "The polar opposite of a book, in fact."

"I can get books on this! Any book in the world," said Jackson. "I don't, though. Waste of time. I've never read a book in my life, and look at me."

They both looked at each other, awkwardly.

He sniffed. "Anyway, it's just a matter of time, love. Right, I'm off to see Bobby—who has finally started making money."

And looks like a broken man, thought Carmen, but didn't say it. The bagpipe music playing popular tunes was doing "I Wish It Could Be Christmas Every Day" and she could hear it from here. God knows what it must be like to be standing next to it all day. Probably like something they did to soldiers under torture.

"But I'm a friendly man. I'll be here when you change your mind."

He glanced around the little bookshop one more time, laughed without mirth, and turned on his heel. Carmen furiously cursed him under her breath all the way down the street, not realizing Mr. McCredie had come in behind her and was standing blinking mildly over his tea.

"How is that helping us make more money?"

Carmen whirled around. "Nothing," she said. "It's fine."

"Did you take anything from Mr. McClockerty?"

"Mr. McCredie! You've spent a year opposing anything modern I attempt to do to the shop, and some shyster turns up with a bunch of sweatshop toot and you're all over him!"

Mr. McCredie looked a little abashed. "She sails with the winter tide, though, Carmen," he said shyly.

"Okay, okay! Well, help me organize the first shelf we're pulling forward from the stacks."

She indicated the polar-themed shelf that was parked near the front, and he paled.

"Really?" he said. "I mean . . ." he stuttered. "It's . . . I mean, there's a lot of books there that mean a great deal to me."

"There are a lot of books in this entire shop that mean a great deal to you," said Carmen. "It really flies in the face of our whole 'we're a shop' ethos."

"I know, but . . ." He stepped forward and picked up a beautiful dove-gray edition of *The Worst Journey in the World*.

"This is the best book ever written," he said to Carmen, who opened it.

"'Polar exploration is at once the cleanest and most isolated way of having a bad time which has been devised,'" she read, then looked up. "Are you really sure you want to do this?"

"'Through endurance we conquer,'" quoted Mr. McCredie, and Carmen knew there was no talking him out of it.

She hauled all the books off the shelves and put them in boxes while Mr. McCredie watched on, aghast, and sold a few books to passing customers who were also extremely interested in what Carmen was doing. Sweaty and cross, she heaved the shelving unit, with no help, over the wooden floor. It was awkward and left a huge dirty mark on the floor. She filled up a bowl with hot water and plenty of soap and set to with a will.

By that afternoon, she thought she had something. She had dusted every book and taken out everything with a white cover of snowy mountains. Then she'd placed them face out, so they joined together, rather cleverly, looking like one long snowy mountain range at the top; a long mural of books. Everything else was carefully filed by expedition—there, at least, she agreed with Mr. McCredie, although she gave more frontage to Scott than he had, given that he despised him for mysterious reasons—something to do with a hot-air balloon, apparently.

She looked at her handiwork later that afternoon with some satisfaction, which was both increased and slightly brought down by someone spotting a large book titled *Dreams of the Distant North*, illustrated with beautiful full-color plates of Arctic expanses, which they immediately took down and paid full price for (nice), but which left her with a huge gap in the middle of the display (less nice). She reminded herself she was a bookseller, not a set designer, and set about finding something else to fill the gap.

The display could be the centerpiece of their Christmas decorations. She needed some penguins (on the shelf below, of course) and polar bears (on the shelf above) and would hang some beautiful stars above it and it would be entirely satisfactory. Perhaps the little train set could run around the top of the shelf, like the *Polar Express*. Although she still wanted a happy Christmas window . . . mind you.

The lighting. The lighting was still awful. And the further back into the stacks they pushed, the worse it was going to get. But the electrics were ancient . . . She couldn't begin to imagine what they would cost to fix.

She was pondering this when she turned around. It was getting dark by four; winter was fully upon them.

Carmen normally didn't mind this as much as some people did. She'd always considered winter a very good time for cozying down, opening a book, shutting out the cold and wet, if you were lucky enough to be able to . . . She thought a little glumly of her chilly bedroom and the dusty, unloved parlor. Well. Anyway. Maybe she'd just hide out at the nice little coffee shop down the road. And then it would be Christmas . . . Suddenly, Carmen felt so lonely. Of course she would be expected at Sofia's. Her parents would be there, and all the children, and presumably Rudi would be, like, totes amazing, and it would be another year. Another year of Carmen being the single add-on, the extra person. When only last year she had been so happy.

She told herself sternly to stop thinking this way. She had had a good day. She was moved in and had started on the stacks. That was the only way through.

A figure stood on the pavement outside, looking disconsolate.

Carmen went over to the door. It was Bobby.

"You've left the shop unattended?" she said, worriedly.

He looked down the street.

"I can see it from here. I have five seconds."

Carmen followed his gaze. One large group of tourists had just departed. Another was at the bottom of the Grassmarket, staring upward at the men above who were putting up the Christmas lights. For a moment, she paused, struck. The theme was white snowflakes with lights in the middle, which meant if you stood at the top or the bottom of the hill, the strands across the street would intertwine and look like a host of flakes coming down, delicate as lace filigree. As the sky continued to darken, Carmen looked up happily, feeling like hugging herself. However tricky things were, there was something like a promise kept: Every year, there will be a festival. There will be tiny lights. There will be joy, and hope. In the very center of the dark, when things seem at their bleakest, there will be firelight and candles and joy.

"Did you say no to him again? He's in a foul mood."

Bobby shivered. Carmen sighed.

"Yes . . . I don't know how long we can hold out, though."

"And what are you doing, anyway?" he said, looking up.

"Trying to increase the floor space, get more things for people to look at," Carmen explained. "But the lighting . . ."

As she spoke, one of the lights buzzed and flashed on and off in a way that normally required a safety warning when it happened in a film.

"Och, that's bad, aye," said Bobby.

"I'm aware of that, thanks," said Carmen, rather more sharply than she intended.

"I mean, it's an easy fix, you just need to rewire the ceiling, get new fittings and fixtures . . ."

"How on earth am I going to pay for that?" said Carmen in despair.

The mournful noise of a bagpiped Kirsty MacColl song drifted up the street. They looked at one another.

"No," said Carmen. "No no no no. Never."

Behind her one of the lights fizzled and popped out.

A stout figure wearing a pair of bright mustard plus fours, Argyll socks, heavy boots, a checked waistcoat complete with fob watch, and a heavy tweed jacket headed up the road.

"What ho!" he shouted.

Carmen looked at him. "Crawford!" she said. "You look like Toad of Toad Hall. We have an illustrated edition; I'm going to show you."

"No need." Crawford beamed. "I know I do!"

"He's not the hero of that book!" said Carmen.

"Of course he is! Poop poop!"

Carmen screwed up her face. "Oh my God, he so isn't."

"Well, I think that's a matter of opinion."

In the back of the shop, lights kept sputtering.

"Well," said Crawford eventually. "Regardless. I came to invite you all to my annual charity Christmas feast! At mine. To celebrate the season!"

"Don't know what there is to celebrate," said Bobby.

"I don't . . . I am not sure we're quite in a position to contribute to charity at the moment," said Carmen awkwardly.

"Come anyway! Don't bring a thing!" said Crawford stoutly. "Tell Bronagh not to bring anything, either; I don't care what that witch says is in her mulled wine, it could fell the Monarch of the Glen."

Carmen locked up, then walked Bobby down the street in case he had any spare lighting fixtures around the back he'd forgotten about.

She surveyed the shop. There were cheap T-shirts with pictures of dogs and "I'm a wee terrier" written on them.

"I don't get it," said Carmen.

"I think it's 'I'm a wee terror.'"

Carmen frowned. "You're selling T-shirts that say your kids are evil?"

"For eleven ninety-nine," said Bobby.

Carmen picked up a set of miniature plastic bagpipes glued to a tartan heart.

"Don't—" said Bobby. It was too late. The bagpipes immediately fell off the backdrop.

"Oh, for goodness' sake," said Carmen. "This is pure *toot*."

She moved past the boxes of cheap, out-of-date Edinburgh rock, and over to a display of tiny tin black cabs, postboxes, and London buses.

"This isn't even *Scottish*," she said. "What even is this? This is tourist tat *from another country*. You might as well stock miniature Eiffel Towers."

"It's for people who are in a rush," mumbled Bobby. "They might only have one day in the UK."

"And they spend it in here?" said Carmen crossly. "Honestly. I can't believe the council allows these kinds of crappy outlets to sprout everywhere."

"Bronagh says they're in league with Satan."

Carmen frowned as she remembered the troop of besuited men and women who came in every second Tuesday, after the council meetings at the city hall, and requested access to the "Special Section" Mr. McCredie kept the only key for.

"They can't be," she said. She thought about it. "Well, maybe the planning committee."

Bobby grunted. "Bronagh seems pretty sure."

Carmen looked around. "The idea that Edinburgh City Council is led by blood-worshipping Satanists is ridiculous and not a thing to say even in jest, Bobby," she said loudly, just in case they were, and somebody was listening.

The bell beeped—Carmen missed its happy clang, but Jackson had installed a system that counted how many people came through the doors, so he could maximize price points at different times of the day. Jackson was standing there, huge, his legs wide in a "power position" he must have learned from some stupid magazine somewhere, his arms folded. He had changed into a purple-and-yellow tartan Carmen had never seen before; his hair was also suspiciously yellow.

"They are a fine bunch of upstanding citizens," he said, also loudly, Carmen noted curiously, "who almost never slit throats or drink anyone's blood. Oh, I see you're here again. Has the old man come around?"

"He has not," said Carmen defiantly. "There have been bookshops on Victoria Street since the eighteen forties. You could buy your serialized copy of a Dickens novel on these premises the week it came out. We were here when the *Scotsman* was just up the hill, when the center of the world for print and books and publishing was Edinburgh. We're not leaving."

"Well, one of you is," said Jackson, curling his lip. "One of you is going on a very long journey."

He rubbed his fingers together, as a man, who appeared to be from the Far East and was wearing a colored baseball cap with the name of a tour company, ran in, staring at his watch. He grabbed, seemingly at random, three Scotland hoodies, three plastic Nessies (which like the bagpipes were covered in badly finished globs of glue), a huge box of shortbread, ambitiously priced, and a canvas bag that said "Hey McLeod, Get Off of My Ewe," which Carmen suspected he probably didn't quite understand. He hurled his debit card at Bobby, who bleeped it—the man didn't even look at the total—then tore out again and jumped back on a huge coach that was idling at the bottom of the street, belching out fumes. The coach had foreign plates: For once, there were no traffic wardens to be seen, and even if there were, it seemed unlikely they would be able to do much about it.

"He just spent more than you take in a day," said Jackson smugly. Carmen had clocked this, too, and now felt slightly sick. Bobby looked downtrodden and sad in front of his boss.

"I've got to go," said Carmen.

"Be seeing you," said Jackson, blowing her a kiss.

Chapter Seventeen

Oke didn't get better all at once. It came and went. Sometimes he just felt horrible, sometimes sleepy, sometimes sick and grumpy. His mother was always there, with a sister or two rotating in and out. He was profoundly grateful to be held, in this cocoon of love, when he needed it.

Mary came back to visit as soon as she was allowed, bursting into his room with a huge armful of books and periodicals, and a vast grin on her pretty face. She threw her arms around him.

"Darling! My darling!" she exclaimed. "Oh my God, what you put us all through."

She wouldn't let go of him and Oke wondered for a moment if perhaps his fuzzy memory had forgotten something about the relationship between the two of them. He remembered them lying back on a car one night, that definitely stayed with him. Staring at the stars. But he hadn't been thinking of Mary, had he? Had he?

He tried to sit up, not very successfully.

"Tell me what happened?" he said.

Mary rolled her eyes. "Don't you remember?"

Her perfume was strong in the small room. He shook his head. "Nope."

"Well, we were having such a lovely time . . ."

Her hand traced down his hand.

"Then you got up and said you felt funny and I said you probably shouldn't have drunk the rum. I thought you were drunk, even though there wasn't much rum." She sounded nervous, reliving it.

Oke frowned.

"Then you were walking toward the privy and you just . . . you just collapsed."

She squeezed his hand tightly. "It was terrifying."

"I'm sorry," said Oke.

"I got Juan-Castillo," she said, "and he looked really serious. We were four days by boat from a hospital. He didn't like the look of you at all. Neither did I. Your eyes were all weird."

"Weird how?" asked Oke.

"Just white. Not nice. And JC thought it might be something worse—we were so deep in the bush, it could have been anything. So he thought better safe than sorry." She lowered her voice. "The insurance was insane. But you must remember the helicopter?"

Oke shook his head.

"Wow! It was amazing. They wouldn't let us both go with you, just me. And then an ambulance brought you here."

He was in a hospital in Brasilia, although the white walls, pale food, heat, and bleeping noises meant it could have been practically anywhere. Oke had hardly noticed his surroundings at all.

"When are they letting you out?"

"I don't know," said Oke. "Apparently I'm well enough to lose the swanky single room."

"Oh, that's a shame," said Mary, who was still sitting on his bed. She tilted her head at him. "Gosh. You were thin to start with . . ."

Oke had already had variations on this conversation, including his nephew informing him that he looked like a boa constrictor balancing on its tail. One sister had said he looked like three small boys in a coat and his other sister had said no, he looked like a pair of pajamas on a coat hanger, so he was used to cheek and knew he'd lost weight. His mother was doing her best to feed him up again.

"I know," he said.

"I'll have to feed you up," said Mary playfully. She still had hold of his hand, and she stroked it thoughtfully. "I make very good brigadeiros."

She indicated a picnic basket she'd brought.

"Are you eating yet?"

Everything tasted of sand to Oke but he was doing his best to choke down the calorific drinks the hospital was feeding him, which tasted of gravel.

"Huh," he said. "Kind of."

Then he frowned. His head hurt. He felt dizzy and faint.

"I need you," he said drily. "Mary, I . . ."

"Yes?" she said. Her lovely face was smiling and eager as she put her hand on his hair and stroked it gently. "I need you" was everything she had been waiting to hear.

"What do you want, my love?"

"I . . . Did you find my phone?"

"No—haven't you got another?"

"Mamma thinks it will hinder my recovery."

Mary frowned. "She's probably right. What you need is rest, not staring at nonsense on the internet."

"Okay, okay," said Oke, who didn't want to argue with anyone. "But I need to ask you: Can you do something for me?"

Then he asked. He had not been sure of much these last few terrible, baffling, pain-racked weeks, but he was sure of one thing. One thing he needed.

"Can you let Carmen know?"

Chapter Eighteen

December

December was fully here, and it was as if a magical curtain had descended on the city of Edinburgh; a black velvet layer, covered in glittering stars. Every window sparkled with lights. Princes Street Gardens were a riot of lights and noise and colors, the huge sprawling Christmas fair in full flood. There were little German houses selling wooden toys and Christmas decorations; sausages sizzling; and rides throwing teenagers around and, pretty ideally from their perspective, into one another's arms. There were glühwein sellers and sweetshops and pancakes and glassblowers; hot chocolate and a Christmas-tree maze and an astonishing miniature railway that ran all the way around the park, where wrapped-up children waved mittened hands at parents wielding phone cameras.

It wasn't just fun, Carmen often thought, wandering down there to the New Town to meet Idra. It was something deeper and more important than that. Especially with everything going on in the world these days. She supposed there was always lots going on in the world; it's just these days everyone knew about it, rather than just their own quarter.

Nonetheless, there was something magnificently defiant in these whirling lights; these dancing teens; the running, excited children full of sugar and shrieking excitement. The lights, the fires, the fun; all of it was like a fist lifted to the sky as if to say, *This darkness will not defeat us. Not now, not ever. We will celebrate being halfway out of the dark.* If you were to fly over Scotland, she mused, the Highlands would be dark, with the people spaced out in the beautiful glens and islands and settlements of the far north; and south, you'd see the quiet borders.

But the central belt, which ran from the great royal seat of Dunfermline, Edinburgh, through Falkirk, Stirling, Glasgow, Kilmarnock, Ayr, these places would shine and glow, end to end: holding the line for Christmas.

She was going shopping with Idra to find something to wear for Crawford's feast. She had Sofia's posh dress but it was more fitted than Carmen felt comfortable with—in truth, it was too small for the amount of feasting she was planning on doing to make up for whatever posh charity Crawford was fundraising for. Probably medals for retired military forces or something equally stupid. She would have looked for something in Crawford's shop, but she was skint, and everything was hundreds of pounds and looked completely insane, like a partridge-feather bonnet with a tweed waistcoat covered in random buckles and a long, tightly fitted women's kilt.

Instead, they were going to hit Primark and buy something jolly. Because it had been, all in all, a tough year. She had to forget about Oke, Idra had insisted, and start celebrating and accepting invitations. And the first one she was accepting was this one.

"But it's just for people who work on the street and Crawford's friends!" said Carmen. "I know them all and everyone is one hundred and owns a broomstick."

"You never know," said Idra. "Someone might bring someone."

"Yes and they will also be one hundred years old," grumbled Carmen.

"That's not true. The coffee bar lot will be coming."

"Yeah. They hate me."

"Stop buying coffee, then."

"Please allow me my one final addiction," said Carmen. "It is literally all I have left. Ooh! Sparkles!"

And she did succumb, both to Idra buying them mulled wine at horrendous expense, as they found out slightly too late, and bouncing giddily through the fair, into the brightly lit shops, where Carmen tried on a dress covered in tulle and gold stars. It wasn't at all what she would normally have bought, being very much a jeans and Breton shirt kind of a person on the whole, but it was, she saw, with the pink in her cheeks brought out by the cold weather and the wine, actually quite pretty. It would be even more so with tights and big boots, so she dipped into her meager bank account and bought it. Sometimes, everyone needs a little sparkle, that's all.

"Good," said Idra. "Are you absolutely sure you can't marry Crawford for his money?"

"I assume," said Carmen, fluffing out her hair in the mirror, "that if he had any money, he wouldn't be running a shop in Victoria Street, because we certainly don't."

In this, however, as in so many things, Carmen was about to discover she had been completely mistaken.

CRAWFORD HAD ONCE told Carmen, "I live just upstairs"—as indeed did Mr. McCredie, and Carmen had been expecting more of the same, although perhaps without the conservatory in the attic.

But in fact, the entrance to Crawford's house was up the steps from the Grassmarket, which led upward to Ramsay Mews, the famous white and redbrick turreted structures that hugged the castle; some of the most expensive real estate in the world. Set in their own private gardens, the grand apartments provided a commanding view over the city below.

"Oh my God," said Carmen, as she entered through an arched, studded wooden door, bundling off her jacket from the cold below. You could smell the frost in the air; it crackled against the lantern light that lined the street. Inside the house it was extremely cozy. "This place is incredible."

"Well, we're not the castle, of course," chuckled Crawford, in what was obviously meant to be a self-deprecating way and came over as completely the opposite. "But you know, we have gardens and they don't."

"So, it's better."

"Well, you say that, not me."

Carmen handed over the second-cheapest bottle of red wine she had found in the supermarket and Crawford looked at it like he would be hard-pressed to feed it to a bullock.

"Oh, *thank you*," he said insincerely. "Now, leave your coat and come into the drawing room."

Sofia always insisted they use "drawing room" for the upstairs sitting room, but it was always clear to Carmen she was putting it on. Crawford, on the other hand, seemed quite at home with it. Duka was an extremely handsome young tattooed man in a white shirt and black trousers standing at the end with a tray of champagne in wide-mouthed glasses.

"I know, I know," said Crawford. "You're going to tell me you should never pour vintage champagne into wide-necked glasses— loses all the fizz—but I'm afraid I just love them too much."

Carmen had absolutely no opinion on such matters apart from "give me some delicious champagne," but she smiled at the gorgeous Duka and took a glass cheerfully.

Oh no, she thought as she entered the drawing room. Some things in life just weren't fair.

The room was wood paneled, with stags' heads, crests, and mediocre watercolors of the glens by minor royals decorating the walls in a completely unironic manner. The front of the room was taken up by diamond-paned windows that took in the entire north side of the city: Princes Street, the New Town, all the way to the Firth and the far shores of Fife beyond, everything aglitter. You could see the lights of planes circling the airport; oil rigs shining like tinsel; great ships going back and forth.

"Oh my word," said Carmen.

Expensive perfume and the scent of something delicious for supper filled the air.

The room was full of beautifully dressed people, not at all just the shop owners Carmen had been expecting. They looked confident and like they all knew each other. She searched in vain for a friendly face—Mr. McCredie was here, but she had seen him over by the bookshelves, humming and hawing and pulling things out here and there, so she knew better than to disturb him. Ridiculously tall Ramsay, their antiquarian dealer, was here, with, unusually for him, none of his children, although his pretty, cheery English wife, Zoe, was here, grinning and having a lovely time. She couldn't be pregnant again, thought Carmen, but clearly she was. Goodness me. Well, the winters were long and cold up in Kirrinfief where they lived. Obviously you had to do something for warmth. A group of people so noisy, self-assured, and beautiful they could only be actors from the Traverse Theatre held court by the fireplace.

Carmen wandered past the huge Christmas tree. It was a vast thing with, to Carmen's amazement and delight, real candles on its branches; a fire hazard, no doubt, but gorgeous nonetheless. Instead of decorations, apart from tinsel, there were actual, full-size toys—a doll, a truck, a zebra, and a bear. It was the oddest, loveliest tree she'd ever seen. And at the very top, crowning it all, sat a robin, looking practically real.

Crawford's wife saw her smiling. "Our grandchildren get to pick their gifts from the tree," she said. "It causes all sorts of panicking, you can imagine."

Carmen could, fervently.

"I think it's a lovely idea," she said. "It's beautiful."

"Thank you, dear."

Carmen was struck by how very like her husband this round, beaming woman looked (whether they'd grown more similar over the years or whether they'd looked like siblings to start with wasn't clear). Crawford's wife smoothed her long tartan skirt over her comfortable hips, and Carmen felt slightly pleased that she hadn't splashed out on one. Carmen drew toward the window, the beautiful view. There was something about the city that emboldened her, its beauty and wildness. She would make this shop succeed. She wanted to belong here so much. She knew about falling in love with people; she'd never realized you could also fall in love with a place.

"Old Father Frost is visiting," observed Bronagh, arriving beside her, clad in green velvet that looked magnificent on her. "Things are changing."

"Things are always changing, Bronagh!"

"Not like this," said Bronagh, shaking her head. "This means cracking, a severing of old ties; a grafting, of new ice, of new ways of moving. It will be cold, so cold. But it will forge a new path."

"That could mean almost anything," grumbled Carmen. "You're being gnomic on purpose."

"Well, if someone was hot and you were cold and that became a difference that separated you from one another," said Bronagh, "I mean, that's the kind of thing you would gather if you knew how to read the signs. Of course, I don't know anything," she added huffily.

"You don't," said Carmen, thinking crossly of Oke.

"But everything changes. The solstice approaches, the world turns in its slumber."

"It's good to see you," said Carmen. "How's the shop doing?"

Bronagh shrugged. "The Edinburgh witches are richer than ever," she said. "The world grows poorer and they grow richer. It's a strong magic."

"Good," said Carmen. "And it looks like Crawford has some cash."

"Oh, this has been in his family forever," said Bronagh, and

Carmen again found herself wishing Mr. McCredie hadn't let his money slip through his fingers. She very much wouldn't mind being a roommate here, in this gorgeous, beautifully heated room. Through the huge wooden double doors, she could see a table laid for at least thirty people, with staff lining up. Carmen sighed to see such loveliness. It made her feel a little like she was pressing her face up against the window of other people's more glamorous lives; that they would all go back to homes of peace and plenty and she would scamper up to the drafty attic, with ice on the inside of the windows, looking dolefully at the dying plants.

Crawford sidled up, particularly resplendent in a plum smoking jacket over his velvet waistcoat, jewel-colored turquoise cravat, and straining purple tartan trousers, with velvet slippers.

"You look magnificent," Carmen said.

He did rather, in these surroundings. Crawford beamed. "Well, I like to show off the shop, you know."

"You're being your own model?"

"I am. Now, come let me introduce you."

A tall, rangy older man with a beautiful swoop of graying blond hair wandered over.

"Are you monopolizing everyone under one hundred years old?" he asked, in the bright refined Edinburgh brogue that sounded almost English.

"Not at all," said Crawford. "This is Carmen, who works with Mr. McCredie at the bookshop."

"Ah yes," said the man, lifting her hand and kissing it. "*Enchanté.*"

Weirdly, this wasn't quite as cringe as Carmen might have expected, and he was so attractive she found herself flushed and giggling, in a way she hadn't for a long time.

"Bertie," said Crawford. "Honestly."

He turned back to Carmen.

"This is the Earl of Rothenhy."

"Goodness," said Carmen.

"Bertie is fine," said Bertie, and Carmen told herself sternly that the hereditary aristocracy was a ridiculous state of affairs that she was completely opposed to in every way.

"It's a ridiculous state of affairs," he whispered. "Crawford only mentions my title because he's trying to sell more stupid trousers."

"These," said Crawford, with some effort at maintaining his pride, "are excellent trousers, thank you very much."

He waddled back toward the servers, his fat bum sticking out in the plaid, and Bertie and Carmen found themselves slightly hypnotized by it; they both giggled, guiltily. Carmen accepted her second glass of absolutely delicious champagne and decided if she was being given a chance to reverse-slum it among the great and the good she was going to enjoy it.

The room was filling up with incredibly well-dressed, sophisticated people talking about wealth funds and oil.

"Good God," said Bertie, "everyone here is *very* tedious . . ."

Carmen was wondering if he found her tedious, too. Because she was very tired of being tedious. Very tired. She looked at him. His long eyes were fixed on hers, highly amused.

"Are they? Tell me about it . . ." she said, in a conspiratorial tone that counted as very flirtatious for Carmen, when Bertie suddenly glanced at the door, and said, "Aha! Until now!"

And Carmen followed his gaze and saw, to her mixture of annoyance and being actually quite impressed, bloody Rudi march into the room. His hair was gelled upward today, in all its bright ginger glory, and he was wearing a rather lovely gray kilt that suited his coloring very well. His green eyes beamed broadly at Bertie, who grabbed him and kissed him full on the lips.

"Rudes, come meet—"

"Oh, we've met," said Carmen quickly.

Rudi gave her a narrow-eyed look.

"Small place, Edinburgh," Carmen went on.

"*Quite*," said Bertie. "Let me go get us some drinks."

He vanished to the bar. Rudi immediately turned to Duka, who was offering tiny haggis pakora canapés.

"Oh, sweetie," said Rudi, "do you work here full-time?"

Duka shook his head and smiled.

"I get off at ten," he said.

"Well, that has just made the evening *much* more interesting," said Rudi, and they exchanged smiles as Duka moved on—without offering Carmen a canapé, she noticed.

Carmen stared at Rudi.

"Oh my God!" said Carmen. "Are you just, like, a full-on McFuckBoi? Is that who's looking after my beloved nephews and nieces?"

Rudi frowned in confusion. "I'm a young man doing what I like in my free time," he said, perfectly reasonably. "I don't know why you're being judgmental about it. I told you I keep my personal life away from your sister's house. I didn't know you were going to be here, did I? I've just bathed and settled a baby, cleaned up three mostly untouched healthy dinners, read four chapters of *The Box of Delights*, and rather felt like a drink. If that's okay by you?"

Carmen felt bad immediately.

"Sorry," she said. "I didn't mean to judge."

He grinned and forgave her instantly, nodding his head at Bertie.

"Having a crack at the earl, were you?"

"No!" said Carmen. Then she shrugged. "He's not bad for an old geezer."

"He really isn't," said Rudi. "Honestly, be my guest, he's too good not to share."

"Oh my God!" said Carmen, spluttering into her drink. "You're terrifying!"

Rudi looked at her. "When's the last time you had sex?"

"Oh yeah, that's the kind of thing I discuss with my *nieces' nanny*!"

"Oh wow, that long?"

There was a pause.

"Yeah," said Carmen, feeling awful.

Rudi shook his head.

"Too bad. You're still young. You know. Just about."

"Uh, thanks," said Carmen, accepting a glass from Bertie.

"What's up?" Bertie said, his hand caressing Rudi's waist.

"You know, Carmen hasn't had sex for, like, *years*!" said Rudi.

"Oh no," said Bertie, looking genuinely sorry.

"It's not years, *plural*," said Carmen.

"She quite fancies a go on you."

"I do *not*," said Carmen.

"Well, happy to oblige, of course," said Bertie.

"You don't have to have sex with me just out of *good manners*," said Carmen.

Bertie shrugged his handsome, distinguished face. "I've known worse reasons. Anything one can do to help."

"You can start by not listening to Rudi," said Carmen and, feeling very pink, went off to find Mr. McCredie by the bookshelves with Ramsay.

"Anything interesting?" she said, as Ramsay burst into a big smile to see her.

"Hey! How are you doing?"

"I've just managed to break out of a spooky Edinburgh sex ring," said Carmen. "Apart from that, fine."

"Oh, the earl is a one-man sex ring," said Ramsay. "I wouldn't touch him with yours."

"You're the one with twenty-one kids," said Carmen. Ramsay beamed happily as he looked at Zoe, who was deep in conversation with Crawford's wife. He was a man who felt lucky every day of his life. His happiness was infectious as they dived into working out if there was anything on Crawford's bookshelf they could theoretically pickpocket and sell for a huge profit, but it was mostly dusty old hunting registers and game books.

"Not looking for pillage, are we?" said Crawford, coming up behind them, and they all put on blank faces and ho-ho-hoed innocently.

THEY WERE SOON to feel even more guilty. Everyone sat down at the long table, gleaming with silver: the cutlery, the candlesticks. The air was scented with freshly baked bread and full of the buzz of lively conversation. A beautiful Cullen skink starter was put in front of them, and wine poured (with little drams of whiskey by their elbows, naturally). Carmen was between Ramsay, whom she liked a lot, and an elderly, red-faced gentleman, who kept falling asleep. On his other side was a beautiful woman who was obviously his wife. The woman she'd seen Rudi with in the shop—she of the sharp bob and red lips—was at the other end of the table between him and Bertie. They seemed to be having a whale of a time, laughing their heads off. *What must that be like?* thought Carmen wistfully.

But then, she'd tried, hadn't she? She'd said that she wanted to have sex with someone, someone she cared a lot about. And look what had happened. Nothing. He'd rejected her. So of course she wasn't going to try that again. Mind you, she looked at the happy, attractive people around her, all of whom were having a good time. Maybe she did have to throw herself back into things; stop wallowing and feeling sorry for herself. At least she wasn't at her sister's anymore, in danger of bringing someone back and risking Phoebe trying to crawl into bed with them at four in the morning. She was free. She was young(ish). She had to enjoy it.

She veered between envy and jealousy and pure crossness at the lavishness of Crawford's life; the obvious fact that he ran his shop as a hobby, as a dilettante, for fun, because he loved clothes—that much was obvious—and was not like her and Mr. McCredie, struggling every day to keep their heads above water.

She looked across the table at Bobby and wondered if he was feeling exactly the same way as her: being invited to something so lavish. The main course was pheasant, roasted with a crispy skin and game chips, with beautiful roast potatoes, deep red cabbage, and a delicious bread sauce, accompanied by a decanted deep red wine called Barolo that complemented everything perfectly. It was as if Crawford was rubbing their faces in it. This world, this house, this room, this dinner, this life: It was beautiful, and the exact opposite of everything Carmen had, which, at thirty-one, was not much. And the opposite of everything Jackson McClockerty wanted: dumbing down, flogging cheap rubbish. Everything here was old. It might be too posh, it might be a little pretentious, but it was beautiful, and loved, and chosen with care.

"Can't we just do a heist on the entire house?" said Carmen. "He'd never suspect us."

"He'd never suspect his *incredibly poor next-door neighbors*?" said Ramsay, grinning. "Are you kidding? If he's got any sense, he's security penned every last teaspoon. And your hands."

"Just one tiny wee heist?" said Carmen. "I bet you know people who could fence stuff."

"That's right," said Ramsay. "Antiquarian booksellers: just one entire Mafioso conspiracy. Everyone knows that. That's why we're all so wealthy."

Carmen sighed and looked at her fork again. "Maybe I could accidentally melt it and then I'd have to take it home."

The pheasant cleared away, Crawford stood up and tinked his very expensive fork against his equally expensive crystal glass.

"Attention, everyone," he said. "Now of course you know I don't invite you around here for nothing . . ."

"No, you make us choke down your underhung pheasant!" shouted someone, to rather drunken laughter, which Crawford ignored.

"As always, we have a cause," he said. "And tonight's is one very close to my heart."

Oh God, thought Carmen. She was going to have to sign up to help sad ponies as well. This was going to be awkward.

"Once upon a time, in my father's day—"

"And good John Knox!" shouted another wag, to widespread hilarity.

"Every shop on West Bow was a bookshop. Paper was traded when they were still burning witches in the Grassmarket. Edinburgh had the highest number of bookshops per head in the world. They spread enlightenment, that gentle revolution of the rights of man." Mrs. Crawford smacked his arm. "And ladies." A younger nonbinary person tugged him on the other side. "Sorry. The rights of all people," he said. "Apologies."

Carmen was watching him, confused.

"And now, we are down to one. One sole reminder of a day when to read books was considered to be the greatest of all achievements; to write and to read the way to a better, more peaceful world.

"And it sounds strange, but more people, I believe, live in peace and harmony than at any time in human history, even if it doesn't always feel that way. And a lot of that has to do with increased mutual understanding of one another. Which we find, often, between the covers of a book. I feel it is no coincidence that often our worst leaders declare that they read the least. So, tonight's fundraiser . . . is to rework the lighting in McCredie's bookshop, clear the floors, and finally getting that old bugger to sell some damn books for a change."

There was some laughter and much applause. Carmen's mouth dropped open.

"And our wonderful Bobby is going to be paid to fix it."

At this, the applause grew even louder and more sustained. Everyone loved Bobby the handyman, everyone had benefited at one time or another from him popping in to fix a broken tap, open a stuck window, or any of the million favors that dwindling stock of useful men in the world get called upon to do every day.

"And hopefully, one day make enough money to *turn off that sodding bagpipe music.*"

At this, the table rose to its feet. Bobby beamed bright pink, truly happy as people started searching in their sporrans for their wallets.

"Oh my," said Carmen, slightly overcome. "Oh wow. This is amazing. This is incredible. I'm almost sorry I was going to steal his spoons now. No, I am. Definitely sorry."

Bronagh caught her eye from across the table, and Carmen remembered suddenly: the good deed. Bronagh must have known, she told herself. The advocaat was just a ruse.

Ramsay grinned. "This is brilliant! This really is. Hey, Erich. You're actually going to have to do some real work, you know."

Mr. McCredie smiled kindly.

"I believe my collections will sell themselves," he said proudly. "And I shall be on the Ross Sea."

"Ahem!" said Carmen.

"With the help of my gracious Carmen, of course."

Chapter Nineteen

Carmen floated back down the hill from Crawford's dinner. It had been the most marvelous surprise, and she was thrilled, even as she felt a little wistful as one part of the party, including Rudi, Bertie, and the geometric bob lady, had departed for Panda & Sons. They had invited her, but she'd panicked, and when she'd said she might come later they'd all snorted and said it was a secret bar, she'd never find it. So she'd let them go, but with a deep aching regret, as they went off into the crisp frosty night, down to the Lawnmarket, the lights glowing above their heads, laughing heartily into the crackling air.

What was wrong with her? Why couldn't she just have fun, like they had? What was she waiting for? Her ex, who was never ever coming back to her? Some kind of stupid, outdated idea of having a sex life with only one person, which seemed to involve not actually having a sex life at all. She was tidying herself away, too young, too early. And she knew it. And so she found herself in bed, slightly drunk, scrolling through old pictures of Oke on her phone—even his faculty shot from the university website, which really *was* pathetic—and composing messages but not sending them. Oh, this was so stupid. She lay back on her bed and stared out of the window at the great moon over the top of Mylnes Court opposite, the very student halls where he used to live. She could practically have touched him.

She lay on her back, propping her head on her hand, lit by moonlight coming in through the windowpanes, making squares on the old heavy blankets and eiderdown. Mr. McCredie had surprised her very much, when they arrived back in together, by handing her, wrapped in cloth, a brick.

"I keep them by the stove," he said. "Put it in your bed for your feet."

She had stared at him, but he had been right. It worked well.

"Oke," she said now, typing, but saying it out loud at the same time, as if to the universe itself. "Oke. I miss you. I miss you so very much. This Christmas . . . Oh you don't care about stupid bloody Christmas. Well, I don't care about that. And I don't care about . . . I mean. I'm sorry. I'm sorry about everything I said about Quakers and everything I said about you, because you really hurt me and, well, I lashed out. And I wish I hadn't. I'm sorry. I miss you, Oke. I love you."

Then she thought about it.

"And now, I am saying goodbye."

And before she could think twice about it, she pressed send and whooshed it to his phone, and then turned over and tried to fall asleep. And as every child the night before Christmas knows, trying to fall asleep is the very worst way to actually get to sleep, and she tossed and turned under the heavy blankets, stared at the stars through the windows where she hadn't drawn the curtains, and fretted to herself.

This can't be it, she told herself. *I can't go on like this. I am going to put him out of my way. Realize I got it wrong. That I lost him. I will move on. Tomorrow will be a new day. Tomorrow I will change. It will be better. It will be different. It will.*

FIVE AND A half thousand miles away, a man twisted on hot sheets. He tossed and turned and muttered her name; seeking a dreamless sleep that would not come.

PART THREE

Chapter Twenty

Carmen must have fallen asleep eventually, because she woke with a start. Cold light was glimmering around the edges of the window. She groped for her phone but couldn't find it. The room felt oddly different somehow. She tried for the bedside light, but that wasn't there, either. She blinked.

The room was very still and it felt as if—she couldn't remember—there was the faint aftermath of music that had not been a dream.

She could hear someone moving around downstairs.

"Mr. McCredie?"

She stood up, pulled on her rumpled clothes from the day before, and slipped out of the room. She crossed the landing to the conservatory window and looked down.

In the first shining moment she saw the whole strange, familiar world, glistening white. The roof of the outbuildings mounded into square towers of snow, and beyond them all the hills of Edinburgh lay buried, merged into one great flat expanse, unbroken white to the horizon's brim.

Despite her broken night, Carmen drew in a long, happy breath, silently rejoicing.

"Mr. McCredie?" she called. "Are you there?" No response. She tiptoed across the house to his room.

But she could hear, as she emerged the sound of his breathing, slow and rhythmical. He was not waking.

And when Carmen looked through the window again, everything had changed. The College of Art seemed to have vanished, although the backs of the walls of the Old Town were still there. The large office block on the south side had disappeared from view. It must be a trick of the light, a trick of the snow. And there appeared to be trees everywhere, clad only in the deep snow that lay untouched along every branch, every smallest twig. They began so close to the city; all around her the trees stretched to the far horizon of the hills.

"Mr. McCredie?" Carmen tried again.

She did not now expect any response, and none came. There was just silence, as deep and timeless as the blanketing snow; the house lay in a slumber that would not be broken.

Carmen went downstairs and pulled on her boots and the old sheepskin jacket that had once belonged to Sofia. Then she went outside, closing the door quietly behind her, and stood looking out through the quick white vapor of her breath.

The strange white world lay stroked by silence. No birds sang. There was only a narrow road around the house now, hummocked with unbroken snowdrifts, with a narrow path leading away down to the marketplace. Carmen set out down the white tunnel of the path, slowly, stepping high to keep the snow out of her boots. As soon as she moved away from the house, she felt very much alone, and she made herself go on without looking back, because she worried that if she did look over her shoulder, she would find that the house was gone.

Carmen heard a faint noise ahead of her.

She stood still. The sound came again, through the muffling trees: a rhythmical, off-key tapping, like a hammer striking metal. It came in short irregular bursts, as though someone were hammering nails. As she stood listening, the world around her seemed to brighten a little; the close seemed less dense, the snow glittered, and when she looked up, the strip of sky over Victoria Street was a clear blue.

She trudged on toward the sound of hammering, and soon

came to the shop. She saw the stone buildings thick-roofed with snow; she saw blue woodsmoke rising, and smelled it, too. She approached the shop that was open to the elements. She stared at the man inside and realized that she knew him. It was Bobby.

"Well met, Robert," she said.

The broad-shouldered man in the burgundy apron glanced up. He frowned briefly, then nodded in welcome. "Eh, Carmen. You're out early."

"It's a new day," said Carmen.

"That it is," said Bobby, and went back to his hammering. Carmen blinked her way toward it. It was impossible to see the end.

"It looks like it goes on for—"

Suddenly Bobby stiffened, and Carmen did, too. She heard a faint noise behind her.

Whirling around, she caught the figure of Jackson McClockerty marching up the street. She could smell the contents of the bag of McDonald's he had in his hand. Quick as a flash, Bobby pulled across the black curtains, so the back of the shop could no longer be seen.

"The girl is abroad," said Jackson, looking at her, amused. She stared back at him.

"Want one of these?" He proffered the McDonald's bag toward her. It smelled good, but just as he did so, Bobby immediately started up a very loud hammering again, and the moment was lost.

"No thanks," said Carmen.

"Suit yourself," said Jackson, taking a large bite. "Hope that doesn't keep you," he said to Bobby. "You've got work for me."

Bobby looked up at him. "Aye," he said steadily.

"Well," said Jackson. "Can't see this working for long. Don't worry. I'll be waiting."

They watched him leave. Carmen shivered. "That guy gives me the creeps."

"Oh, he has no power over Victoria Street," said Bobby. "Not in the end. Remember that."

He headed back into the shop. "Come see this," he said, pulling back the curtain.

"You started after last night?" said Carmen.

"No time like the present," said Bobby. "I still have to work the day."

He checked something, then commanded her to stand back. And then he flicked a switch.

Among every stack, more and more, going back, were beautiful ancient hanging pendant lights, metal, in a smart dark green color. They came on one after another, back and back.

"Oh my God," said Carmen, who never went that far back, and had never managed to count the stacks in the dark. "It's huge!"

"There's more," said Bobby, leading her through. Sure enough, off to the side there were cave-like indentations in the very rock itself, ancient hollowings-out. Mr. McCredie had filled those, too, with maps and tomes and vintage illustrations.

"Oh my God!" said Carmen. "This is mad."

"I would strongly suggest a no smoking policy," said Bobby. "I've got you a couple of fire exit signs from the hardware shop, they're covered by Crawford's kind, posh friends, too."

"My God," said Carmen. "It's literally an Aladdin's cave."

Bobby smiled. "It is. God knows how you'll sort it."

"I think," said Carmen, "I'll need to take everything I can out to the front—everything Christmassy and wintry. And lots of children's books and lovely editions. Then for the rest, until I get a chance to get to it, I think we might just let people explore. Discover treasure for themselves. I want them to feel its magic, too. Bobby. Thank you thank you thank you thank you."

"Bronagh said that the frost would change things," said Bobby.

"She also said the ghost of a brokenhearted fisherwoman in Leith cursed the path her man walked upon, and that's why they can't finish the tram extension."

Bobby scratched his head. "Yeah, that makes total sense actually."

But Carmen did feel different.

THEY MADE THEIR way to the little sitting room at the back. Mr. McCredie was already seated with his tea in front of the blazing fire.

"Good morning," said Carmen. "I thought I heard you earlier."

Mr. McCredie frowned. "It's very bright in here."

"Uh-huh," said Carmen. "We discussed this, remember?"

He nodded. "And I have to say," he said, as if surprised, "it makes it a lot easier to read."

EVENTUALLY, CARMEN MADE hand-painted signs that pointed an arrowed route around the store to stop people banging into each other in the narrow gaps between the stacks. They went counterclockwise, in the hope that they would end up popping out neatly at the cash desk, ready to buy or at least better conceal whatever it was they were stealing. And this in itself worked reasonably well, apart from a few people stuffily telling her that this wasn't Ikea, thank you. More commonly, someone would arrive at the cash desk and realize they did, in fact, want to purchase the eighteenth-century *Illustrated Weekly News Guide to Verified Sightings of Mermaids*, or some such, and make their way back, only to discover that they could not find said book again amid the thousands and thousands of tomes; that where they'd thought it was full of *A Lavish Guide to the French Court Ballet of Louis Quinze* or a book of Victorian dress samples or a horrifyingly high stack of apocalypse literature, from atom bombs to zombies, as if the books themselves were on the move; detectives visiting fairyland and cricketers going to sea.

Oh, the fun of that first morning! The shock on the faces of the regulars, realizing there was a whole new world to explore; like a dream in which there is a door in your house you have never opened before. Ronald, a railway fan, found a huge vintage transport section and his eyes widened. He took out his phone, then quickly put it away again.

"What are you doing?" asked Carmen.

"I was going to put a picture on my train enthusiast website. But they'll only all come here and ruin the place."

"Do it!" said Carmen, but Ronald shook his head firmly, marching toward the locomotives section.

"Well, at least tell me the website," bellowed Carmen after him, taking a photo anyway.

"I've already said too much," said Ronald stiffly before stroking in a slightly too-affectionate way a full set of 1967 trans-Pennines timetables.

Tourists, too, were dumbfounded, excited to be able to explore back into the rock and asking if she'd found any plague victims there, then looking disappointed when she shook her head. So Carmen took to shrugging, as she hadn't one hundred percent proved there weren't any plague victims down there and, by the way, had they seen the plague section?

Two DAYS LATER, Carmen was happily looking at the new layout, and then, occasionally, out into the snow. It was beautiful, and people were traipsing up and down Victoria Street, slipping, heading up and down to West Bow and taking lots of photographs. All was as it should be.

At lunchtime, exhausted but cheerful, she stood back and looked at the shop. The difference was remarkable. The space just went on and on. Then the doorbell tinged and, extending her joy even further, the children poured in.

"Auntie Carmen!" Phoebe yelled, dashing over, knocking over an entire pile of farting bear books on the way. Carmen didn't mind.

"My darling," she said, as Pippa and Jack filed in with shy smiles, Rudi bringing up the rear.

"You're working the weekend?"

"I help out where I can," said Rudi, who looked absolutely none the worse for wear from whatever he'd been getting up to in his spare time. He even smelled lovely, of some sharp tobacco and citrus aftershave, when Carmen got close enough to sniff him.

"Are you sniffing me?"

"No," said Carmen. "But if I was . . ."

"Penhaligon's," said Rudi.

"Sofia is paying you how much?"

"Oh, not mine," said Rudi. Carmen gave him a look and he grinned back that irrepressible grin she couldn't help returning.

"Oh my *goodness*," came a voice. It was Jack, who did not normally express excitement in a bookshop. "Is it a maze? You have a maze here now?" He didn't stop for an answer but bolted into the stacks.

"Uh . . ." Carmen twisted around, but he'd already disappeared.

"This looks incredibly cool," said Rudi. "Well, for nerds. It's like Disney for nerds."

"Thank you!" said Carmen, for whom this was the highest compliment imaginable. "I am so happy to see you all!" she added to the children. "Pippa, how are your tests going?"

"Well," started Pippa self-importantly, "Oliver J and Oliver P were saying, 'Pippa, you mustn't think you're going to come top anyway because sometimes boys need to come top, too.' And I said boys never come top, and they said well watch out for it this year."

"Are they twins?" Phoebe wanted to know.

"Don't be so *stupid*, Phoebe; they have the same name."

"Oh yes," said Phoebe, and Carmen instinctively tucked her arm around the little girl's shoulders.

"So I said anyway I will come top and if I don't then I will tell on you for when you were looking in the girls' toilets," finished Pippa in a rush, beaming.

"That sounds reasonable," said Carmen. "Smart *and* strategic."

Pippa gave her a look as if she didn't trust whether Carmen was being sarcastic or not.

"How's your boyfriend?" Carmen asked.

"Oh, I told him he wasn't trying hard enough, so he's buying me something expensive for Christmas," said Pippa.

"*What?*" said Carmen.

"You have to demand the attention you deserve," said Pippa.

"You're in *Primary Seven*!"

"When you're right you're right," said Rudi, giving Pippa a high five.

"It's not about the gift," explained Pippa. "It's about the care and attention to your needs."

Carmen rubbed her head. "I'll bear that in mind."

Jack came tearing back through the exit behind the cash desk.

"Wow!" he said. "Okay, this shop is so much better now."

He held up a book he'd found on Second World War aircraft. It was called *New Aircraft of Today*.

"Aha," said Mr. McCredie, bustling through. "Now, let me show you what's interesting about this. The Spitfire, you see . . ." And he launched into a learned disputation about Birmingham, finishing, eventually, with, "Now, you must take this book away and let me know what you think."

"You must not!" said Carmen. "You must buy it with some of your parents' money, which they have loads of!"

Mr. McCredie looked sorrowful so she mimed someone whooshing through the snow at him to remind him of his Antarctic commitments, although she'd never been skiing so she wasn't terribly good at it. But he cottoned on eventually.

"Ah yes," he said.

"I've also got some books about a farting bear," said Carmen hopefully, "at Christmas."

Phoebe picked up a copy, frowning, and opened a random page. "'*So, Mr. Bear. Do not worry; of course you are still welcome to our vegan Christmas feast even though you love to fart. Farting is normal, even at Christmas!' said Mr. Snake."* She looked at Carmen. "They are inviting a bear around *just to do farting*?"

"At Christmas!" said Carmen.

"But snakes lie on the ground! The bear would fart, like, downward at the poor snake."

"I don't think snakes can smell," said Jack, who was profoundly interested in crawling and slithering animals of all kinds.

"Well, that's why they don't mind the farting, then," said Carmen.

"That's not very fair on the penguins," said Phoebe, studying the illustration. "Penguins are even more at bear bum height than snakes."

"Do they stop the bear farting with the penguin's beak?" said Jack, interested.

Carmen flicked through it. "No, we learn a lesson about doing more yoga. Okay. Oh, and being kind to people with IBS. Huh. That took a swerve."

"Can I see your new room?" said Phoebe. "My room has new fairy lights now."

"Except you keep leaving them on in the daytime and letting the battery run down," said Pippa.

"I do *not*! Oh, I do do that sometimes," said Phoebe, who found almost everything about being eight quite challenging. "I miss you being downstairs," she continued, and Carmen was intensely gratified. "Except now we have Rudi! And he is *brilliant*!"

"*And* he plays soccer," interjected Jack.

"And he knows a lot about the bassoon," said Phoebe.

"He knows a lot about the pink oboe," said Carmen, smiling sweetly in Rudi's direction, who stuck out his tongue.

SHE LEFT MR. McCREDIE in charge, told him not to get lost in the stacks, and led the children through the caves toward the steps.

"I'll need to start locking this door," she said as they went through the stairway. "Stop people wandering up."

"Or just fill it with more books," said Rudi. "Let them keep wandering."

Carmen smiled. "Gosh, we probably could," she said. "Just carry on and on, books for miles, on and on forever. Right across the city."

They ascended, past the rooms piled high with books from all over the world; on up into the roof of the house, towering over the Lawnmarket.

"This'll keep you fit," observed Rudi, who couldn't hold the balustrade, which was on the left of the little staircase. He looked around the many doors. "And it's just him?" he said in wonderment.

"And me, now," said Carmen.

He shook his head. "All these years?" he said. "You know how many homeless people there are in Edinburgh?"

Carmen did, in fact, know, having dated Oke, who had an interest in this kind of thing, but she wasn't thinking about him. When she'd recovered her phone, she had checked it, just once, to see if he had got back in touch, and of course he hadn't. But then the world had changed, because the snow had fallen. So now it was time to move on.

They reached the top floor at last, the children's little boots clattering on the wooden steps, and revealed the conservatory garden. The children gasped. Outside the snow had completely carpeted the roofs and balcony and was piled high against the French windows.

"It's a fairy garden!" said Phoebe, enchanted.

"I think those plants are dead," said Pippa, rather more pragmatically. Rudi whistled through his teeth. Snow had started gently falling again, covering the glass roof.

"Wow," he said. "This is . . ."

"Amazing! I know!" said Carmen.

"A mess," said Rudi. "These poor plants . . . Look at you, poor little poinsettia."

He picked out a handful of soil. "Well, they've been watered, but that's not enough. This soil is barren. It needs to be completely dug up, replaced. It needs good mulch, fertilizer. Blood and bone."

"That sounds disgusting."

"No worse than your average sausage."

"Fair enough," said Carmen.

"What's wrong with sausage?" said Phoebe.

"Never you mind," said Rudi. He looked at the pots again, and wiped some dust off a leaf with his good arm.

"Hey, kids! Who wants to grow some lovely things for spring?" he said.

"Can we grow flowers?" asked Pippa.

"Yes," said Rudi.

"A Venus flytrap?" said Jack.

"No," said Rudi.

"A dandelion?" said Phoebe.

"That's not a flower; that's a weed!" said Pippa.

"But I like them!"

"It's a weed!"

"We will grow many things," said Rudi. He looked around once more. "Try to keep everything watered, and I'll bring them over with stuff soon, yeah?"

Carmen nodded happily. "Yes please!"

"I love your new fridge house, Auntie Carmen," said Phoebe.

"Come whenever you like," said Carmen, kissing her on the head.

"Ugh, don't do that; you'll eat nits," said Jack.

"She will *not*!" hollered Phoebe.

"Okay, come on, you monkeys, let's go," Rudi interrupted smoothly. "We've got to get to the Meadows for Jack's soccer practice."

"And hot chocolate," whispered Phoebe.

"Won't they cancel for the snow?"

"Well, if they do we will have a massive snowman building competition on the Meadows. And crush all-comers."

They clattered down the stairs. Carmen felt a tug. She would like, too, to be going to the Meadows to build a huge snowman, then have a hot chocolate. But she had to get back to work, then come home, on her own . . .

Her optimistic mood was fading. At the bottom of the stairs, Phoebe threw her arms around her.

"Can you come and have hot chocolate?"

Rudi looked at her inquiringly.

"Not today, sweets," said Carmen. "I have a lot to do. But soon."

"And we will come back soon, and we will make you a garden," said Rudi sincerely, and she looked at him, sure that her gratitude showed in her face.

Chapter Twenty-One

Okay, Carmen thought, waking yet again into the stillness and magical air that proved that the snow had not left the city. Okay. To work. In her beautiful big new shop. The children had made paper chains and she would hang them everywhere on the new shelves. Any leftover lights she could beg, borrow, or steal now snaked their way around the new layout.

Just a few days in, it was already obvious that the stacks were working, although not in the least how Carmen had expected. She had tried to organize them thematically—there were, for instance, some absolutely splendid biographies of people Carmen had never heard of: generals, female weavers, St. Kilda inhabitants, and old music hall stars, so she bunched them together.

There was a beautiful church section, which must have come from some ancient cathedral sell-off, something Carmen couldn't quite imagine. But there were exquisite illustrated Bibles and missals; oil-painted books, even though when you opened them they turned out to be *Tales of the Saints for Children*, and those tales of the saints seemed to involve a lot of cutting bits off themselves, or falling down dead in useful circumstances. Carmen glanced at a particularly brutal full-color St. Agatha, and decided not to shift it to the children's section just yet.

And the classics section . . . Carmen cursed herself—and then, more sensibly, cursed Mr. McCredie—for not making more of it before. It was huge. Here were beautiful early editions of anything and everything: *Waverley*, *Sunset Song*, Dickens, Austen, Trollope,

Coleridge, Eliot, and everything imaginable in between in any format you could think of.

So everything was more or less, if not in order, at least in the spirit of the shop. But it was more than this. Every stack contained something—just a little something—that would snag your attention as you browsed and render itself irresistible.

The classics had a copy of *Was Jane Eyre a Murderer?*, a book that tried to detect real literary crimes, and a copy of *Thursday Next*, about an imaginary literary detective, who did likewise. The sensational map section had books on the politics of borders, written before the current borders of the world; books from the 1940s that were extraordinarily prescient on the future of the Middle East; and beautiful illustrated poetry books about the possible existence of Australia. Every time she tried to clean or tidy up, Carmen found something to grab her attention. In the church stack, it was a book of beautifully illustrated marginalia from illuminated manuscripts: where bored monks had scrawled graffiti, or drawn angry cats, or set little quizzes for each other.

And it wasn't just Carmen who got caught like this. People would come in looking for a tourist guide to Edinburgh, set off down the stacks, and reemerge forty-five minutes later, babbling about the mile-long railway tunnel that still existed under Leith Walk, or that The Caledonian Hotel was secretly a train station. People would come in for the latest children's book, and leave with a full set of math examination papers from 1913.

Mr. McCredie was an infuriating man in many ways, thought Carmen, serving one slightly glazed-eyed but happy customer after another, but he knew his books.

"I feel like it goes on forever," said the professor, whose hair was green today. "How . . . how could you have been hiding it away all this time? The world needs to know about this."

"They do!" said Carmen. "Please put us on Instagram."

"But then it won't be our secret place." She frowned.

A bookish young couple in tank tops came in, cackling and ex-claiming and treating the maze as their flirting zone. And an older man, unkempt, his clothes very worn and with holes in his shoes, huddled in a far corner, simply keeping warm.

"Christopher Pickle," said Mr. McCredie gravely, when Carmen mentioned him, guiltily wondering what she should do. Mr. Mc-Credie vanished toward their new poetry stack and came back with a thin, ancient volume of poetry titled *The Long Dark*.

"The most gifted poet of our generation," he said, glancing in the man's direction. "The world proved not ready for him. But he has a place here."

And after that, Carmen posted a little stool next to the end of the poetry stacks, and Christopher Pickle came in often, scrib-bling feverishly in a little book, nodding his head in gratitude.

A FEW MORNINGS later, a wild woolly-looking man came charging out of the stacks. Carmen hadn't seen him come in. She eyed him suspiciously.

"When did you get here?"

"I am absolutely not sleeping in one of the rooms off the stacks," said the man. "Although if I was, I would say you should put more wood on the fire before you shut."

Carmen frowned, but not before she wondered if it was warmer in the stacks than it was in her aerie. At least the books would act as insulation, wouldn't they? Also, which room off the stacks? How far back did the books go? She could follow the pathway to the sit-ting room and the stairs, but behind that there was no lighting and she didn't even know what was there.

Perhaps the books carried on underneath the entire city; with steps down from the library, under the Mound, millions of mil-lions of words and papers, filling the Leith tunnel all the way to the sea. She liked the idea of it.

"But I would definitely like this," he said, putting a vast book

Carmen had never seen before on the counter. "Which I have just found now, at this exact second," he added quickly.

Carmen wiped the dust off it with a yellow cloth. The cover was a huge spreading drawing of a place she knew—the Ormiston yew. It was "An Intimate History" of a tree that had stood, near Edinburgh, when Jesus was born. The Romans had known it. The Jacobites had hidden in it.

The book was beautiful and Carmen had never heard of it. The tree had been a passion of Oke's and suddenly her memory of him, and them together, poured through her like ice water.

"I'm sorry," she said, her voice choked. "It's . . . it's not for sale."

"I don't think anyone has touched it for thirty-five years," said the man.

"That's because it's *not for sale*," said Carmen, her voice sharper than she'd intended. The stacks were wonderful, but not everything they uncovered was welcome.

"Huh. Okay then," said the man, lifting his rucksack on his back. "Also, you should do room service."

And he stomped out of the shop, and Carmen crossly hugged the book and planned to take it upstairs before someone else tried to take it from her. Not that . . . well. She'd just keep it out of the way for a bit, that was all.

THE PHONE RANG late one morning. Carmen mentally prepared herself for bookshop phone conversations, which normally went along the lines of, "I want that book I've seen on TV—it's purple?"

She'd got quite good at this game, in fact, and was often surprisingly accurate on what the book shows were talking about that week, much to the surprise of the caller. But it was nice, knowing a happy David Nicholls book was going to make its way to an equally happy recipient. Sometimes if it were a book she had taken a terrible dislike to because of some inexplicable reason, mostly about beautiful women abandoned in swamps or torn apart, she would recommend something she reckoned the caller would genuinely enjoy much more, and that worked pretty well, too.

"Hello? McCredie's?"

The line crackled. They had to replace the phone. Carmen wondered if there was anything left in Crawford's charity fund. She doubted it. Not that she wasn't grateful; she truly was, but if she'd known they were going to be the recipients, she'd probably have drunk less of his expensive champagne.

"Hi, yeah?"

Americans.

"Uh-huh?"

"Hi, yeah, this is the production office?"

The film! Carmen had forgotten all about it.

"Yeah, we're going to do, like, a launch party in Edinburgh? And we'd like to use the shop again?"

Carmen thought quickly. "Well, it's getting close to Christmas . . . That's going to be very expensive."

The voice paused.

"We're going to do an international launch and press call, to the world's media, with famous film stars and a red carpet . . . and you want to *charge* us for it?"

"Worth a shot," said Carmen cheerfully.

"Oh well, in that case, we'll just ask the town council to shut the entire street and we'll do it in front of your shop," said the person. "They will, you know. They'll stick a marquee right in front of your entrance. For days. And shut off the road even to foot traffic."

"I know," said Carmen with a heavy heart.

"They already offered us their Traffic Warden Militia for security."

"Okay," said Carmen. "If I let you use the shop will you mention us in the publicity?"

"Yes."

"Will you over-order on wine and let us keep some of it?"

"No."

"Will you order some whiskey that nobody will drink and let us keep that?"

"I'm . . . That can probably be arranged."

"We'll do it," said Carmen.

Chapter Twenty-Two

Plausible deniability, Mary thought to herself. And he'd forget he'd asked, probably. Sin of omission, she simply wouldn't mention it. Or if he asked her straight out . . . well, she'd say she didn't know who he meant. He'd been delirious.

Of course Mary knew who he meant. Oke had mentioned Carmen throughout the research trip. He probably didn't even realize he'd been doing it. He'd be talking excitedly about the trees of Scotland then he would say, "I went to see them with Ca . . ." and then he'd trail off and stop talking. It wasn't hard to put it together. It was an unusual name in Scotland, plus she ran a bookshop so it was easy enough to google her, but when she did so she realized she'd come across her already: Carmen followed Mary on Instagram. But she hadn't liked a single post. *Interesting*, thought Mary. *Very interesting*.

She wasn't *that* pretty, Mary thought. Okay, so she had dark hair and pink cheeks, but she was plainly short and quite round. Her Instagram was mostly shots of a bookshop and pictures of books and to Mary's delight there were absolutely none with Oke in them. There had, in fact, been loads, but Carmen had taken them all down in a fit of pique in March and couldn't bear to put them back up again.

So, she obviously wasn't suffering at all and basically absolutely did not deserve someone as great as Oke, Mary justified to herself. After all, if she missed him, she'd have got in touch herself. She, Mary, would have been utterly frantic if she didn't know where

Oke was. She would have torn the country apart looking for him. Carmen, on the other hand, was posting pictures of children planting bulbs in pots, and lots of bookshelves.

There didn't appear to be a website for the shop she worked at, so that was weird. Well. She'd tried. I mean, she could DM her on Instagram, but loads of people didn't look at their DMs. Maybe her DMs were blocked. Who knew if that would even get to this woman? They'd broken up. They'd absolutely broken up. That woman didn't give a crap what was up with Oke. She didn't care. She didn't deserve him. And Mary had loved him for such a long time.

Mary did not pass on Oke's message. Surely he would forget, she thought. Surely. She'd get him better and he would forget, and realize what was best for him.

Chapter Twenty-Three

The trailer for the film landed shortly afterward.

Carmen went to Sofia's so they could all watch it on the huge-screen TV. It came up as "Coming Soon" on the big streaming service and she'd taken Mr. McCredie with her. Back at Mr. McCredie's house, they had settled into a comfortable evening pattern of eating a simple meal—it was rather helping with her post-party-bag recovery phase—and reading in front of the fire, which Carmen was finding both restful and occasionally completely terrifying, as if she'd gone to sleep one night and woken up aged seventy-two.

Mr. McCredie was utterly bamboozled that somebody would have a screen that size in their house and kept trying to discuss confidential legal matters with Sofia, who was technically his lawyer, and who kept trying to shush him. The girls were bouncing up and down on the sofa in excitement and baby Eric was bouncing because he liked bouncing.

"I think we should have been in it," Pippa was complaining. "I could have played my bassoon."

"Well, I don't think it could make it any worse," said Jack, who had already seen the trailer on his phone and was bored of it. It was very much not his kind of film.

Jingling bell music played over a sunny, snowy city.

"This holiday season," came a deep American voice, "travel to a land beyond imagination."

The sisters looked at one another.

"Do they mean this actual real land we're standing on right now?" said Sofia.

"Sssh!" said Carmen, who felt some ownership toward the movie, seeing as it was filmed in the shop, and was taking it personally.

"Hi. I'm new in Edinbo-row," said Genevieve with her mound of very shiny hair, stepping out of a London bus onto the Grass-market.

"Weel, bonny lassie, weelcome to Scotland, to be sure, to be sure. I'm Lord McEarl," said Lind, who was wearing a full kilt, except it was a hunting tartan paired with a Bonnie Prince Charlie jacket, which made Carmen's teeth hurt.

He was standing in front of the shop, though, and everybody cheered. There was some fake snow here and there on the ground, even though the bright golden light made it perfectly clear that it was obviously being filmed in the middle of the summer.

"And why do you no coom into ma wee sleekit book shoppy just here?"

"No thank you, I don't think books are very good," said the woman. "I like clothes and shoes and I think men who sell books are soft."

Large mystical pipes that sounded clearly Irish to Carmen swelled as the scene cut to the beautiful woman in a minidress walking down the cobbles in the dark, wearing a pair of gigantic heels that looked alarmingly ready to break her ankles, and coming across two red-haired men having a fight.

"Naw, but GEE MEE ALL YOUR HEROIN," shouted one.

"NEVER! FREEDOM! I'm GONNA DAE A MURRRRR-DDEEERRRRRR," shouted the other.

The beautiful Genevieve would have looked distressed if her face hadn't had too much plastic surgery and she couldn't actually make many facial expressions, but she held up her hands.

"Dinnae worry, my bonnie brave wee lassie," said Lord McEarl, appearing out of a side alley. "Why yes, hard drugs are our scourge, but it remains a beautiful and mystic land."

He did some rather murky punching and the two men immediately ran away, holding their faces with one hand and shaking their fists at one another. This was the only bit Jack liked.

The Irish pipes were back and suddenly the pair were soaring above Loch Ness in a hot-air balloon.

"Aye, she's just doon there," said the man, pointing at the badly Photoshopped head of a monster. That was Phoebe's favorite bit.

"Hiya, Nessie!" she called out cheerfully.

Then the scene cut again and they were somehow pulling a huge fir tree up Victoria Street.

"It is from one of my many estates," said Lord McEarl. "But I am lonely there. It's a terribly sad and lonely life, being a millionaire landowner in Edinburgh."

"Oh no!" said the brunette.

"Och aye!"

Then it cut back into the shop. A slightly smaller cheer this time from the assembled.

"Why yes, this *did* belong to Mary, Queen of Scots!" Genevieve was saying. "We have an entire 'Books that belonged to Mary, Queen of Scots' section just over there! *Some* still have blood on them from where she got her head chopped off!"

The music changed again to something jaunty and suddenly a roomful of charmingly diverse Scots, from all backgrounds yet somehow attired in full Highland dress, all joined in laughing with her heartily.

"This Christmas," came the deep American voice, "travel to a land of wonder and mystery . . ."

"Well, you can't," pointed out Sofia, "because the trains are all on strike and the ferries don't work."

". . . and discover the true *heart of Scotland*!"

The words *HEART OF SCOTLAND* came on the screen in tartan lettering.

"I thought the heart of Scotland were those stones you spit on on the ground," said Jack, looking confused.

"That's the Heart of Midlothian," said Sofia absently. "And don't spit on it; it's dirty."

"Only if you lick the ground after," said Jack cheerily.

"But I don't understand," said Mr. McCredie. "Does that woman work in our bookshop?"

Sofia and Carmen looked at one another.

"You know how moving pictures work, though, right?" said Carmen, slightly worried that he really was losing his marbles. He had been clutching a letter all day and looking confused and she didn't like it.

"Oh! Of course," said Mr. McCredie. "She's an actress."

"She's an actor," said Carmen. "Yes."

"Right. I . . . I thought it might be a documentary."

Carmen and Sofia exchanged glances again.

"They just waved at the Loch Ness Monster from a hot-air balloon," said Carmen.

"Yes, yes," said Mr. McCredie. "I wasn't really watching. It's terribly loud."

"Do you not remember them filming? In the shop? In the summer?"

Mr. McCredie frowned. "I reread *Moby-Dick* over the summer. And it was *just* as marvelous as I remembered. Did you know—"

"Okay," said Carmen. "Well, I'm glad I brought you, then."

There was a noise outside: Rudi arriving at the basement door.

"Rudi!" shouted the children in a way they hadn't really ever shouted for Carmen, she couldn't help but notice.

Rudi popped in.

"Hello!" he beamed. "What's up? You going to the South Pole yet, Mr. McCredie?"

Mr. McCredie sighed. "Not quite yet, no," he said.

Carmen winced slightly. There were more people coming to the shop, that was true, but they had so many more lights on and a new heater at the back, and although it barely shifted the thermometer, their power bill had immediately leapt from "just about manageable" to "sell a kidney."

"But it's all right. I'm going to Jackson McClockerty's Christmas party. He says he absolutely has a way to make it happen for me."

"*What?*" said Carmen, who couldn't believe her ears. "What are you talking about? We are bending over backward to make it happen! We're going nuts!"

"Well, Mr. McClockerty came to see me again and said he can guarantee the trip—buy me a ticket, he said."

"But I've been working my ti—head off! And what about Crawford doing the fundraising dinner? It might just take a little longer, that's all. The Antarctic isn't going anywhere."

Mr. McCredie held up the letter. Carmen took it and read it. At first it didn't make any sense.

"This is what . . . insurance?" she said. Mr. McCredie nodded. "I don't get it."

"I'm seventy-nine, my dear," said Mr. McCredie simply. "They will insure me this year. They won't insure me next. It's either now or never."

There was a silence.

"But after everything we've done," said Carmen.

"It's all a drop in the ocean, my dear," said Mr. McCredie. "I think Jackson will have to get us to the finish line."

"But he'll ruin the shop; we've been through this!" said Carmen in disbelief. "I am working day and night to try to sort this out for you! And you don't do anything; you just sit in a corner reading and complaining about the metric system."

"It's just such a clinical way of describing our beautiful earth . . ."

"It means nothing agrees with each other . . . Oh my God, forget about the fricking metric system. You can't give in to this guy! You've seen what he's done to Bobby! You know he just wants to ruin everything and I'm only doing it for *you* and you are doing *nothing* except marching about talking about polar bears."

"That's the No—"

"Penguins, *sodding penguins*!"

There was a silence in the room, and Carmen realized that a) she was bright red in the face and was shouting very loudly at an old man, b) Mr. McCredie looked cowed, but not as if he were backing down in any way, and c) everyone was staring at her. Phoebe was looking scared; Sofia never shouted. Carmen felt herself flush even hotter. She didn't like looking out of control in front of Rudi, either.

"Well," said Mr. McCredie, standing up, "I didn't realize you felt so strongly."

"I can't work for that guy!"

"Well, I thought you worked for me."

Carmen bit her lip. "For now I do."

They looked at each other. Mr. McCredie's large blue eyes looked hurt. "Oh," he said.

"It's going to work," said Carmen. "With the new stacks. Just give it time."

"I *don't* have time."

"Carmen, please," said Sofia. Carmen looked down. Phoebe was holding her hand, suddenly.

"Don't be cross, Auntie Carmen," she said. "I don't like it when people are cross."

"I'm not cross," lied Carmen. "I'm just standing up for myself."

"Are you sure you're not being a bully, Auntie Carmen?" said Pippa.

"No!" said Carmen. "I'm just . . . I'm just trying to do what's right, Pippa. Everyone's just trying to do what's right."

She felt exhausted suddenly. All the jubilation for the new stacks, about getting the film company to host a party at the shop, and the thrill of seeing the trailer had faded away. All the work she'd put in. Was it all going to waste?

"Is the shop going to close?" said Phoebe sadly.

"No," said Carmen.

"It may have to change," said Mr. McCredie.

She looked at him.

"What?" he said, in his kindly manner. "Aren't you always telling me I have to face cold hard facts?"

Carmen folded her arms. "And aren't you always telling me that there are many, many things more important than money?"

Chapter Twenty-Four

It is quite tricky having a fight with someone when you then have to accompany them back to the home you both share. They were quiet en route. As soon as they reached the Lawnmarket, Mr. Mc-Credie scuttled downstairs, and Carmen made her way upstairs, still furious.

She felt so downcast, not least because Sofia had obviously been irritated with her for fighting in front of the children. But also because she thought—she absolutely did think—that this could work. Okay, so everything needed a coat of paint and more dusting than she could get around to at short notice.

But also, she didn't even think people minded that so much. The old rugs she'd dug up for the stone floor were worn, but they were interesting, and there was an absolute sense that there was hidden treasure in the shelves—who knew, maybe even a copy of the rare and valuable *Up on the Rooftops* somewhere. That would be like a EuroMillions ticket, she reflected ruefully. Probably not worth counting on.

But there was a thrill in getting lost among the dark twists and turns of the bookshelves; finding the magic and mystery section deep in a side cave, cut into the rock.

Funnily enough, the person who sorted her out was Rudi. He brought the children over the next day.

"What?" she said, leaning out of the window. Rudi laughed.

"GARDYLOO!" he shouted. "You look like a washerwoman."

"SEE," SAID RUDI, after the children had pounded around the house again—they absolutely adored it—and they were settled upstairs with Garibaldi cookies, a cookie nobody liked but Sofia was going through one of her phases and this apparently was some kind of meaningful childhood sugar compromise.

"What, you can have a cookie, but it's horrible?" said Carmen.

"More or less," said Rudi.

"Makes sense," said Carmen.

"This is horrid," said Jack, taking four.

"Okay," said Rudi. He unpacked his bag. Inside was a weed-spraying contraption, fertilizer, leaf polisher, and a beautiful red-and-yellow watering can, as well as several packets of bulbs.

"Merry Christmas," he said.

"Is this going to involve a lot of me running about carrying cold water?" Carmen asked.

Rudi patiently turned to the children and explained what they had to do to look after the plants and, pretending just to be polite, Carmen listened in and overheard him as he explained the growing cycle, how much water the poinsettia needed, what to do with greenfly, and how to make a lovely tasty mulch—"like dinner for the tree," as Phoebe put it.

"Rudi is a very good nanny," said Pippa, standing next to Carmen, who offered her the last Garibaldi ("No thank you," so Carmen ate it herself, despite not liking it one tiny bit).

"I see that," said Carmen.

"You should ask him for help."

"He's not *my* nanny!"

"Yeah, but he's just kind of good in general."

"Huh," said Carmen.

"So," said Rudi, turning around, "you know what you should do?"

"Is this something you and Pippa have cooked up together?"

"Pippa and I are actually a crack secret problem-solving team," said Rudi, and Pippa beamed with pleasure.

"Do you mean a couple of nightmare nosy parkers?" said Carmen.

"I mean that, too," said Rudi.

"Huh," said Carmen.

"Well," said Rudi, "you know I'm invited to Jackson McClockerty's famous Christmas party?"

"*You're* invited?" said Carmen. "Do you know, like, everyone?"

Rudi shrugged. "Well, I get around."

"*Clearly.*"

"Rudi has lots of friends," said Pippa. "Like me. We're very alike in many ways."

Carmen bit her lip so she didn't reply to this and Rudi caught it and grinned very quickly.

"So," said Rudi.

"So, what?"

"So, you should come with me. Keep an eye on Jackson; see what he says to Erich."

Carmen never ever called her boss Erich, nor even thought of him as an Erich.

"Then we can either persuade him out of it or just keep them apart."

"I honestly thought we were in the clear," said Carmen. "I never dreamed . . . I never dreamed he'd listen to that awful man."

"He's got more explorer blood in his veins than he looks."

"He's got more *ungrateful* blood in his veins than he looks," complained Carmen.

"What are you paying in rent again?" said Rudi.

"Shut up," said Carmen quickly.

"Come on," said Rudi, smiling, "it's a really good party."

"Your definition of a really good party," said Carmen, "is probably quite frightening to me."

"Okay," said Rudi. "Well, stay at home with your Frosties, then."

"We're not allowed Frosties," said Phoebe sadly. Carmen felt ashamed. The first thing she'd done after she left Sofia's house to perk herself up was to buy a large box of Frosties. She'd need to hide it somewhere.

"I don't want to give him the satisfaction of going to his stupid party," said Carmen.

But she remembered how it had felt going to Crawford's; the feeling that she had been missing for so long. Going out. Dressing up. Having fun. She'd left all her friends behind on the west coast; Idra worked every night. Staying in and reading books was lovely in its way, but . . .

Living in the center of town didn't help, either. Every night it was absolutely flooded with people: people dressed up in full kilts, sparkly gowns, or black tie, going for large dinners at the smart Witchery restaurant, or going dancing in the Grassmarket; work lunches tumbling out of restaurants in hysterics; silhouettes of parties in the windows of the many apartment buildings she could see from the house. People kissing in every close and secret stairwell of the city. It felt as though the whole of Edinburgh was having a great street party to celebrate Christmas, and there she was, on her own in her room, staring at the stars, night after night.

"Someone I hate in my class had a stupid party and I had to go and I hate him," said Jack. "It was an 'invite everyone' party."

All three of the children groaned.

"What?" said Carmen. "It's nice to invite everyone!"

"It *isn't*," said Phoebe fiercely. "The horrible people come."

"Phoebe, you're eight. There can't be that many horrible eight-year-olds."

Rudi and Phoebe snorted at exactly the same moment.

"Oh," said Carmen. "I thought it was just because I liked you so much they were all like that."

Phoebe looked placated.

"Anyway," said Jack, "I went to his stupid party because Mom made me. And I ate all his sausage rolls. All of them. I didn't even talk to him at all. I told Mom he wanted plasticine."

"What's wrong with plasticine?"

"*Nobody* wants plasticine."

The girls nodded in agreement.

"You spoiled toads!" said Carmen. "I loved plasticine!"

She remembered too late that she had enjoyed trying to stuff it up Sofia's nose and wandered over to examine the plants, which were indeed looking shinier and a bit less gray and close to death than they had done earlier.

"Well," said Jack, "I'm just saying. Go and eat all his sausage rolls."

Rudi nodded solemnly. "And save the bookshop."

"I think actually you should sell Nessies," said Pippa.

"Me too," said Phoebe.

"Don't you start," said Carmen. "Okay. I will. I'll do it."

"I'll pick you up at seven," said Rudi, sotto voce, as he ushered the children out, leaving Carmen completely discombobulated. Was this . . . a date? No. Surely not. Not at all. Definitely not.

And what if it was?

Chapter Twenty-Five

"The nice ginger?" said Idra, frowning.

"Don't say ginger, it's gingerist."

"What? How?"

"I don't know. But it is."

"It isn't! That's the color of his hair! That's literally what it's called! What am I meant to say, nice Pantone 21c?"

"It's not a date," said Carmen. "Well, it might be for him, he's a massive FB. But it isn't for me."

"Why not?" said Idra. "I like him. Why can't it be?"

"Well, you have a go, then. He lives at my sister's and he looks after my nieces and nephews."

"Were you planning on going at it in their living room?"

"Well, no, obviously not."

"In that case, I don't know what your problem is."

"My problem is . . ." began Carmen, then realized that her list of problems was so long and comprehensive it wouldn't really be appropriate to get into, and they'd be very late for the party.

"Never mind," she said. "Can you make me look fierce, please?"

"And it's in Jackson McClockerty's house?" said Idra.

"Uh-huh. How come *everyone* knows him?"

"His millionaire's house in Barnton?"

Barnton was a smart area of north Edinburgh, with leafy avenues and large houses.

"Uh-huh," said Carmen.

Idra grinned. "I think I'm going to take the night off and come," she said.

"What?" said Carmen. "Why?"

"Extra young female, trust me, he won't mind," said Idra. "And I want to see what his house is like! He's famous! He's always in *Hiya* magazine! Scotland's entrepreneur!"

"He's, like, fifty," said Carmen.

"Nothing wrong with fifty," said Idra. "I like the mature gentleman."

"You obviously haven't met him, then."

"Don't you want me to come?"

"Oh, I *do*," said Carmen, who hated her bestie working nights. "Although I'm slightly worried that I'm not even invited and if I turn up with a posse it will look like I was totally desperate to come to his stupid party when, in fact, I hate him."

"Oh, I thought you'd think I was muscling in on your date."

Carmen had also been thinking that. A little bit.

"It's not a date! I . . . don't think. No, it isn't. Anyway, Rudi gets around."

Idra raised her eyebrows. "Well, I think I'm going to come anyway. You never know who you're going to meet. And the restaurant is solid wall-to-wall moms' nights out from the local schools."

"Oh, that must be nice?" said Carmen absentmindedly, tracing on a black flick eye. Before Crawford's party, she hadn't dressed up for ages. It felt weird. The sparkly dress would have to come out again.

Idra looked at her as if she'd gone mad.

"Are you kidding? They're *moms*. They all work, they haven't been out for months, they're raising kids, they're *crazed*. Mentalists. Everyone is drunk by six thirty. I always put extra tissues in the ladies' because there *will* be crying."

"I thought Edinburgh moms were fancy?" said Carmen, thinking of Sofia.

"Ohhhh, they are. Some of them. They are hideous professionals on moms' nights out. They show up ecstatically greeting everyone, who are delighted they've attended, order bottles of prosecco, let everyone get comfy, don't even take a sip. Then when everyone is settling in, they jump up and say, 'So lovely, got to go,' fling down not quite enough cash, and fuck off, leaving everyone else completely trapped and drunk.

"And," she added ominously, "they wear *cream wool coats*. In *Edinburgh*. In *winter*."

"Maybe Bronagh is right about them being witches," said Carmen. "I never believed it, but now I'm starting to."

"Makes sense," said Idra. "Now, sit still. I am sticking eyelashes on you."

"It's like having a spider gummed to you," complained Carmen.

"I would think that's as close as you've been to getting off with someone in a long time."

"Oh God, that is very depressing."

"Yes, having a spider in your eyes is as close as you've been to sex in—"

"Stop it! I mean it."

"Well, do you think Ginger is up for it?"

"I think Ginger would be up for it with a fox terrier."

"Well then!" said Idra. "Why not?"

"My sister . . ."

"This, for once, has absolutely nothing to do with your bloody sister. It's the weekend. He gets time off. He can come back here." Idra frowned. "Can you put the heating on? It's freezing."

"I know," said Carmen. "There isn't any heating."

"Also all your plants are dead. It's a bit spooky."

"Exactly," said Carmen. "Even if I was inclined to bring him home, which I am absolutely not, and even if he didn't mind . . ."

"Because . . . fox terrier . . ."

"It's still . . . not exactly a shag pad."

"Oh, I don't know," said Idra, looking around. "It's rather lovely. You could light the fire?"

"I don't know how. Mr. McCredie lights the kitchen fire. I might burn down the house, plus it might be a bit, 'Hey, guess what, I lit this fire so I could lure you back here! For shagging!' Like wearing good underwear."

"Why don't you wear good underwear? Every day?"

"Because that turns it into bad underwear," said Carmen.

"So you buy new underwear, you massive dag."

"Okay, Miss Moneybags."

"Nice underwear isn't being a *moneybags*. It's basic self-care." Idra tugged Carmen's graying bra strap from under her T-shirt. "Seriously."

Carmen pouted. "I'm not wasting good stuff!"

"Your good stuff will all be eaten by mice by the time you ever get to it! You wearing this is a *guarantee* you won't pull."

Carmen looked down.

"I mean, do you want to pull or not?"

"I did," said Carmen. "And now . . . now I don't know how I feel about anything."

"You've lost your confidence," said Idra, but not unkindly. "You need to get it back. Need to do your best. Oke really kicked the stuffing out of you."

Carmen stared at herself in the mirror. Her dark eyes were wide; the fake eyelashes definitely made them stand out more.

She sighed.

"You're the one that thinks you have to get back to it, aren't you?" said Idra.

"I know."

"You're going to go for a whole year without . . ."

"It's perfectly common," said Carmen quickly.

Idra rummaged through Carmen's underwear drawer. They had been friends for a very long time.

"Christ," said Idra. "This looks like a PE Lost Property box."

She eventually fished out a neat black Lycra bra and some black panties.

"Better than nothing," she said. "Well, not better than actually nothing but it's pretty chilly out there."

"What are you wearing?" said Carmen. Idra pulled back her sharp black suit jacket top to reveal a cerise lace strap, and her trousers to show a matching thong.

"You wear a thong? Like, on purpose, for extended periods of time?" said Carmen. "Maybe it is you who's the witch."

"They're very comfortable when you get used—"

"No way," said Carmen. "It's your bare ass against your trousers all day. I refuse to believe that's comfortable."

"Okay," said Idra. "It makes you walk sexy and get attention."

"Thank you," said Carmen. She vanished into the freezing bedroom to get changed and came out in the sparkly dress. Idra added bright red lipstick and a large gold-colored necklace, and slicked back Carmen's dark hair.

"There you go," said Idra. "You look like *Cabaret*."

"Is that good or bad?"

"Very good." Idra put her arm around her. "Darling," she said in her deep voice. "You know. I think it's time."

"It is time," said Carmen. "I know."

"You want to be back to yourself, don't you?"

Carmen nodded.

"Well, this new foxier version."

"Well, quite."

"So," said Idra. "Game face on. Let's go. It doesn't have to be the ginger. It can be anyone you like. I just want to see you bubble again. Consider it a Christmas present to yourself."

Chapter Twenty-Six

The TV on the ward was tuned to DownFlix and Oke was dozing. He couldn't believe he was so sleepy; he felt a hundred and six. His mother was preparing food and his sisters were coming in, he knew. And Mary was going to be about; she was always there, asking him questions, chatting with his mother in an officious kind of way as if they had a lot to prepare. He overheard bits of conversations but was never quite sure, really, if he had heard them or simply dreamed them. The line between *his* reality and *actual* reality was still wobbly, a permeable membrane he didn't quite know which side he was on.

It was warm in bed, and he could see a bright sky outside, glowing summer, so he was surprised when the television started up a Christmassy bell-ringing jingle. He squinted his eyes. He had never paid any attention to Christmas before; it was something strange that took place far away from him, like people celebrating Eid or Chinese New Year. Nice for them, but not relevant to his daily life; something that just washed over him.

But last year it had been so central to his experience of being away, being somewhere new; such an important article of faith to the people around him. He couldn't deny, he respected it, obviously, as he respected all good things people loved and took joy in, but, if he was utterly honest with himself, he had enjoyed it, too. The dream of rebirth, embodied in a baby. It didn't seem so bad to celebrate a little, to display joy, even if being excited was, normally, not at all his way and certainly nothing to aspire to. But he had taken pleasure in the excitement of others, of the children, and of course of Carmen, whose face had shone at the choir singing carols, whose eyes had flashed like stars at the lights crowning the glorious city.

The jingling on television continued, and he found his eyes reluctantly focusing on the set.

"This holiday season—travel to a land beyond imagination," intoned a voice.

Then as Oke watched, more and more startled and confused, straining at the drip in his arm to lean forward to get a better look, a large red London bus pulled up on the cobbles—just outside the Christmas bookshop.

Oke blinked. He couldn't . . . What was he looking at? Was this real?

"I know this place," he croaked.

The nurse who was in with him smiled nicely, as if he was a child. "Of course you do, sweetie," she said and went back to looking at his chart.

"Is Carmen . . . ?"

He stared at the screen, his confused brain unable to make sense of what he was looking at. "Carmen?" he said. But the brunette on the screen wasn't the brunette he was looking for. Why was she serving behind the counter? He swung his legs off the bed.

"Oof, come on now," said the nurse. "None of that."

But Oke, although thin, and wobbly on his feet, was strong, and he walked forward, pulling the drip behind him as the camera swirled around the very familiar streets of Edinburgh. He wanted to touch the television; wanted to push his fingers up against it. He could almost feel a cool breeze come from the screen, smell a subtle hoppy smell from the last remaining brewery in the city, up by Haymarket, that sometimes came to you on the breeze at unexpected times of day.

He could almost feel the chill of the easterly winds swooping down the long rows of steps that made you shiver and pull your clothes around you and cram your hat further down on your head, looking forward to getting in out of the wind to a cozy bar or a warm library or even just the Scotmid supermarket where, he had learned to his surprise, even though he considered that he came from a friendly country, he had never lived anywhere where the checkout assistants had opinions on every item of your shopping, and it was actually the depths of rudeness not to share your plans for the rest of the day with them.

He closed his eyes, opened them again. Now there was a couple kissing in front of Edinburgh's Christmas market and he sighed slightly, so sure, for a moment, he could step into the screen, find himself exactly where he needed to be. So far from this over-hot, listless, stultifying summertime that never ended, into the cold, bracing air. He knew he would feel better. He would. If he could just get away from this heat.

"Hey, hey, hey," came a voice, as Mary entered, concern on her pretty face. "What are you doing up, *mea amor*?"

"Oh, he's doing okay," said the nurse, as if Mary had implied she was neglecting him.

"You are," said Mary in a singsong tone, as if speaking to a very small child. "Well done, you! Aren't you a big brave boy?"

Oke was still staring at the TV, which had finished the trailer and was now showing something baffling about dinosaurs entering a dance competition.

He stepped backward and sat down, reaching for the lukewarm water glass beside his bed and taking a long pull.

"There we are, well done," said Mary. Oke frowned; he felt light-headed, but still more alive than he had done in some time.

"I forget . . . I know I've been a bit delirious," he said.

"You've been ill," said Mary, patting his hand. "Don't worry, baby. I'm happy to look after you."

She leaned her head against his shoulder, then lifted it again as it became clear he wasn't particularly responding. He was still staring at the screen.

"Did I ask you to . . . did I ask you to contact Carmen?" he said. "I think I did. In Scotland?"

It was not easy for Mary to do this. She had been raised to be an extremely truthful person, to see telling the truth as the best thing she could do under almost all circumstances. She was not a bad person. She was madly in love with Oke, who was ill, and the last thing, she reasoned to herself, the last thing he needed was to go haring back to the other side of the world pursuing some absolute flibbertigibbet of a girl who had made him very unhappy. It would set him back and be bad for his health. She couldn't do that to him; she wouldn't. By any measure, the best thing for Oke would be to go home to his family, where his sisters could look after him and she would be just next door, maybe even taking a sabbatical from college for a little while so that she could look after him as a trained nurse should. And then, one day, hopefully, they would get married. That was absolutely what he needed and that was doing the right thing for him, for her, for the community, and probably for Carmen, who should probably stick to . . . Well, Mary's grasp on Scotsmen went about as far as Groundskeeper Willie on *The Simpsons*, so probably someone like that.

So she lied.

"Oh yes," she said. "Of course I did, I got in contact. But I haven't heard back."

Oke, still staring at the television screen, was conscious suddenly of a deep stabbing feeling in his heart. She hadn't even . . . she hadn't even got in touch. He was not a man inclined to feel sorry for himself, but he'd been in the hospital—extremely ill, according to absolutely everybody—and she hadn't even bothered to check how he was or get in touch with him at all. She didn't care. He had preferred it when she was angry.

"I see," he said carefully.

"Do you want me to prompt her?" said Mary. "I'm sure she's

very busy. I mean, they have some crazy fuss over there this time of year, don't they? I don't really know what they do, but I think it's a bit over the top. She's probably just forgotten."

This was a twist of the knife. Oke shut his eyes, turned his head away from the television. "No, it's okay. Thanks, Mary."

Mary put her hand on his shoulder. "I cannot wait till you get home. Everyone is going to spoil you rotten. Especially me. It must be soon now, look at you, you're better every day. Now you just need feeding up."

She playfully patted his flat stomach and he flinched slightly, which didn't go unnoticed by Mary. She put it down to him having had doctors crawl over him for weeks, sticking tubes in him, and told herself not to be daunted. Once he was home and safe and she was looking after him, everything would be all right.

"When do you think we can discharge him, Nurse?" she asked. The nurse still had his chart and looked at it.

"As long as he takes his medication, it'll be pretty soon . . . I think they wanted to get some weight on him."

"He's always like this," said Mary, giving him a possessive little pat and a giggle. "I'll try my best to feed him up!"

The nurse shrugged. "Well, he's getting better every day. As long as he promises to convalesce properly . . ."

"Of course he will!" said Mary. "We're all here!"

Oke looked around, puzzled. Why was Mary talking about him like he was a child? His head still felt a little fuzzy and full of cotton wool. What were they talking about? What did they mean?

"It's all going to be great," said Mary.

"I'll have the specialist check him out tomorrow," said the nurse. "But you seem to have it all under control."

Mary beamed.

Chapter Twenty-Seven

Rudi was not displeased in the slightest or discomfited to be picking up two women instead of one; quite the opposite. Carmen wondered what it must be like to feel so at home in your own skin, even when he didn't have the same amount of skin as other people. He was making Idra laugh by pointing out cold and miserable teenagers clumping through some of the most magnificent streets in the world, glued to their phones and dragging their feet on the cobbles at the awfulness of their extensive holidays.

"Rudi is being charming," said Carmen, in the back of the cab he'd hailed. "He does that."

"Nine sisters," said Rudi. "Can't help myself."

"A man who actually likes women," said Idra, arching her eyebrows at Carmen. "Interesting."

"Rudi likes *everyone*."

"I do," said Rudi. "Oh! Look, Phoebe's sent you a message."

He unlocked his phone and played the voice message.

"Hi, Auntie Carmen! We hope you have fun tonight at the party! With Rudi! Is he your new boyfriend?"

"He is *not*," came an authoritative voice off-screen. "Oh my God, Phoebe, don't be *disgusting*. He's our *manny*."

"Shut up, Pippa. You don't know."

"Well, I do know, actually, because I have a boyfriend and you will never have a boyfriend."

"*Shut up. I will have a boyfriend!*"

"Who will be your boyfriend?"

"Maybe . . . Peebles."

A shriek of fake laughter from Pippa, and genuine laughter from Jack. Carmen frowned.

"Who's Peebles?" said Idra.

"Next door's dog," said Carmen. "Oh God, Rudi, turn it off. I hate it when they tease her."

Rudi's voice could be heard on the message suddenly.

"If you have someone as good-looking, loyal, and cheerful as Peebles in your life, that will be an absolutely excellent choice. Smart thinking, Phoebe; well done."

Carmen felt herself softening. It was very hard for her not to warm to anyone who was nice to her niece.

They turned up a cul-de-sac marked "PRIVATE ROAD NO PARKING" in a suburban area of Barnton. The road was lined with yellow no-parking cones. Obviously the inhabitants of the street took their "private road" status very seriously indeed. There were also large "WARNING CCTV" and "NEIGHBORHOOD WATCH" and "WE DO NOT BUY OR SELL FROM THIS DOOR" signs everywhere, which made Carmen feel like she was misbehaving even though she hadn't done anything.

At the end of the cul-de-sac sat the largest house on what was effectively a small private estate. In Edinburgh the houses are often grand, but they tend toward the traditional: tall, narrow town houses, like Sofia's, austere and gray and symmetrical, or large Victorian homes with enormous bay windows, in which sat grand pianos or rocking horses or, this time of year, enormous Christmas trees decorated tastefully, with warm white lights and tartan ribbons.

This house, though, was something else. It had obviously been built around the 1980s, before planners started putting in at least tiny sops to the built environment of the old city. It was low and sprawling and absolutely vast, and reminded Carmen of that old TV show *Dallas* that her grandmother used to like. There were completely incongruous Greek columns across the front, on either side of a squat door that didn't seem quite in proportion to the rest of the house.

A huge driveway was lined with even huger cars, most of them massive Range Rovers, plus a low-slung, bright pink sports car, and was fully lit up with a Christmas display. It was extraordinary. Hundreds and hundreds of colored lights flashed on and off, leading from an illuminated ten-foot snowman to bright candy poles. On the roof was a Santa Claus and sleigh, which looked like it was probably visible from space. There was fake snow strewn across the grass and an American light-up mailbox. "Jingle Bells" was blaring from speakers embedded in the garden. Carmen rubbed her eyes.

"Ow," she said.

"Whoa," said Idra.

They climbed out of the taxi gingerly.

"Oh my God, the kids would love this," said Carmen.

She suddenly felt quite sorry for them and the exquisite taste-fulness of Sofia's decorations, which they weren't allowed to touch, and the tree, which did not contain the cruddy baubles they made at school, but instead very expensive matching ornaments from Harvey Nichols. There was a second, smaller tree in the kitchen that was meant to be more "homemade" and "rustic" and con-tained their school-based efforts and paper chains, and all of the children secretly complained mutinously that it was the crap tree.

"I love it," said Idra, and when Carmen looked at her, "Oh, don't be a snob! Your snotty sister and being in the New Town have done a right number on you! You weren't like this at all back west."

"Is that true?"

"It is," said Idra. "I would have loved this house when I was small and I love it now and you're being a snot box. Who secretly loves it. Don't you think, Rudi?"

"I think anyone who tries to make merry is a blessing to the world," said Rudi, and Carmen suddenly stopped. That sounded exactly like something Oke would have said. She glanced at him but he seemed to be completely sincere.

"So, let's absolutely take full advantage of their hospitality and go bat-shit bananas," he added, which didn't sound like Oke at all.

"I don't—"

Idra grabbed her arm, and the three of them stumbled up the icy pavement.

Chapter Twenty-Eight

The doorbell jangled, to nobody's surprise, "I Wish It Could Be Christmas Every Day."

"You can just program that right in," said Idra. "In fact, I think I'm going to do it. And leave it up all year. Just to be annoying."

"It's already annoying," said Carmen.

"Stop grumping up this party! It's going to be perfect!"

A woman opened the door. She was dressed in tiny red-and-white hot pants, a red velvet bikini top trimmed with cheap white nylon fur, a Santa hat over her bright blond hair, fishnet tights, and high-heeled shoes.

"It is!" Rudi beamed as Idra and Carmen's mouths dropped open.

"Hiyas!" said the girl cheerfully. Carmen couldn't help comparing how pert the girl looked to herself, even though she was the one at the party and this girl was working at the party in a really demeaning outfit. This had to stop, Carmen told herself for about the zillionth time.

"Come in, yous," said the girl, opening the door wider, revealing a houseful of people—and several girls dressed up in the sexy Santa outfit—behind her.

The house was absolutely stifling. Sofia's house was always comfortable, and if you needed to get toasty, you went next to the AGA. Mr. McCredie's house was completely freezing at all times but you could dive down to the kitchen when the fire was lit or go into the shop itself, which was warm. Carmen had, she realized, just got used to it. Edinburgh was a cold city on a cold coast of a cold country. Its beauty came from its austere glacial bareness in the winter; its clean gray lines and cold glory; punctuated by cozy golden auras of light and joy and comfort.

This was something altogether different. The house was indeed vast, with a slightly hilarious double staircase going around an incredibly tall Christmas tree. It was three meters at least, entirely silver, decked with lights that blinked on and off at high speed in a way that Carmen thought was going to give her a headache.

"Ooh," said Idra. "I want to go and stand at the top of the stairs and call someone a bitch!"

"I want to descend in a huge super-bitch ball gown while a hush falls," agreed Rudi.

The Santa Claus woman had spirited away their coats and reappeared with glasses of bright red fizzy liquid which, on examination, turned out to be some sort of gruesome combination of mulled wine and champagne. At first sip it tasted like cough medicine. On fourth sip it also tasted like cough medicine, but you'd stopped minding, because you were drunk.

Carmen looked around. There was a plethora of well-fed, ruddy-faced bellowing men who looked incredibly pleased with themselves, next to thin, nervy wives, occasionally quivering like terriers. Everyone was drinking very quickly. There was a large, merry-looking pianist in a rather tightly fitting dinner jacket playing extremely elaborate covers of Mariah Carey songs full of twiddly-diddly bits, which Carmen assumed, correctly, made the pianist extremely expensive.

She was glad she was wearing the dress—at first she'd thought it would be too bare, but it was tropically hot; she could already see damp patches on the expensive shirts of the louder men. She could smell cigar smoke, too, and the noise levels were insane, until there was an *ahem* at the top of the stairs.

"No way," said Idra. "Someone's going to ask which of these bitches is their mother or something."

It was Jackson McClockerty, of course, dressed in bright red Stewart tartan trousers that made his bum look frankly enormous, as if it was about to float into the air like a pair of balloons. He'd also donned a frilly white shirt and a preposterous Bonnie Prince Charlie jacket and waistcoat fiasco, all far too tight—there was no way the huge square gold waistcoat buttons would ever do up.

"Welcome, one and all, to my humble abode," he boomed. Everyone cheered and laughed, and Carmen, looking around, could see people spray crumbs over the thick pile carpet. She wondered who would be cleaning that up.

His wife was dressed—Carmen couldn't tell if it was on purpose or not—as a huge purple Quality Street, the hazelnut caramel. Her dress was tight and had a layer of tulle over the shiny bodice spraying up into her face. Her hair was bright yellow, she had blinding white teeth, and her eyelashes and breasts both stuck out for miles. Her eyelashes grazed Jackson's head every time she turned to look adoringly at him. It made Carmen feel slightly jealous of the two of them, and slightly cheered to think that Jackson undoubtedly thought his wife was the most beautiful woman on the face of the planet.

"Tonight there will be some live music . . . featuring me!" said Jackson. Normally Carmen would expect laughter if someone announced something like that, but here there were only cheers. Well, maybe everyone appreciated his largesse.

As they clapped, and a professional-looking photographer took photos, more people appeared behind them, squeezing into the hallway, so they made their way through into the vast sitting room. There were cream leather sofas everywhere with hot fuchsia pillows embroidered with slogans like "Live Laugh Love" and "There's no IN without GIN" and "BELOVED DOGMOTHER LIVES HERE!" and "Rules of the house—Laugh and be kind! AND DRINK GIN!!!" There were two white fluffy dogs with bows on their heads, yapping and snarling at each other or at anyone who came past them, in the large arched room that led to the back of the house, where huge French windows were fringed with the most flowery, drapey curtains Carmen had ever seen. There was a full pelmet with golden pom-poms hanging down from the hilt. Carmen was still hypnotized by the curtains when Idra grabbed her arm and handed her a new pink drink accessorized with a candy cane.

"You have to try these," she said. "Minky's own Christmas cocktail, apparently."

"Who's Minky?" said Carmen.

"Oh, it's Jackson's wife."

"She's called Minky?"

"No! She's called Melinda but all her close friends call her Minky, apparently, so we are to as well. I got papped!"

"But I haven't met her," said Carmen.

"Well, she makes drinks like this," said Idra.

Carmen looked around. "Where's Rudi gone?"

"Oh, he's met a bunch of people he knows."

"I bet he has," said Carmen, slightly wistfully. She had lots of friends, too, she told herself. Except they lived on the other side of the country and she had been really crap at keeping in touch with them for the last year. They all had babies now and she could barely like their Instagram posts, never mind send them lovely presents.

"He's leading a conga."

Carmen smiled. "Oh God, if he wasn't so sweet he'd be completely insufferable."

"Well, he can't exactly follow a conga," said Idra. "He'd keep missing the turns."

"Idra!"

"What?"

Carmen hated people mentioning Rudi's arm, Idra noticed, even though Rudi didn't mind it at all. Interesting.

Carmen tried the drink. It was sticky, sweet, nauseating, and hit you like a punch in the face. "Good God," she said. "Does Jackson have an undertaking business on the side?"

She took another sip, then sucked on the candy cane. It tasted slightly better the second time, especially on top of the cough syrup/champagne aperitif. "Come look at this," said Idra, who already had the absolute layout of this party. Through an archway covered in Anaglypta—something Carmen thought had more or less disappeared when her grandmother died—set out in a conservatory was a vast buffet.

"Not the prawn ring, then?" said Carmen, her mouth starting to curl up.

"Oh yes," said Idra. "Look! They also have individual arctic rolls!"

"I love arctic roll!"

"Christmas puddings with a whole orange inside for some reason!"

"Oh my God."

"*Gold-leaf* salmon!"

"Truffled truffles!"

They couldn't help it: They both burst out laughing. Carmen had been brought up on a totally normal housing estate, but Sofia going to university then moving to Edinburgh had meant she had watched her sister become obsessed with classy things: organic food, wooden toys, and all sorts of other affectations Carmen found pretentious.

But this was pretentious in a completely opposite way. It was, in its over-the-top bounty, the most ridiculous thing Carmen had ever seen, and it made her feel oddly queasy. There was just so much. She saw an extremely well-fed man in a golfing sweater, his color very high, heaping mound upon mound of roast beef—more than a normal human could possibly want to eat—onto his plate. He also piled on foie gras (from a big tub that said "BEST FOIE GRAS" on it, just in case you thought it might be something not quite so illegal), salmon, and, Carmen saw as waiters ferried them back and forth, a mass of fresh hot chips.

"Oh Lordy," said Carmen. "I don't like this. A sausage roll would have been fine. Actually, maybe just some chips." She looked around. "I don't think Mr. McCredie's come after all. I'm not sure whether that's a good sign or a bad sign. Or maybe he had a sip of the punch and passed out. Or maybe he's lost somewhere looking for the library."

Idra's eyes narrowed. "Bronagh isn't here, either. You don't think she's up to something?"

"What, and Mr. McCredie is avoiding it because of that?" Carmen snorted.

The two little dogs—whose names were Brandy and Whiskey, Carmen figured out from people shouting at them—were cavorting underneath the vast white tablecloths, waiting for people to drop food, which they did, continuously, even as they heaped more onto already heaped plates.

"Okay, I'll give you this one; this is gross," said Idra. "He should take this to the Grassmarket Project."

"Maybe he will take the leftovers?" said Carmen. They looked at the throng brandishing their plates.

"I don't think there will be any," said Idra.

"I'm going to pocket some for Christopher Pickle," said Carmen.

A man with the largest, fuzziest blond mustache Carmen had ever seen, an expensive-looking suit, and ridiculous loafers sidled up to Idra.

"Hey, babe," he said.

"Hey," she said. "Nice costume."

The man frowned. "What do you mean?"

Idra tugged on his mustache. It stayed put.

"Oh," she said. "Ooh."

"Movember," said the man, looking at himself in a huge mirror on the wall that had "LIVE! LAUGH! FOREVER!" blazoned across it in scrawly black letters. "But I liked it and decided to keep it."

"I like it, too," said Idra.

"*Idra!*" hissed Carmen.

"Can I stroke it?"

At this point Carmen gave up, took a sip of her drink, and wandered back to where Jackson had now appeared on a large stage with a huge PA set up. It was going to blow the windows out.

"EVERYONE FEELIN' ALL RIGHT?" Jackson screamed into the microphone, having suddenly adopted an American accent.

"Yeah!" shouted everyone back at him, having suddenly adopted American accents also.

"I said, you feeling ALL RIGHT?" shouted the fake Bruce Springsteen. Minky was standing by the side of the stage, gazing at him with total adoration in her eyes.

"YEAH!"

"Okay then!"

Behind him, three bored-looking session musicians picked up their instruments.

"And a one . . . a two . . . a one, two . . ."

Carmen had been expecting "I Wish It Could Be Christmas Every Day" or "I Saw Mommy Kissing Santa Claus."

Instead, a pulsing drum beat broke out and Jackson lowered his brow, ran his fingers through his freshly highlighted hair, kicked his leg to the side, and started singing a deep, groaning version of "Like I Love You" by Justin Timberlake, complete with hip thrusts and tips of his tartan fedora.

Carmen's mouth dropped open again. She stumbled backward in case anyone could see her about to collapse in absolute hysterics, particularly as Jackson started the sexy slow rap. Everyone else seemed to be getting into it as the light show started. On the other hand, everyone else was completely and utterly stocious, and after two of the special party cocktails, Carmen was feeling slightly woozy herself. She was certainly losing control of her emotions. The room was full of rich golf club men dancing about as well as rich golf club men usually dance, and the noise was ear bleeding. Carmen was desperate for some fresh air; she couldn't bear the smell of perfumes clashing, the scented candles overpowering everything, the sweat and breath that was a combination of champagne and caviar (i.e., a kind of fish bubbles), as well as the manic overheating. She headed back to the front door. Outside was a motley collection of younger people smoking furiously and trying to keep warm. Rudi was among them, not smoking, but making one of the girls laugh by wrapping her neck up in a long scarf, one end in his teeth.

Suddenly Carmen felt a piercing note of jealousy. Why did nobody tease her like that? Now the girl was laughing uproariously and putting the scarf around Rudi's neck, pulling him close. With his pointed eyebrows and chin, he looked rather like a naughty faun, Carmen noticed.

He looked up, sensing her eyes on him, and spotted her. His face split with glee.

"Don't tell me you're not enjoying Gubbins McTimberlake in there?" he said. Carmen shivered. It was shockingly cold now she was outside.

"I felt a headache coming on," said Carmen. "I don't know why. I used to love parties."

"I love parties!" said the girl with the scarf, aware she was losing Rudi's attention. Rudi smiled at her.

"Oh, Crystal, you do. Shall we head back in and dance?"

Crystal immediately grinned and headed back inside.

"Give me a second," he called after her.

"Don't be late!" she said, blowing a kiss at him as she left.

Carmen looked at him. "Well, I'd say you're in there."

He smiled. "She's a good girl, Crystal."

"Uh-huh," said Carmen, wondering why she felt so gloomy. She was a good girl, too; had been a good girl for much, much too long.

The rhythm juddered out of the house, but you couldn't hear Jackson doing his sexy singing, so it didn't sound too bad. The snow had stopped, leaving a pretty white layer on top of the fake stuff already strewn around the garden, and hiding the bulk of the huge house and its four-car garage behind them. It could almost be rather romantic in the cul-de sac. Carmen found herself moving closer to Rudi. She couldn't pretend she didn't know what she was doing. She knew she was a little drunk. She didn't know where Idra was. Rudi was grinning, looking at her patiently.

"You look very pretty in that dress," he said, and Carmen blinked, realizing it had been a very long time since she'd had a compliment from a man. She'd often had them from Phoebe, particularly if she was wearing something very flowery and long that made her look like an Amish maid. But not from a man.

She grinned at him, realizing she had completely forgotten how to flirt. At all. And then, she thought something else: What would Sofia think of her flirting with her manny? No doubt she considered him her own personal property. She'd roll her eyes and look disappointed but unsurprised. This made Carmen feel stranger than ever. Why? Why did everyone else get all the fun and all the laughs? Even those people in there, enjoying the buffet and the music, were just having a simple good time, rather than fretting constantly like she had, all year long.

She inched forward, taking a long sip from the drink she was holding.

"You know that stuff is actually drain cleaner?" said Rudi.

"You disapprove?"

"Absolutely not!"

He held up his own glass, which was a martini glass with a martini in it. "Fortunately, I knew Jackson was rich enough to have invited his own barman."

"Where?" said Carmen, who had looked around the party for anything to drink that wasn't a cocktail, unsuccessfully.

"The VIP area."

"This party has a *VIP* area?"

Rudi grinned. "Obviously!"

Carmen shook her head. "Don't tell me, it's in the downstairs lav?"

"Jungle room," said Rudi seriously.

"They have a jungle room."

"They do."

Carmen started laughing again. "Bet you wish you could get a manny job here."

"Their dogs are their children," said Rudi, grinning. "Plus, I think Jackson already has a bunch he never sees from his first two marriages."

"Oh *God*," said Carmen, "why did I come to this? I'm never going to get near him. And I wanted to appeal to his better side, so that he would stop making big offers to take over the shop. And also he obviously just *loves* being him. He doesn't have a conscience. Why would he?" She sighed.

"What did you think would happen?" said Rudi.

Carmen shrugged. "I thought . . . I thought I'd make him see the positive side. That having lovely shops in Edinburgh helps bring people into his shitty shops."

Rudi laughed. "Well, I can see how that could make a compelling argument."

"But now I realize," Carmen went on, "that actually, from the look of this house—he loves that stuff. He thinks 'See You Jimmy' hats really *are* hilarious! He thinks a little plastic sign that says 'A spoiled Highland terrier lives here' is the best gift anyone could ever be given!"

"I think I saw one of those in the kitchen."

"Yeah, me too," said Carmen. "He's going to make a huge bid and take the lease, isn't he? Right out from under us. He's going to take all the councillors out to dance around the annual sacrifice and they'll waive his business rates."

"Which is something the council would *never ever* do," said Rudi loudly.

"Mr. McCredie can't hold out for long. He doesn't *have* long."

"On the plus side," said Rudi, "the VIP bar make good martinis. Here, try this."

His drink was sharp and strong and had a twist. She took a gulp and gasped.

"There we go," he said. "Now, how about I smuggle you into the VIP area . . . ?"

"I do not want to go to the jungle room, thank you."

"Aren't you at least going to try?"

The sound of someone strangling "Mirrors," but strangling "Mirrors" in an intensely serious and well-meaning way, greeted them each time the door was opened and closed. Carmen glanced inside. Jackson was singing it to Minky, down on one knee, completely out of tune, the backing band in their low-slung jeans looking more bored than ever. Minky was clasping her hands together in pure delight.

"No," said Carmen sadly. "I don't think . . . I don't think it will work. I think I tried . . . and I've failed."

"Well then, how about we liberate some champagne and break this joint. Unless you want some more gold-leaf salmon?"

Carmen made a face.

"No, quite right. We'll find somewhere else."

The sliding glass doors at the back of the huge house were suddenly pulled open, framed by the girls in the sexy red Santa costumes. Carmen had felt a flare of excitement as Rudi had suggested they leave. What did he mean? Where were they going? It always felt that there was an aura of fun around him; the sense that anything might happen. No wonder the children adored him. Although for quite different reasons.

"We can still have some fun," whispered Rudi, in a voice that suddenly was very clear in its intent.

And there and then, two cocktails down, months of sadness and stress behind her, Carmen decided. What was the worst that could happen if she threw caution to the wind? No doubt Idra was arm in arm with the mustachioed blond by now, obviously thinking nothing of it.

"What about Crystal?" she whispered.

"Oh, she can come, too, if she likes."

"No she can't," said Carmen, more forcibly than she meant. Rudi looked at her with those elongated, almost amber eyes, a smile on his lips.

"Okay then," he said, and he took her left hand with his right, and squeezed it. Carmen trembled, and not just because it was cold.

The music had subsided, and the crowds were spilling outside.

"And now," Jackson was shouting, "it's time for the great . . . *illuminations*!"

Chapter Twenty-Nine

Orchestral music started from a vast stereo system: something very loud and very familiar from aftershave advertisements. Jackson stood in the back doorframe, looking very sweaty.

"Now!" he shouted.

Everyone clapped and cheered as a vast fireworks display was set off in the back garden. Then, they set off a new corner of the garden with illuminations that made the front yard look totally pathetic: a full Santa sleigh, complete with eight reindeer with flashing red noses; a bizarre golden nativity scene where everyone had bright orange halos; Santa's grotto, with sexy green and red flashing elves; and overhead the fireworks whizzing and banging in time with the music. Carmen blinked at the spectacle. Inside, Brandy and Whiskey were going absolutely insane with yapping, as was every other dog in the neighborhood, of which there were clearly many. They threatened to drown out the music.

Suddenly a huge rocket went up and off, and as it was heading downward, *bang*, a huge snow castle from *Frozen* was illuminated in the garden. It was as tall as the house, with thousands of glittering white lights flashing on and off. The crowd gasped as it flickered on once, twice, the fireworks showering down white sparks—and then, with a sharp crack, it went out.

The other illuminations went out.

The lights in the house went out, and the music turned off very sharply. The neighbors' lights went out, on both sides. The lights on the other side of the back garden, far away though it was, went out.

The only remaining sound was the increased ferocity of the yapping and the howling of the dogs, and a sole woman—possibly Minky—screaming. Everyone else stood in paralyzed silence.

RUDI WAS RIGHT behind Carmen, holding a sparkler that was the only light visible. It lit up his impish face.

"Quick!" he said. "It's going to be mayhem."

And they darted through the house, pausing only to liberate a bottle of champagne from the conservatory, ignoring the dogs, who were now up on the buffet table, scrapping over a huge honey-roasted ham.

The floor was littered with food and drinks that had been carelessly dropped and trodden into the expensive carpet; the streetlights outside had gone off; and they didn't stop going through the spooky place until they found the front door. They grabbed their coats with a phone flashlight Rudi held in his teeth, as the hubbub of people in the garden behind them grew louder and more raucous. Many people, it turned out, were rather annoyed and belligerent, despite having their bellies stuffed and alcohol poured down their throats.

"Quick," said Rudi. "The mob are going to turn."

They hurtled out into the pitch-black cul-de-sac, only the occasional lights of passing drivers illuminating the suburb, where the woods that surrounded it now closed in, ominously.

Neither of them could stop laughing, stumbling up the Queensferry Road. The traffic lights were out, too, which meant the normally busy junction was completely gridlocked, just people stuck, honking at one another.

"It's a very long time till morning," said Rudi, deftly sticking the champagne bottle between his legs and popping it with one hand.

"That is quite the party trick," said Carmen.

"Darling, you have *no* idea."

Carmen quickly called Idra, who told her that everyone was going mental, but she and the mustachioed Hendrik were perfectly safe and making a picnic to take home. Carmen recommended avoiding the ham.

Taking swigs from the bottle, they waved at other stranded, giggling partygoers who were shuffling through the snow on both sides of the street. The whole city, it seemed, had been chucked out: of its golden bars and expensive restaurants; of noisy house parties, now silenced; and of beautiful hotels where elevators no longer worked and televisions had switched off. There were sirens in the air. As they reached higher ground, Carmen turned around. Overhead was a very bright full moon, and there was one shining diamond of light in the city: She realized she was looking at the Western General Hospital, undoubtedly running off emergency generators. She gave a brief thanks that it was all right; that everyone there was safe. Then they scampered across the road and plunged upward, ever upward, into the old part of the city. Neither of them mentioned the direction they were taking.

But it wasn't to Sofia's house.

Chapter Thirty

Carmen felt full of naughty misgivings as they arrived—quietly, although she couldn't imagine you could wake Mr. McCredie; he wasn't anywhere near the top floor. Or if he slept at all; he probably stayed up all night reading books about how to skin a seal. She flipped a switch—the lights were out all over the city, it was true. It looked as though Jackson had sucked so much power from the grid, he'd done for it. Carmen didn't mind. She was nervous as all hell, and happier with a candle.

Rudi, of course, wasn't nervous at all, for which she was profoundly grateful. Instead, he giggled and looked in various cupboards until he found two flat-bottomed glasses and an incredibly dusty bottle of whiskey. He looked at Carmen and frowned.

"What?"

"This is . . . this is ancient. I mean, if he's got another one of these that he hasn't opened, he could probably sell it and fund his entire voyage, save all our problems."

Carmen rolled her eyes. "Don't."

Rudi fit two glasses into one hand. "Can you manage the candle?"

Carmen did, and lit the way up the many stairs, conscious—she couldn't help being conscious; every nerve in her felt shredded—of him following her. It had been so long. So incredibly long. Maybe they'd changed it. Maybe she'd forgotten how to do it. Maybe Rudi did loads of exotic things and she wouldn't know what any of them were. He was so experienced and might want to do weird bendy things with kitchen implements and . . . Oh Lord.

Up at the top of the house was something extraordinary: The full moon was shining right through the conservatory glass. It was as bright as if the lights were on.

"Hey, hey!" said Rudi. "Look at this."

He went over to the plants, putting down the glasses on the marble-topped table. He put his hand inside the largest pot and withdrew it with a smile.

"You've been watering!"

Carmen smiled. "I have."

"You're going to bring it all back to life," he said, looking around.

"There are a lot of things that need bringing back to life," said Carmen, swallowing hard.

They both took a sip of the sweet, smoky whiskey, looking out over the darkened rooftops of the power cut, and the great huge light of the hanging moon. From far below you could hear, distantly, joyous shouts of happy revelers, undeterred by the cold and the snow, candles lighting up the Grassmarket as they had done some endless time ago. It was unearthly and extraordinarily beautiful. Carmen could still feel her heart beating, nineteen to the dozen.

Slowly, carefully, Rudi moved toward her. He looked more serious now, less impish, and was not being his usual jolly self, but quiet and calm, as if she was a nervous creature. Which, in truth, she was. She absolutely was.

She turned, her fears and worries bubbling to the surface.

"Oh, Rudi," she said. "It's been . . . it's been so hard."

She was suddenly terrified she was going to cry.

"It's been so long," she said. "I've . . ." She shook her head, then laughed with a slightly hysterical twinge, which was better than crying, at least.

"I've totally lost the habit. I don't know what I'm doing. I don't know what I'm meant to be doing. Everything went so wrong. I feel . . . I feel like this is the first time. Like I have to start everything over again."

It might have been the moonlight; it was unlike Carmen to feel able to expose herself like this, to be completely open and honest about exactly how she felt.

"I feel like I've been in hibernation; hiding away under my clothes. Just working. And ignoring other things. Just a big ugly ball of worry and nonsense."

"Everyone feels like that," said Rudi soothingly.

"Sofia doesn't."

"I'm sure sometimes she does," said Rudi. "Or maybe she feels like a burned-out crazy person."

"Hmm," said Carmen. "Is that the one really rich, successful people get?"

"Don't think about Sofia right now," said Rudi. "Don't think about anything."

He moved toward her and, very gently, stroked her hair. She realized that, apart from Phoebe crawling on her from time to time—which happened less and less as she got older—she had been starved. She was hungering for physical contact.

Nobody touched her. She missed that. She had missed the very simplicity of being touched. She had been so lonely; so cold.

She leaned her head into his hand, just a little. He moved closer; again, so slowly, as if she were something fragile, liable to disappear.

"I don't know how to do, like, fancy things and swings and stuff . . ." said Carmen, her voice still tremulous.

"Swings and stuff?" said Rudi, his voice amused as always.

"Well, weird stuff."

"No such thing as weird stuff," said Rudi, turning her around. "There are just such things as humans, and bodies, and what they both want—or what they all want. Together. It's meant to be a bit of a joint enterprise. And it's always different. And it's always new. And it's always the first time. That's the fun of it."

He moved slowly closer, and she reached up and kissed him.

And to her absolute surprise, it was like a very first kiss: gentle and soft. His arm closed around her back; her hands clasped behind his. It wasn't remotely odd, in fact, except in how un-odd it was. The moonlight, the whiskey, the cold, cold night. She felt herself melting against him; as if she had been carrying a huge burden: of being sexless; unwanted; nobody caring for her, and her pretending she didn't care.

And now this man was here, telling her and showing her that none of that was true. That it had been a story she had told herself.

"Look," said Rudi softly, breaking off, his voice sounding breathy. He pointed to the glass window; they were reflected in it. "Look at you," he said.

He moved away, moved over to the old spotted mirrors that sat behind the huge cheese plant. He tilted it so it, too, reflected Carmen in its old soft grain, the candlelight flickering; the moonlight beaming.

Then he stepped back behind her and took hold of the zip of her dress. Kissing the back of her neck, he unzipped it to her waist, and she shivered, but not from fear, not even from the cold, because she didn't feel cold anymore.

"Look at yourself," he urged again, until she turned her head. She saw her breasts spilling over the top of her bra, the creamy flesh pale as marble in the moonlight; the curve of her back and her dark hair falling softly on her neck; the soft swell of her hips, where the dress sat.

"Can you see?" said Rudi in her ear. "Can you see what is so lovely about you?"

Carmen swallowed hard. "Uh."

"Can you?"

She nodded, still looking, as Rudi carried on kissing the nape of her neck, putting his arm on her shoulder, holding her tightly against his body. Carmen stared at the reflection.

"You are so lovely," he said. "You are so fine. I cannot imagine why you ever thought there was anything wrong with you."

And Carmen realized immediately why he was so extraordinarily successful with men and women both. It had nothing to do with physical attributes and everything to do with a man who was observant, and who knew how to listen, and who was kind.

And who could respond; she felt him stiffening behind her, felt, as he moved his mouth to the side of the neck now, but still gentle, still incredibly slowly, how very reassuring he was. He was never too fast, but never leaving her in any doubt of where he was going, and what he wanted. There was tenderness in his kiss, but no hesitancy. She glanced at them both in the old soft mirror once more and believed it: They were beautiful; her hair so dark, his glinting red and gold in the strange pale light. And she felt herself responding in return; as if waking up from a long sleep. His body against hers; his warm lips; his firm, yet gentle, stroking arm. She thought of the bulbs he had planted in the ancient pots; the children he was helping raise; the joy he grew and spread around him wherever he went, trailing behind him like the sweet notes of a pipe.

She wanted almost nothing more now than to turn around; to press against him, feel him skin to skin. Pull him against her; stumble into the bedroom; feel his hand unhook her bra; feel his soft lips on her breasts. She wanted him, suddenly, very badly indeed. She very nearly did whisper, "Come here." She very nearly did put her hands, trembling, impatient, to his belt, pulling the buttons off his shirt; feeling his strong, wiry chest against hers; pulling at him, fiercely, making him gasp. She felt power, suddenly, coursing through her brains; felt warm and frenzied and alive.

Her body did not let her down. Her body did not betray her. But, turning, she caught, in the reflection in the mirror, the spirited flare of the tiny candle, burning bright; sending a line of smoke into the night. And she remembered. A low voice. That gentle wisp of an accent. The deep belief in everything he said.

"I want . . ." she said. "I want sex . . . to be something sacred to me."

Rudi kissed her with increasing fervor.

"Well, how about we start with 'not bad' and take it from there?" he suggested.

But she knew, deep down, however good he was making her feel, he was not the one. Not the one she wanted, not right now. However much she should probably get back on the horse, or break her duck, or whatever it was people said. This had been wonderful. Amazing. And a lot of her did want more—a lot more—from this mischievous man.

The very deepest part of her did not.

And she pulled away, and turned to him, and looked into his slanted bright eyes.

"Thank you," she said.

He blinked back into focus, came back to himself, then looked at her, with infinite understanding, and a slight smile on his lips, now puffy and pink.

"No way!" he said, his eyes still glinting with merriment.

"No way what?" she said, sad to break the spell.

"No way you're about to tell me to go home!"

"I'm . . ." Carmen looked confused. "I don't know what I'm doing."

Rudi stood back immediately. "Oh no! I thought I was quite good at checking for consent. Although on the whole I prefer 'wild enthusiasm.'"

She smiled at him. "Oh, believe me, I am very, very enthusiastic about you."

"Uh-huh, yeah, whatever, you were thinking, *Well, that's all fine. I think I'll just wait for the person I really like now.* You are being *very Catholic*, Carmen Hogan."

"I am not!" said Carmen.

She looked up at him, then glanced at the stars and glanced back. It was a night for honesty.

"Well," she said, "maybe you're right. I'm sorry. I am very grateful, though. For making me feel . . ."

The sentence ran out.

"No. Just for making me feel. Thank you."

"You're welcome," said Rudi.

"I'm sorry if I led you on . . ." said Carmen.

"You never need to apologize for not wanting to have sex with me," said Rudi. "Unless it's a ginger pubes thing, in which case you're being a bigot."

"It's not!" protested Carmen honestly. "I love your hair. I love your freckles. I love your lovely hand and I love your rounded nubby arm, and believe me, I really really love your mouth." Rudi smiled beatifically. "Everything about you is completely fabulous. I just . . . I just . . . I am ready. Thank you for showing me. I am ready. And I want the next thing. But the next thing for me . . . it isn't being a kind of charity case for you."

"You could never be that," said Rudi.

"But I think . . . I think I'm ready for a one-woman man," said Carmen. "Even if it's not the one I really wanted. I think he was right. And I want the whole deal. I want . . . spiritual connection and . . . God. I don't know. Sofia's stupid underfloor heating."

"Personalized doorbell?" said Rudi, grinning, handing her the whiskey, and wrapping a blanket he whisked off the sofa around her shoulders.

"Babies," said Carmen. "School shoes. Batch cooking. Radiators. A milkman! Not like that. I mean, just someone to deliver milk. In bottles. I'm pathetic. I'm probably more conservative than Pippa, and she thinks her school should bring back corporal punishment."

Rudi nodded, puzzled.

"And . . . I don't think you're the person for that."

"Well, I fucking hate radiators," said Rudi, and Carmen burst out laughing.

"I don't think I'm built to be a party girl anymore. Someone spoiled me for that."

"You," he said, pulling her in and kissing her on the forehead, "are built to be a whatever-you-want girl."

He looked at the old clock on the wall and grimaced.

"Oh no, you can stay!" said Carmen. "Just . . ."

"Just," said Rudi. "Not a problem."

And they leapt under Carmen's blankets, which were freezing and made them both yelp, and then they huddled up together, and spooned for warmth. Carmen had not felt so safe and comfortable in a very long time; and she slept incredibly well, barely moving, Rudi's beautiful red hair on the white pillows, his left arm propped by her shoulder; his right arm stretched around her curved stomach; the stars and the moonlight white through the high window. The snow, when it came later, fell softly and blanketed the world, muffling any sound from outside; and Carmen slept the most soothing night she had known in a long, long time.

Chapter Thirty-One

Carmen woke, at first unsure as to why she felt so peaceful and happy. For just a moment she thought Oke was there. Just the tiniest fraction of a second. Then her eyes opened fully and she nearly sat bolt upright. It was Rudi! Rudi in her bed! Oh my God! What had she done?

Her heart was racing but gradually calmed as it all came back to her. They hadn't slept together. It had been okay. It had been fine. Better than fine. She hadn't messed up anything; it had been nice, in fact. Lovely. He shifted slightly in his sleep and his arm tightened on her. He smelled good. They did say that about redheads. He gradually came awake and kissed the back of her hair instinctively. She smiled.

"Morning," she said.

She could tell it was taking him a moment to figure out where he was, too.

"Good morning, gorgeous," he muttered.

"Ha! Have you forgotten my name?"

His eyes opened and sparked to life.

"I have not! And clearly you are gorgeous."

The mocking edge to his tone was back and Carmen was glad. He squeezed her shoulder.

"Mmm, it is so lovely and warm in here," he nuzzled. "But I have to move, otherwise . . ."

"What?"

"Boy-things will happen," he said. "Inevitable. You are irresistible. Sorry."

Carmen squirmed away.

"I need to pee anyway," she said.

"Me too," said Rudi, frowning. "It's a very confusing situation down there."

The immediate problem was that it was utterly arctic beyond the glorious warmth of the blankets. Every time one person moved another piece of the eiderdown around themselves, the other yelped.

There was no help for it. Together, they scooched to the end of the bed. Carmen put her arm around Rudi's shoulder, and his hand held the blankets together around them.

"We're going to have to jump," he said. "Together, so we don't lose any of the trapped heat. I mean it. This is going to take teamwork."

"But what about peeing?" said Carmen.

Rudi rolled his eyes. "It's called a penis and stuff comes out of it," he said. "You can close your eyes."

Carmen laughed. "I mean, I don't want to pee in front of you."

"What is this, eighteen ninety-six?" he said. "Also, I spend my life changing the diapers of members of your family. I am immune, believe me."

Giggling, they hopped off the bed together and shuffled toward the door. The bare floor was utterly freezing beneath their feet. Then they gasped. Beyond the bedroom door, the attic glowed white. Ever more snow was piled against the large glass conservatory window, reflected back in the old mirror. It was bitterly cold, but astonishing; the light turned the entire top floor into a vast white space, the green plants stark against the light; a true winter garden.

"Wow!" They stared at it.

"This is amazing," said Rudi. "Now you cannot tell me you miss Sofia's basement."

"I miss not having to dress as a yeti every time I want to brush my teeth," said Carmen.

They shuffled, still giggling, over to the tiny bathroom—the power was back on, Carmen noticed—then took turns to hold up a blanket barrier over their near-naked bodies, while each one performed their ablutions, brushing their teeth and swearing loudly about how freezing they were. Then they rolled themselves into the blanket again and hopped back, hysterical, wondering how they were going to make coffee and Rudi explaining how he'd had a grabber, actually, at one point, like a hook, and how it had given everyone conniptions while not being much use but he did use it sometimes and Carmen had stared at him and he had explained he hadn't actually killed people with it, it was for picking up mugs, and she frowned and said, did it do other things, and he had said, see, that's why he didn't wear it anymore, stupid questions like hers, and yes it was very useful for pirate adventures, until they found they were laughing so hard they couldn't breathe, and he pulled her laughing face toward his and kissed her gently on the forehead and said, you are so brilliant, Carmen Hogan—and that was the exact moment the children found them when they burst into the upstairs rooms, come to inform Carmen that it had snowed lots and lots, and could they all go and play immediately.

Chapter Thirty-Two

There was silence. Carmen froze. They were both half-naked under the blankets and only had their underpants on; neither of them could drop it. The children's mouths were open. Sofia clattered up the stairs just behind them.

"Children, you should knock—"

She came to a standstill at the top of the stairs. Her mouth fell open, too.

"You should," said Carmen tremulously.

"Go and wait downstairs," said Sofia quickly to the children. "NOW."

She never shouted. Phoebe opened her mouth to protest, but Pippa grabbed her roughly and pulled her away. Jack backed carefully to the stairs, nearly tripping on his way down. Carmen and Rudi, roped together by the blanket, didn't move.

"I can't . . ."

Sofia just stared at them. The shock and horror in her face made Carmen want to shrivel up and die. Instead, of course, what it did was bring out her combative side.

"I don't remember just telling the kids they could run up and down and go anywhere they wanted," she said.

"That's literally exactly what you said to them," said Sofia. "You said they were welcome anytime. Oh God. Oh God."

"Oh, it's hardly a pornographic film set," said Carmen.

"I knew you were after Rudi!"

"Excuse me, this is *none of your fucking business*," said Carmen, flying off the handle. She dropped her end of the blanket.

"Well, it literally is," said Sofia, "as he's my employee. Jesus, what are you thinking, Carmen? Is this revenge?"

"It's a free country," yelled Carmen, going pink.

"Yes, it is for you!" said Sofia. "No responsibilities, nobody to think about except your own damn self. Then you break up with him for nothing, just like you did with Oke, then he leaves, then I lose the best nanny I've ever had and I'm back in the crap again, thanks to you."

Carmen's mouth dropped open.

"There are two hundred and fifty thousand men in Edinburgh. Please, please, *please* have any one of them that won't mess up my kids when it goes wrong."

Carmen turned and attempted to walk with dignity into the bedroom, which isn't easy when you are only wearing skimpy black underpants, trying to hold your stomach in, and have goose bumps all over your body. Especially when you're doing it in front of your sister and she is wearing a beautiful fake-fur black coat, her hair is newly blow-dried, and she looks fresh and lovely with a gorgeous baby strapped to her front.

Carmen shut the door behind her—rather leaving Rudi in it, she realized—and punched her pillow very hard several times. Then she grabbed a sweater and a skirt, threw them on, and opened the door again with a flourish. Sofia had gone.

"Bollocks," she said.

Rudi winced. "It's okay," he said. Then he screwed up his face. "She is never in a million years going to believe we didn't do it, is she?"

"I know," said Carmen, half laughing suddenly despite herself. "Oh God, do you think she might sack you even though it's all my fault apparently?"

"She's a lawyer," said Rudi. "There's no morality clause in my contract. We could sue her and take her house."

"Ooh!" said Carmen, but it wasn't funny, not really.

"Anyway, no, I don't think she can, but I'll offer to leave if she likes. It's not hard to find a job."

"I'll bet," said Carmen. "I'm so sorry. It didn't sound like she wants you to leave. Just for me to die in a ditch."

Rudi patted her shoulder. "Oh God. What shall I tell the kids? Do you think this is one of those 'when two people love each other very much' things?"

"I don't know," said Carmen. "They get sex ed at school."

"We didn't have any sex!" groaned Rudi. He glanced at her, one eyebrow up.

"No!" said Carmen. "That won't make anything better, will it?"

"It would make one thing better."

"Get dressed!"

He disappeared obediently onto the landing where they'd left their clothes. Carmen stared out of the window at the snow, pondering. They opened later on a Sunday, so she had some time. If she turned on the immersion heater, she figured, she could have a nice hot bath. In about ninety minutes. She sighed and turned it on anyway.

Rudi came back into the bedroom shortly after, all dressed, doing up the buttons on his jacket in that nimble way she so admired.

"Ach," he said, pulling her to him. "Stop worrying. Worse things happen at sea."

"They do," she agreed, still feeling utterly miserable. The children meant so much to her. What if she wasn't allowed to see them?

"It'll all look the same in a year."

"A *year*?"

"A week. I mean, a week."

Carmen's phone rang. She bolted to it, then looked at the number.

"Sofia?"

Carmen shook her head.

"Worse."

Rudi frowned.

"It's our mom."

She refused the call. "Ugh, Sofia always does this: gets her side of the story in first."

"Huh," said Rudi.

"Do you think . . . do you think it will harm the children?"

"Not if we're honest, I suppose. You said they've done sex ed? Thank God it's not a Catholic school."

"Nooo," said Carmen. "Far more progressive. Mind you, Phoebe asked me if you had to have sex lots of times to make a baby and I said, sometimes, and she said, yeah because you have to make the hands and the feet and the fingers and the head . . ."

"She thinks . . ."

Rudi screwed up his face.

"I think she thinks you build a baby out of sperm."

He put his hand on his head. "Oh God. Then *perhaps* this will provoke a useful conversation?"

He picked up his phone. "How long do you think it will take Sofia to cool off?"

"Six to eight months," said Carmen.

Immediately, Rudi's phone rang. Sofia's name flashed up.

Carmen made herself scarce in the bedroom as she heard Rudi's tentative "Hello?"

There was the murmur of voices, nothing raised, even though Carmen strained to hear through the door. Then something that sounded like "uh-huh" and "yeah, okay" and finally, the phone hung up. She gave him about 0.3 of a second.

"Well? What? What? What's happening? Are you fired? What's up?"

Rudi held up his hand. "All right, calm down. Well, I'm not sacked. Although she did ask me if I wanted to go. Which I don't. This is a good job. I like those kids. You should see some of the possessed wolverines I've wrangled in my time."

Carmen smiled. "They are brilliant, aren't they?"

"So. Anyway. No. I have to talk it over with the children and tell them it was innocent."

"It *was*!"

"Well, yes. And then, she says, if they're okay with it . . ." His voice trailed off.

Carmen looked at him beadily.

"There's something you're not telling me."

"What do you mean?"

"Is that all she said?"

"Uh, why?" said Rudi, looking slightly uncomfortable and checking the time on his phone.

"What else did she say? Tell me, I mean it."

"She said . . . she said . . ." He sighed. "You've really wound her up."

"Yeah, she made that clear," said Carmen, rolling her eyes. "What did she say? I need to know; I've got to face her if I want to see the kids again."

"She *might* have said you did it on purpose as revenge and I wasn't to take you too seriously."

"She said *what*?"

"Oh my God," said Rudi, to himself. "I have sisters. The fundamental rule of having sisters is don't ever get between any *stupid sisters*. What is wrong with me? Nothing. She said nothing at all."

"So you are completely fine and I am bad Carmen pulling you into my evil web and ruining everything for revenge just because she kicked me out of her stupid basement?"

"I wouldn't—"

"Oh God," said Carmen. "She's such a horror show."

"I mean . . ." Rudi looked incredibly awkward.

"Oh no, off you go," said Carmen, very upset. "Off you go back to Sofia's perfect world that won't get absolutely ruined by Carmen ever touching it or coming near anything."

"That won't happen," said Rudi. "I'll talk to the children."

"I'm probably barred from going anywhere near them."

"She's just had a shock. She'll sort herself out."

"Whatever," said Carmen. "She seems to have sorted herself out pretty quickly when it comes to you."

"It'll blow over," said Rudi.

Carmen still looked sad and pouty there, though, in the beautiful winter garden room. Rudi came over to her and squeezed her.

"Do you want me to stay?" he said.

"No!" said Carmen. "I want you to go and de–freak out my nieces and nephews. As soon as possible."

"Okay," said Rudi. But he stayed a moment longer.

"It was nice, though."

"It was nice up till the screaming started," said Carmen.

"Well, anytime you fancy a different type of screaming . . ." said Rudi.

Carmen gave him one of her looks. "You are incorrigible."

"Thank you!"

Chapter Thirty-Three

Oke woke just after midnight. The hospital was quiet, or as quiet as it ever was—hurried muffled footsteps, far away; quiet whispering voices up and down the corridor.

But something was different. His head felt different. Clear. He knew, deep down, for the first time, that he was better. The drip had been removed; he was now on oral medication. He was eating, his dreams hadn't even been delirious, or at least, he didn't think so.

He couldn't, that was true, think back much on what had happened in that room, in that hospital bed. It was a blur, much of it.

But he knew who he was. He knew where he was and what had happened—malaria, he assumed, virulent and very serious when caught so far away from the beaten track. He could easily have died. Many did.

He opened the old window. Warm air swirled in, smelling of diesel and vegetation. The sounds of the city drifted up to him: music, motorbikes zooming this way and that. He looked out. It was home. It was beautiful. He thought of his mother's face, so concerned, and his sisters. He loved his family deeply. But the thought of being taken home, fed, fussed over, worried over . . . and Mary worried him, too. He knew what she thought and what their families thought. Everyone in their community would be delighted; everyone would approve. It would be easy.

But Oke had always wanted more. He was lucky to have solid roots, he knew, but he wanted to stretch out his branches, to explore new soil, always. He couldn't help it. He dreamed of distant horizons, and, now, of colder worlds.

He stared at the moon a while longer. The stars weren't visible from the pollution of the city, but he knew they were there.

He paced around the room, feeling fitter, drinking water. He felt like a caged beast, trapped inside the hospital. Restless, he felt strong, and in absolutely no mood for sleep.

He turned on the TV. The film trailer was showing again. He stared at it. Then he turned around in the empty room, took a deep breath, picked up his bag . . . and walked out of the hospital.

Chapter Thirty-Four

Carmen went downstairs and cranked the shop into life. It gave her some small satisfaction to watch the rows of new lights ping on, back and back, making her feel like the master of a large domain. She turned the window lights on; the little train set started up on its snowy tour, which never failed to draw a crowd. In the other window, the doll's house filled with mice had, over the year, had a bare tree added, studded with sparkly lights, and a vintage car from Mr. McCredie's attic.

The morning's trade was brisk; young families were up and about in the cold wintry air, delighted to find somewhere open that now had browsing space.

"Hello!" said an older man with a long beard, clearly either a professor at the university or someone who would dearly like you to ask him if he was a professor at the university. He was wearing a tweed jacket and a heavy Fair Isle sweater, with a tweed cap.

"I'm looking for a book I hope you know. It's purple."

Carmen smiled. Finally, she had an answer to this. One of the first things she had done with the new space was to put random books that she couldn't place properly into a large display done by color. Some book purists had complained about this, but children particularly loved to see the rainbow in front of them, and it jollied up a dull corner. Plus, it was somewhere to direct people with impossible questions.

She pointed to it.

"You'll find our purple just in the back corner, sir."

Looking slightly surprised, the man wandered over. Next was a woman with a large Christmas shopping list (which was helpful), but who had forgotten her glasses (which wasn't) and wouldn't let Carmen look at the paper, which meant quite a lot of patience. As she was dealing with another customer and keeping half an eye on someone's baby doing a taste test on the board books, the young nerds in love slipped in again, giggling and holding hands, and vanished into the stacks. Carmen rolled her eyes. Although to be fair, it was Rudi who had noticed that there was wild mistletoe growing up the side of a tiny holly plant outside in the winter garden and suggested she prune it. She had hung sprigs of it at every junction, much to the approval of Bronagh, who told her she would dream of her true love, which was unhelpful to say the least. Plus, she didn't want to squish what they obviously thought was a lovely naughty romance. It just wasn't very practical and she didn't want the other customers who loved to run into the stacks—specifically, children—to be confronted with anything . . . unsettling. Because she'd had quite enough of that for the moment.

Still, it was nice to be busy. She sold a beautiful purple wine guide to the man with the beard, who said it wasn't exactly what he was looking for, but it did look nice and purple, didn't it, and she agreed, with feeling. She sold a whole hardback edition of the Cazalet Chronicles to a woman who gushed so fervently over it, with Carmen's full agreement, that the woman behind her in the queue, who'd only been buying an *Each Peach Pear Plum*, got sucked in and ended up buying a full set, too. She promised she would come back in and let them know what she thought, which made Carmen smile, because she would, and the cycle would begin again, as it always did with Elizabeth Jane Howard's books. Carmen thought of her and her ex-husband, Kingsley Amis, who had downplayed her literary ambitions, as a version of Mozart and Salieri from *Amadeus*, one's name growing stronger and resonating through time, one fading away to nothing.

She thought wistfully of the children and wondered what to do.

Rudi would sort it out, of course. Would he? And they would be fine? They would hardly be scarred for life, would they? And why did Sofia have her panties in such a twist? She couldn't bear not having everything her own way, and it just wasn't fair.

More people bustled in after cozy crime novels to curl up with in front of the fireplace with a glass of sherry; for great big long family sagas to sink into like a warm bath; for the friends they ran into again, delighted to see them, year after year—Stephen King, Ian Rankin, Sophie Kinsella—for the new and the different that Carmen cheerily steered them to—Percival Everett, Bonnie Garmus.

People lingered over the happy Christmas displays: *Little Women* in four colorways: green for the Jos, red for Megs, dove-colored for Beths, and blue, of course, for Amys, sitting under a tiny gingham wreath of their very own; a beautifully decorated, ornate chest Carmen had purloined from Mr. McCredie's hallway, filled with copies of *The Box of Delights*; a huge wall display of *The Snowy Day*, a book so crisp and graphically designed that it looked like it had been written yesterday.

The fire crackled in the grate at the back of the shop, and their new dog welcoming policy had increased footfall well beyond what Carmen had believed possible. It seemed having a dog had somehow become the law while she wasn't watching. She didn't mind at all; she had rarely met a dog she didn't like, and a sales rep had rewarded her for making a large order of Blair Pfenning's *How to Heal Your Dog at Christmas*. It was a book of the most gigantic rubbish that recommended, effectively, petting your dog. But which bore on its cover a picture of Blair, hair blow-dried becomingly, wearing a country-style sweater and cuddling up to an exquisite chocolate Labrador, both of them wearing Santa hats and showing very white teeth. The book had flown off the shelf, and it meant Carmen had a box full of Blair Pfenning dog treats, which she took great pleasure in handing out, particularly to the scruffiest, ugliest rescue mongrels she could find, and taking a picture of them for the shop's Instagram page, tagging Blair in it. She didn't tag him in pictures of any of the good-looking dogs.

It was, in fact—and much to her surprise—a happy, busy day. Apart from carrying on ringing up sales and greeting regulars with a smile pasted on her face, Carmen didn't know what more she could do.

Mr. McCredie came down with his tea in a proper cup, as usual. He looked at her.

"We're doing well!" she said.

"But . . ." he said, looking so sad.

"And I'm paying you rent, don't forget!"

"Yes, but that comes out of the takings, ultimately, so it doesn't change very much."

"It doesn't?" said Carmen. "Perhaps I could . . . uh. Quickly set up an online shop?"

"Could you?"

"Ten days before Christmas?" said Carmen. "Not really. Remind me in January. Last January," she added gloomily.

"I don't know what an online shop is," said Mr. McCredie.

"It means you send books all over the world."

"But we do that already!"

"Yes, if people send you actual physical letters," said Carmen. "We need an email address and a website and . . ."

Mr. McCredie nodded, then brightened as a customer came in and asked if they stocked anything on the old Edinburgh railway station at The Caledonian Hotel. It was an unbelievably niche subject by any standards, and therefore one at which Mr. Mc-Credie was delighted to hurl himself. He may not be going on his trip, she thought, but opening up the stacks had still been a good thing to do. She must thank Crawford again when she saw him. It had been such a good turn he had done her—or the street, as he insisted on saying, waving away her thanks. It would keep them going, through this Christmas and beyond, even if they couldn't make Mr. McCredie's wish come true. Oh, and she owed Bronagh a good turn, she remembered. Huh. She'd add that to her very long to-do list.

She sighed, then, as a customer dinged their way out and they were temporarily quiet. She listened. Something was missing. What was it? It is much harder to spot something that isn't there than something that is, and she finally realized it was the bagpipe tunes from down the street.

Bobby must have turned them off, which meant he was on his way somewhere—and just as she was thinking that, he appeared.

"Hello!" said Carmen, suddenly remembering that she hadn't seen him at Jackson's party. "Your evil bagpipes have stopped!"

"Haven't you heard?" said Bobby. Carmen shook her head. "You know that blackout last night?"

"I do indeed," said Carmen, tactfully refraining from mentioning where she'd been when it had happened.

"It was at Jackson McClockerty's."

"Was it?" said Carmen neutrally.

"He overloaded the entire electricity grid! Set his house on fire!"

"He did *what*?" said Carmen, looking up quickly.

"Yeah! He's got one of those huge places down in Barnton, apparently. Quite modern, though. So it went up like paper."

Carmen shook her head. That couldn't happen. Mind you . . . She thought of all the pine, the plaster pillars, the flammable rugs covering everything, and, of course, the knickknacks displayed everywhere.

"Oh my God!" she said. "Oh my God! Is everyone okay?"

She remembered the sirens screaming through the black night. So that was where they'd been going.

"Oh yeah—he had a lot of people there but they were all out in the garden watching some fireworks." Bobby shook his head. "God. Imagine him squeezing all this money out of us and out of people buying all sorts of his crap, then spunking it all on fireworks and parties and nonsense."

"Imagine," said Carmen, biting the inside of her mouth.

"He says it's ruined. That there's nothing left."

Bobby looked down at the ground. "So anyway, a bunch of us are going to go down later on, help him out . . ."

"You're kidding," said Carmen. "You're going to help that awful man?"

"Well, he's part of the street," explained Bobby. "I'm not saying I like it. I'm just saying, that's what we do here. We help each other out. We always have."

"He doesn't help! He's *the baddy*!" said Carmen.

"I'm just saying," said Bobby. "You don't have to come."

"You're all going?"

And sure enough, as she tidied up at the end of the day, she saw Crawford, Bronagh, Dahlia from the coffee shop, and sundry others troop into the hardware shop and come out armed with buckets and brushes. They clambered into Crawford's gleaming, huge Jag, while he shouted futilely at a traffic warden who was giving him a ticket, even though he had been parked up with his hazards on letting people get in his car for under fifteen seconds.

Carmen stared at them, then turned back to look at the empty shop, its lights extinguished, with only the cold, lonely room above. She thought of Bronagh's good deed.

"WAIT FOR ME!"

Chapter Thirty-Five

Carmen fiddled with her phone all the way down the road, looking and looking to see if there was something from Sofia, i.e., a groveling apology. Nothing at all. She must still be absolutely furious. She messaged Rudi to ask him what the hell was happening. The three dots seemed to type for ages.

Well, came up finally. Pippa came and told me we weren't really suited and she knew about these things because she has a boyfriend.

Oh God she's right again, tapped back Carmen, annoyed. Rudi sent a laughing emoji.

> Phoebe on the other hand thinks we're getting married, and we're going to have to let her down gently. She wants you to come back and share a room with me but not to have any other children because we've got them.

> I am tempted to do that just because of exactly how much it will annoy my sister.

> Can't think of a better reason to get married.

> What about Jack?

Jack doesn't give a rat's fart.

Good, good.

Carmen stared out of the window. The Christmas shoppers were out in force on George Street; queuing up outside The Dome restaurant, with its vast, over-the-top but glorious decorations: lights wrapped up huge towering pillars; trees and bows everywhere. You couldn't really say you'd had an Edinburgh Christmas if you hadn't had a fish tea at The Dome. Up and down the road you could see children gasping at the fairyland; generations of moms and daughters out nattering together; bobble hats and large brown paper bags from Zara and Primark and John Lewis, rolls of wrapping paper poking out the top. Everywhere was excitement and people looking forward to a sit-down and a cup of tea or a glass of prosecco.

They had to turn off because a full quarter of the street length was taken up with an ice rink. Music played, and the sound of children alternately giggling or yelling filled the air, along with the scent of sausages and mulled wine. The austere gray buildings of the Georgian New Town were sparkling with light, beating back the dark—for now, in mid-December, it was almost always dark. It was lovely. It made Carmen feel lonelier than ever.

What about my sis? she typed. There was a long gap and a lot of dots and reversing dots, as if Rudi was writing something then deleting it. Finally.

I'd leave it a couple of days.

Carmen closed her eyes. God. Christmas Day was going to absolutely suck. If she was still invited, that is.

Turning into the cul-de-sac, it was quite a shocking sight.

The ugly house was still standing but it was soaking wet and the smell of waste and burning was incredibly strong. The pine doorframes had been burned away; the pillars had had all the paint burned off them. The garden was just full of blackened crap, smoke still drifting from the frazzled illuminations. Carmen gave Bronagh a hard stare, but she was gazing out of the window, humming a tune like a very innocent person would do.

Jackson was standing in the doorway, looking around, absolutely dumbfounded. He was still a big man, but the confidence and chutzpah had completely gone. His ponytail had come out, leaving his curly mullet bedraggled down his back, and he was wearing, of all things, a Dryrobe, presumably bought for some cold-water swimming passing fancy; he was about the right age to buy all that kind of nonsense. Probably had five grand's worth of cycling gear in his shed as well, thought Carmen, uncharitably.

He looked up as they approached, then frowned. "What . . . what are you lot doing here?" he said. "If this is about rent, it's not a good time."

Crawford shook his head. "We're here to help, of course."

"I've brought brooms!" said Bobby.

Jackson blinked. "Oh," he said. Then another, "Oh."

"What?" said Crawford. "I thought you'd have an army of helpers."

"What about . . . what about your friends?" said Carmen, looking around. There had been hundreds of people here last night. Hundreds of people drinking his drink, eating his food, and treading on his carpet.

Jackson snorted. "They made themselves pretty scarce," he said. "Funny, that."

Carmen suddenly found herself feeling sorry for the man, which was ridiculous, seeing as he was trying to do her out of a job, or at least a job she liked.

"Still, at least Minky is—"

"Minky's gone to her mother's," said Jackson, his face looking uncharacteristically downbeat. "She said she didn't sign up for this."

Carmen remembered the rapt look on Minky's face, just the previous evening, when Jackson had serenaded her. Goodness.

"Well," she said, clapping her hands together. It was freezing outside. "Better get started."

IT WASN'T MUCH warmer inside. The electrics were completely fritzed, but there were paraffin lamps set up everywhere illuminating the mess: black piles of old food; broken glass absolutely everywhere; furniture filthy and useless, if not occasionally melted. Bobby's sturdy brooms and buckets were the best thing for it, but the house was completely unlivable. Carmen grabbed one of the big black trash bags, and they all got started.

"Are you insured?" she asked Jackson when they found themselves side by side.

"Well, technically I am," he said. "But also, apparently, technically, setting off fireworks next to a garage full of below-code synthetic material is, I dunno, illegal or something. But it'll be fine. I just need someone to offload everything for the insurance."

He looked slightly unsure of himself for the first time ever.

"Yeah. It'll get sorted. I'll find someone to take it."

"Edinburgh City Council won't come and suck your blood or take your immortal soul or anything?" said Carmen jokily.

He looked at her, suddenly, with a haunted expression.

"I'm joking," said Carmen hastily, tying off another trash bag. "So, where are you staying?"

He shrugged. "I'll check into a hotel, I suppose. Caledonian is pretty nice, right?"

Well, you can't be doing that badly, thought Carmen to herself as he named the single most beautiful and expensive hotel in the city.

"All your stuff . . ." said Carmen, looking around at the melted tchotchkes.

"Ach, it's only stuff, isn't it?" said Jackson.

After some fairly grueling work in the kitchen, they lined bag after bag up on the pavement—they could really do with a dumpster. It was tough, and Carmen found herself warming up and even sweating, despite the freezing air.

The dumpster turned up eventually, and they started heaving stuff in.

The neighbors came and watched them fill it, but never once offered help or a word of condolence; uncommon for Scotland, where most people pitch in to help whether you wanted them to or not, and certainly have advice to give you in most circumstances.

"Jackson," said Carmen finally, wiping her brow, "did you invite the neighbors to your party?"

"Neh," said Jackson. "Stupid stuffy posh buggers. You'd think they'd like a bit of half-decent music or the sweet sound of a flashy car once in a while; but nope, it's moan moan moan all the bloody time."

Carmen shook her head. "You are incorrigible."

"I don't know what that means," said Jackson. "That sounds like a stupid book word."

"It is."

"How big are the suites at The Caledonian, anyway?"

Carmen rolled her eyes and moved into the office, which hadn't been open at the party. It was covered in fake oak paneling that was now becoming unstuck, with a huge fake antique desk, and bookshelves full, Carmen was horrified to discover, of empty covers of "old-fashioned style" books, like the cartons her parents used to have to hold VHS tapes.

"What on earth have you got in here?" she said. This room must have been closed off from the main fire; it was relatively untouched, including the large computer and three screens. "This looks really sinister. Is it where you spy on people?"

"What? No," said Jackson, following her in. "It's where I run my business. A modern-day business that actually works, rather than some stuck-together handwritten quill nonsense like what you do."

"Yes, but you actually have a quill," said Carmen, laughing at an elaborate oversize gold-plated quill sitting on his desk. It looked utterly ridiculous.

Jackson sniffed.

"I can't believe you bought *empty books*," said Carmen. "You know, I could have given you a good price on books people didn't want in pretty bindings. Then at least they would be real books."

"I tried that," said Jackson, indicating the wall behind with an actual bookshelf. "They're bloody heavy."

Carmen smiled and went over. She couldn't help it; she couldn't pass a bookshelf without having a glance, didn't know how to. Jackson picked up the gold quill and turned it over in his hand, as if he was seeing it for the first time.

"Got this when I made my first mill," he said, almost quietly. Carmen bit her tongue. The books were a motley selection, bought for the color of their spines—ancient red, green, and brown—rather than any subject matter.

"You know," he said, "the only people who came to help . . . the only people who gave a shit . . ." He paused. "Were a couple of people who wanted the dirty details to pass on to the papers."

Carmen didn't say anything.

"And that was it. Nobody. The only people who came to *help* were you. You're my true friends." His voice thickened. "You're . . . You actually . . . thought about me."

Carmen felt increasingly awkward. "You'll be all right," she said.

"Och aye—I've got money," he said. "But . . . but I thought I had a lot of friends."

"You've got us," Carmen found herself saying.

And suddenly, she spied it. And she let out a squeak of excitement.

Chapter Thirty-Six

She pulled the book down from the shelf slowly and carefully.

"So . . ." Jackson was going on, and Carmen was trying to listen, but she couldn't help being overexcited.

It was an old hardback. Not, she knew straightaway, a first edition. But almost better: a small house, illustrated, limited edition. It was large, an A4 format, and illustrated beautifully and expensively, with full-color paintings of the city.

"Oh my God," she breathed, quickly wiping her hands and putting the book down carefully.

"What?" said Jackson, walking over.

"Don't touch it!" yelled Carmen.

"*Up on the Rooftops*? What's that, then?"

"It's a book written for children. Quite a long time ago. It fell out of print . . . but people never forgot it, not really."

Jackson shrugged. "So what, it's worth something?"

"It is," said Carmen. "You're very lucky. It's not the original edition, but the illustrated edition . . . The artist went on to illustrate all sorts of things. Oh my God, it's got the original map plates."

Her fingers went to her mouth. "I need to tell Mr. McCredie . . . I've never seen one in real life."

"What's it about, then?"

"It's about three children, Wallace, Michael-Francis, and Delphine. Delphine escapes onto the roof of her London apartment and gets kidnapped by the Queen of the Nethers, and the boys need to rescue her without their feet touching the ground."

Carmen's voice grew dreamy. "They have to go across London on roofs and cranes, till they get to Galleon's Reach."

"That sounds rubbish," said Jackson.

Carmen looked at him severely. "You're right," she said. "You would hate it."

"You take it, then," he said casually, heading out of the room.

Carmen looked up in shock. "What?"

"Well." He looked shrewd for a second. "It's not worth, like, a million quid or anything?"

Carmen shook her head. "Oh no, no, nothing like that. No. But it's worth a little."

She wrestled with her conscience. If she said it was worth twenty pounds, Jackson would be none the wiser. He wouldn't give a toss. Even if she said it was worth fifty pounds he might be in the mood for generosity. But she would be lying, and she would be stealing. And the book . . . the book meant more to her than that. She looked at the cover. It was a glorious painting of the children, and their one-legged pigeon friend, Robert Carrier, scampering up the dome of St. Paul's Cathedral. She sighed. And she told the truth.

"A few thousand," she said.

"For a *book*?" said Jackson. "Who cares that much about *books*?"

"Lots of people," she said.

"Really?" said Jackson. "Huh."

He looked at the book, then he looked at her, standing in her overalls, dirty washing-up gloves on, a trash bag in one hand. One of the only people in the world who'd come to lend him a hand.

"If I let you have this, you aren't going to let me take over the lease, are you?"

"I can tell you," said Carmen, "that if you did take over the lease, I would be the biggest thorn in your side and pain-in-the-ass employee—and possibly sitting tenant—that hell could devise as punishment for you."

"You sound just like my ex-wife."

"All your ex-wives would appear to you as heaven and sweet honey to a bee," said Carmen quickly. "And the sharpest serpent would appear as mild to you as a summer's kiss."

Jackson smiled and shook his head.

"Go on then," said Jackson. "Don't tell anyone about my good nature, ever."

"Not a word," said Carmen. "I'll keep telling them you're a prick, like I do now."

"Merry Fucking Christmas," said Jackson.

Chapter Thirty-Seven

As soon as she could break away, Carmen hopped on a bus and sped back to Mr. McCredie, constantly staring again and again at the extraordinary good fortune that lay in her bag. The cover shone, gilded, as if it had been painted yesterday; the children perfectly brought to life, climbing the great dome. She didn't want to open it in case she cracked the spine, but it was incredibly frustrating.

The bus huffed and puffed its slow way around as usual and Carmen, impatient with the traffic, the trams, and the usual full-up Edinburgh roadworks, jumped out at the top of Queensferry Road and tore along the pavement, almost gibbering with excitement.

Her cheeks were red and the freezing air was tearing at her lungs in the dark as she ran, but she didn't care. She ran past the crowds of valiant drinkers, braving the outside air in the Grassmarket: laughing and hollering, eating hot dogs from the Christmas stands, warming their hands on glühwein in thin plastic cups. Past the pubs and restaurants, stuffed to the gills, condensation on the windows and dripping down the roofs onto jackets and pink faces and laughing heads. Full pelt past kitchens preparing venison and turkey; chipolatas, cabbage, warm nutty mushroom roasts, and perfectly plated smoked salmon with champagne or deep red wine. Past the Salvation Army brass band, shaking a tin, the old melodies transformed into something even sweeter and richer by the soft brass intoning "Once in Royal David's City," as crowds came down Victoria Street, with bags and with children, togged up warmly, riding on shoulders; with dogs with tinsel in their collars. Everyone, it seemed, was out and about on this happy day, as she hurried on up, toward Mr. McCredie's bookshop, her red scarf flying out behind her.

She was watched, rather mournfully, by a painfully thin, very tall figure, underdressed for the weather; his hands clasped around a cup of tea. He was standing at the bottom of the Grassmarket, just emerging from the coffee shop; completely unnoticed by Carmen as she flew by.

MR. MCCREDIE WAS at the desk, fiddling sadly with a tartan cloth Nessie, whose pin eyes had already come untethered and were lying there, creepily, on the top of the desk, when Carmen burst in.

"Goodness me," he said mildly. "And also, don't be noisy; I think there are people kissing in the stacks."

"Well, *tell them not to*!" said Carmen, not for the first time. "Oi! Nerds! Cut it out!"

She dashed up to Mr. McCredie, unable to stop the smile on her face.

"What?" he said. "Look, Carmen, I don't think this is so bad—"

"Forget that," said Carmen, swooping the Nessie off the desk and straight into the trash can. "Look!"

And, as the two giggling nerds crept out behind them, she opened her backpack and revealed the treasure within.

Oke peered in the window; dark outside, but such a warm glowing light within. He saw how they had expanded the shop—it would be Carmen's idea, he knew. It looked beautiful; full of tempting, gorgeous covers, lovely editions; books everywhere. The little train pootled around its merry way; the mice in the window were having dinner, he saw, with tiny plastic molded dishes of fruit and a large roast chicken.

And Carmen and Mr. McCredie had their heads together, poring over something—he couldn't see what, but Carmen was giggling and exclaiming, and Mr. McCredie was shaking his head in astonishment and delight.

It didn't take much to discourage him.

Oke turned away. His head hurt. He had had a very, very long journey and was utterly exhausted. Spoons had welcomed him back with open arms, so that was something, but he had pushed himself too far—not to mention the fact that his entire family was now utterly furious with him. This was something he was going to have to deal with sooner or later but he couldn't quite think about just now. He would sleep on it. It would be fine.

Seeing her again had shot a fire through his heart; had cracked him open worse than the illness had. Seeing her happy was worse. Mary had been right. Of course she was too busy to contact him; he was a deluded, crazed fool. Stuck in a city that didn't want him, far far from home.

Chapter Thirty-Eight

Tuesday was the day of the film party. Carmen looked at the list that the organizing team had sent over. It had been on her phone, and she'd only glanced at it in passing. But now she was paying attention and realized it was utterly ridiculous. By the time it hit noon, caterers were already milling about, asking anxiously where the ovens were, traipsing up and down the stairs and generally getting in the way.

"Popcorn . . . lots of mini cakes," the publicist said, making notes. "And Santa Claus turns up at seven."

"Santa's coming? Who for?" said Carmen. "I thought this was a work party?"

"Everyone loves Santa," said the woman dismissively. "Hire in some children. Who cares? Right. We'll be putting a big tree outside, have the choir singing around that. Marshmallows are coming . . . hot chocolate . . ."

"Wow," said Carmen, feeling sad.

Every song she heard on the radio seemed to be about being with loved ones at Christmas . . . about love and family . . . She thought of Sofia. Even if she felt she'd done nothing wrong, she should reach out. Also, she still needed to do her good deed. The Jackson one had benefited them all so outrageously, it really couldn't count.

She owed Sofia so much, she knew. Who else would have taken her in, for a year? Blessed her by opening up the full world of her family to her. And even though it hadn't been what it looked like, from Sofia's point of view she supposed seducing the best nanny they'd ever had in front of the children could look pretty bad.

Okay. She was doing it. She picked up the phone.

SOFIA DIDN'T ANSWER. Oh God, was she still so cross? Bugger. Screwing up her face, Carmen called Pippa's number—the phone Pippa wasn't really supposed to have while still at primary school, until Sofia had crumbled exactly the same way as every other mother in the world.

"Auntie Carmen? Auntie Carmen, I need to change my Christmas list. I would like to sponsor a donkey for the poor people."

Carmen smiled to herself. Pippa didn't sound terribly traumatized, it had to be said.

"Well, that's great, Pippa. Of course, I'd be delighted to do that. Are you sure you wouldn't also like a little thing just for you for being so generous?"

"Oh . . . well . . . *maybe*," said Pippa.

"Put Auntie Carmen on speaker," came a voice in the far distance.

"No, she wants to talk to *me*!" Pippa said regally. "For advice on her disastrous love life, probably."

"I did call all of you," said Carmen.

"Oh," said Pippa and pressed a button.

"Hi, everyone," said Carmen, clearing her throat. "I just wanted to say, I'm really sorry you guys came in when Rudi and I were having a sleepover. We won't do that again."

"But are you getting married?" Phoebe wanted to know.

"No," said Carmen.

"So you're not going to get married to Rudi and you're not going to get married to Blair and you're not going to get married to Oke," said Phoebe. "Oh, it is very sad you are not getting married to anyone, Auntie Carmen."

"I'm fine with it," said Carmen. She could hear Rudi sniggering slightly; he would be walking them home from school on this crisp icy morning.

"Mommy was very disappointed in you," said Pippa importantly.

"Well, that's something I have just learned to live with all these years," said Carmen tightly.

"Are you coming to our concert?" said Phoebe, and Carmen's heart melted. Not about the concert, particularly—that was interminable and super boring even when it was your own kid performing—but that she was still invited.

"Wouldn't miss it for quids," she said.

"Phoebe's got a solo," said Pippa. "We are really, really hoping she doesn't completely stuff it up."

"And are you coming for Christmas morning?" said Jack, interested as to when, exactly, presents might be happening.

Carmen had been avoiding thinking about it, entirely on purpose. She couldn't bear to sit there with an atmosphere. And, of course, be single Carmen, yet again, while her parents would be cooing their heads off over baby Eric and she had to try to look interested as the children ripped the paper off their bounty. And she would have to say thank you for some stupid yoga trousers or something. The temptation to hunker down in bed with a bottle of champagne and a box of chocolates was very strong.

"We'll see," she said. "But don't worry; I have *very big* presents for you."

Carmen's liberal belief in plastic and flashing lights for children—diametrically opposed to Sofia's love of the handcrafted and wooden—meant that the children thought she was the doyenne of gift giving. Previous hauls included a Girl's World, a Slushy Machine, and an Evel Knievel, so she had a bit to live up to.

"Yay!" said the children.

Carmen got to the meat of the call.

"You know if you like . . . there's a party tonight for the film, and I didn't think that children were invited, but it turns out they are. They're having singers and things . . . You could come if you like?"

"That sounds boring," said Jack.

"Yeah, true," said Carmen. She looked at the delivery list. "The only reason I am asking you is because they are doing a lot—and I mean a *lot*—of cakes. *And* there might be a very special guest!"

"OKE?" said Phoebe immediately.

"NO!" said Carmen.

"Patrick?" said Jack, mentioning his small friend from the Highlands.

"Oh, that's a good idea; I'll ask them."

"Is it Santa?" came Phoebe's shy tones.

"I couldn't possibly say," said Carmen.

"But he isn't at work yet."

"Well, maybe in Edinburgh he starts work early."

"He isn't—" Jack started, but both Pippa and Rudi silenced him so quickly Carmen thought he'd been garroted.

Carmen's voice lowered. "Just ask your mommy," she said.

THE FILM COMPANY did nothing by halves. There were cameras filming cameras. There was even an itty-bitty red carpet that led out onto Victoria Street, meaning people did, as people will, line up to take a look at it. Inside were lines of very good-looking staff with hot chocolate and mince pies (vegan, tragically, it being the film industry). Carmen was already calculating how many politely spat-out bits she'd find in napkins scattered around the shelves the following day. There was a brazier outside you could toast your own marshmallows on. The children, Carmen knew, were going to like that a lot. If they were allowed to come.

The fireplace was blazing at the back of the shop in the little nook, and there was now so much more space for people to thread their way through. It looked, too, like everyone was coming. From 5 p.m., various half-familiar Edinburgh faces filed in. It was Baltic outside, the snow frozen into harsh ridges you could walk along; the thermometer well below zero. Carmen took coats politely with a large smile, then hurled them into a huge inchoate pile in one of the vaults. She figured if people were having a bad time and wanted to leave early they might get cross when they had to search for their jackets, but it wouldn't matter, and if people were having a good time, they wouldn't care.

The noise clattered higher and there were excited flashbulbs outside. The star of the film, Genevieve Burr, had arrived, her elegant legs appearing from the taxi. As ever, Carmen stared at her, fascinated. She seemed too perfect to exist in the real world. Her long, perfectly shaped legs, her tiny waist, immaculate white dress, high cheekbones, perfect skin. It was really quite dazzling. She smiled for the cameras, turning to her best side—although they were both, clearly, her best side—stuck out her leg, bent her arms to her hips, and acted as though this was the single best night of her life. Ushered into the shop, finally, she lit it up, as everyone turned around, happy to be in the presence of such beauty and direct-to-streaming stardust. She looked at the mulled wine with a puzzled expression on her face, as someone somehow magically produced a glass of champagne for her. She took a tiny sip, then grimaced.

Lind Stephens, the movie star, arrived behind her. The cheers and clapping and flashbulbs weren't *quite* as loud for him, and he obviously noticed: His granite jaw looked a little tight.

"Hello, Genevieve, good to see you," he said. "Are you putting on weight? Ooh, have you got a role in a realistic film?"

Genevieve would have scowled if her face had been able to move that much. As it was, people were taking lots of pictures of them together, arms around each other, so they both plastered on wide grins.

"Are you going to have a big party for your sixtieth?" hissed Genevieve.

"I'm nowhere near . . . Oh, hi, yeah, hello!" said Lind.

Carmen regarded them with amusement. They didn't quite

seem to be having any fun yet. On the other hand, Crawford and Ramsay had just arrived, Ramsay's head bouncing off the ceiling as ever, two of his menagerie of children, Patrick and Hari, alongside him prattling nineteen to the dozen. Bobby and Bronagh and Dahlia were there, of course, making very loud remarks about how successful they thought films set in bucket shops or magic shops or coffee shops would be. Even Idra had made it, gorgeous in a gold gown that perfectly matched the mustache of Hendrik, to whom she appeared to be joined at the hip.

And there was Rudi, impish as ever in a green woolen hat that set off his red hair marvelously, shepherding the children up the street. Carmen's heart leapt with joy. She had long made fun of Sofia's clothing policy for the children, who basically, as Carmen pointed out, were dressed like evacuees rather than in comfy tracksuits and hoodies. Jack wore shorts and long red socks every day of the year to school.

Just them, she saw, her face falling a little. No Sofia. Just the children, like some kind of weird divorce handover.

But even so, seeing them walk merrily, bickering, entwined, up through the snowy cobbles—the girls in their matching double-buttoned coats and Fair Isle caps, white tights, and party shoes and Jack in his shorts, his hair pressed down firmly—her heart just about burst. Mr. McCredie stood behind her.

"*The vale of tears is powerless before you*," he quoted softly.

> *Whether Christ is born, or is not born, you*
> *put paid to fate, it abdicates*
> *under the Christmas lights.*
> *Monsters of the year*
> *go blank, are scattered back,*
> *can't bear this march of three.*

THEN THEY WERE upon them, loud and full of cheer and excitement; making quite pointed remarks about the vegan mince pies, but enjoying the marshmallow fire very much; and absolutely delighted to see Hari and Patrick. Hari was charging through full of news, and Patrick was looking around rather prissily and opining that he had quite a lot of information on how much faster than the speed of sound Father Christmas's sleigh had to travel and how Christmas Eve was actually thirty-one hours if you managed the time zones properly. Meanwhile, the Edinburgh Boys' Brigade choir was doing their best "Carol of the Bells" out in the snow. The chatter and photos and snapping levels inside the party were high and the film had, apparently, been quite the hit on Instagram, which could only, Carmen thought, increase people coming to have a look. It was okay. This year had been hard—so hard.

But as she looked into the happy faces of the people around her, and cuddled Phoebe, who was very worried someone was going to touch the mouse doll's house, she couldn't help feeling happy. Next year would be better. The shop would be on an even keel, they'd expanded, Mr. McCredie would get his wish—indeed, he was already wearing his reindeer hat, which always indicated when he was in a festive mood—packing had begun.

And then, suddenly, walking up the hill, Carmen saw the very person she was longing to see.

It was Sofia, Eric in the sling.

Carmen looked at Rudi, grinning.

"Oh yeah," he said. "She was just parking. You know what those traffic warden bastards are like. Takes all your stealth and cunning."

"I do know," said Carmen, and went and stood at the door.

"I'm sorry," she said immediately. "I didn't do it to piss you off." She examined her conscience thoroughly. "Okay, well, maybe about five percent."

"No, *I* came to say sorry!" said Sofia, almost teary with relief. "It was none of my fricking business. And neither is your job and neither is your love life and I am so so so sorry I kicked you out and then yelled at you, and that makes it all my fault!"

"You didn't kick me out," said Carmen. "I needed to go. I did. And I love it here. It's . . . uh, bracing."

And she did love it, she realized. Perched in her little aerie. She had some gardening books and was looking for Rudi and the children to help her with plans for the spring. They would grow the bulbs. They would make something beautiful out of something cold and withered.

Sofia grinned and they hugged as Eric demanded to be let out of the sling and allowed to crawl dementedly about the room eating things off the floor. Rudi came over and removed him, smiling at both of them.

Chapter Thirty-Nine

"We nearly sent the police! *Mea amor*, my darling, we've been so worried! Mary is frantic! Are you even in your right mind?"

Oke swallowed. "I'm so sorry, Mamma. I really am."

"Everyone is so worried about you! The hospital staff were looking everywhere! And all that money on flights, Obedience."

"I know," he mumbled. "I'm sorry. It was rash. I don't know what I was thinking."

"You haven't been well," said his mother, softening immediately at the sound of her beloved only son. "You really haven't. I don't think you realize. Darling. Come home. You are missed."

"But I have my job starting back here . . ."

"You can get a job anywhere," she said. "Come back and work for the rain forest mission. Goodness knows it needs defending. Spend time with us, with Mary. There is such a good life waiting for you here."

"There is," said Oke, looking out of his window. Spoons was tapping furiously on his laptop. He was so pleased to have Oke back, even if he did have to give up the frozen mice fridge.

The lights of Edinburgh refracted in the frost were gorgeous. The big wheel of Edinburgh's Christmas market turning, full of excited children and flashing lights and the familiar sounds of Edinburgh's most famous radio DJs telling you repeatedly not to fall out of the window. He opened the window a crack, much to the annoyance of Spoons, who liked the room tropical and for him to be able to work in shorts that showed off quite a lot of hairy backside whenever he bent over, and who said keeping the room hot was fair for "the majority of, uh, living things that had an opinion on it." He could smell the icy air, hear the laughter and screams from the fair, the giggles and the local accent that he loved.

He bade his mother good night. He knew he should go home. This coming and going was bad for him, was bad for his future. He could stay here, but it was cold and expensive, and the person he'd come back for hadn't even cared that he'd been in the hospital.

His feet led him. The conscious part of his mind refused to admit that he was going one last time, for one last attempt. No. He was just trying to clear his head, to think about what was next, that was all. He had felt a lot stronger after sleeping for twelve hours and eating a hearty Mylnes Court Scottish breakfast: potato scones, square sausage, haggis, and black pudding. Although without that weird red gloopy stuff they smothered perfectly good beans in.

Physically, he felt well. Emotionally was another matter. He passed silently through the crowds, one of the few people not wearing a Christmas sweater adorned with reindeer, a sparkly diamanté outfit, a light-up headband or armlet. They had the joyous pink cheeks of people intent on celebrating a wonderful time of year. He went past the tired shoppers on George Street, and on into the West End, where the snow sat so quietly in the private circular gardens of Moray and Ainslie. If you ignored the cars, you were looking at a scene that had not changed in two hundred years.

He found himself out the other side of the bustling Queensferry Road, on the street where Sofia's perfect house stood; where he had been so happy the previous year.

The trees in the windows were lit up beautifully—one up, one down, perfectly aligned, their warm white lights sparkling—as were the two outdoor trees at the top of the steps, and the huge wreath. It was beautiful.

But the house itself was closed and dark. There were no lights indicating the children running around the back of the kitchen, or begging Carmen to curl up with them to watch *The Muppet Christmas Carol* just one more time. There was no baby rolling on the floor; no Jack tearing up and down the stairs like a herd of elephants; no girls making paper chains and squabbling their heads off, just as his own sisters used to squabble when he was a child. The house looked like a doll's house, sterile and empty: devoid of life. He sighed and turned away.

Just past The Caledonian Hotel, a large man in a purple tartan suit was holding open a taxi door.

"Come on, Minky; we'll be late and you won't get your picture taken with Lind," he said to a woman with huge lips, who was pouting and tugging down a gold lamé dress.

Oke took the long way up and around the castle, on King's Stables Road, its dour car park making the street quiet and dark, the cliff towering above him. He pounded the pavements, cold, but not feeling it; slipping occasionally on the ice underfoot.

It was like the queen's house in *Alice in Wonderland*, though. However much he walked away from it, took a different direction, he found his feet inevitably leading back toward the central street in the entire city. The center of commerce and Edinburgh life since there had been an Edinburgh, more or less; since Dùn Èideann had pushed itself up and out of the rocks, a thousand years before.

Even as he felt himself approaching, he couldn't help it. His feet strayed on up the hill. He could hear the music and see the blinding lights of a festival he barely understood; happy noise and music everywhere, all emanating from the tiny windows of the little Christmas bookshop.

Chapter Forty

Carmen winked at Christopher Pickle as he slipped out of the stacks, and passed him a full plate of sausage rolls. She thought perhaps vegan sausage rolls were better than nothing. Christopher Pickle objected quite noisily that they weren't.

Carmen tilted her head when she saw Jackson and Minky arrive, larger than life.

"Hello," she said. "Don't touch any electrical equipment."

Minky had found Lind and was touching his arm in a way he was clearly appreciating.

Jackson looked around. "Waste of good footfall, this place."

"Don't start!"

"No, no. Anyway, I'm getting out of that business."

"Are you?" said Carmen happily. "Really? That's wonderful! Even for Bobby?"

"Turns out brooms are, like, quite useful," Jackson admitted. Carmen beamed.

"He reckons he can get some branded Edinburgh ones. Him and Bronagh are going to do witches' brooms," said Jackson.

"Except mine will work," said Bronagh in passing.

"And rugby balls on the buckets," said Bobby stoutly.

"Is that a thing?"

"Commemorative rugby buckets are definitely going to be a thing."

"Great!"

"Anyway," Jackson went on, "there's loads more money in American candy. Loads more."

"Noooooo!" said Carmen.

"But I've still got a load of half-charred tartan toot on my hands," said Jackson. "Hey ho."

Minky came over, dragging Rudi, who put his right arm on Carmen's shoulder for balance. She rubbed her cheek on it affectionately.

"You know," Minky announced, "Rudi's never seen a suite at The Caledonian before."

Carmen looked at him. "You *wouldn't*," she said, aghast, then burst into peals of laughter.

Rudi looked impish. "I *do* like a nice hotel suite," he said.

Still laughing, Carmen glanced up. It was as if a ripple had passed her by, or someone had walked over her grave. She looked out into the dark night but there was nothing but a flapping coat, walking past the entrance; the ghost, she thought, of other years. She shivered.

THERE SHE HAD been, as lovely as ever, so full of passion and fire this time with a handsome young man, her arms around him, laughing. Yesterday had not been a one-off. Carmen was happy. She was happy. It was done.

"YOU WILL COME on Christmas morning?" said Sofia anxiously, once the children had consumed as much hot chocolate as any human being could reasonably be expected to take on, and she was slightly concerned that Phoebe might choke if she had any more marshmallow.

Carmen looked at her and smiled. "I am going to spend the morning lying in bed on my ass, pleasing absolutely myself," she said. "But I will come in the afternoon. Of course I will."

"So we get *presents around two!*" said Jack.

"Yes, not stupid Santa presents!" said Phoebe. "*Real* presents!"

The two sisters looked at each other and Carmen mouthed "sorry" but Sofia took it in good part.

"Good," said Sofia. "I'm so glad."

And they hugged and emerged onto the street, to a long line of flashbulbs and paparazzi, as their exit coincided almost exactly with Genevieve's. Pippa, Carmen couldn't help noticing, had posed instinctively and rather well.

As SOON AS he got back to Mylnes Court, Oke started looking up flights. Of course everything was fully booked. Because it was bloody bloody bloody Christmas. Of course it bloody was.

Chapter Forty-One

The last week flew by. The bookshop was in every newspaper because of the party and the film, so they had a stream of people taking pictures outside and then, often, coming in and buying a book as well. Both she and Mr. McCredie sold and sold and sold, but the nicest day of all was when a very old woman came in, walking with the aid of two sticks. Carmen immediately found her a chair to sit down in, wondering what she was looking for, and was surprised to learn that she was Mr. McCredie's client for *Up on the Rooftops*.

When they brought out the box they were keeping it in for safe-keeping, she let out a little sigh. She was English, Carmen realized.

"This was exactly the one I had," she said. "The exact same one. Me and my sister. She's gone now," she added. "But we thought we were just like Wallace and Michael-Francis; that we would have been just as daring and brave even though we were girls."

She sighed. "My sister talked to pigeons for years afterward. Years. Just in case."

She turned the pages carefully with gnarled fingers.

"It was a gift from my father. He brought it home for us one evening. And then he went to France."

Carmen, listening hard, brought her over a cup of tea.

"You know everyone still talks about Dunkirk," said the old woman. "But they talk about the boys who went home."

She swallowed hard. Mr. McCredie, very unusually for him, patted her a little on the back of her raincoat.

"I also lost my father in the war," he said. Carmen looked at him. It was so rare that he mentioned his father. She was proud he could do so now.

"Well," said the old lady, dabbing her eyes briskly with a cloth handkerchief. "I am . . . I am very pleased. It feels . . . This feels . . . like happy times come to life again. Like stepping back into that life. And now I shall read it to my own great-grandchildren. Because that's what books are, aren't they? A coming home."

"I think so," said Carmen.

"I'm not going to let the fiends touch it, though. They're absolute bastards."

"Quite right, too," said Mr. McCredie. And they watched her disappear into the dusk of an Edinburgh afternoon.

"Well, well, well," said Mr. McCredie, suddenly perking up like Grandpa Joe in *Charlie and the Chocolate Factory*. "I *believe* I'm going to finish packing!"

Carmen grinned at him. "I suppose you are. When does the boat leave?"

"Boxing Day, Leith Docks."

"I'll come down with you. I think we can probably shut the shop."

"I think we probably can."

He looked up.

"I don't think I say thank you enough, Carmen. Thank you."

"You're welcome."

He handed over a small package.

"What's this?" she said. "Can I unwrap it now?"

"You may."

It was a quill: made of a long feather, personally sculpted and as different from Jackson's hollow gold one as was possible. It was such a kind and thoughtful gift from a man who, with all his frailties, had shown almost infinite patience and kindness toward her.

"That's from a giant petrel," he said. "One of the most beautiful birds of the Arctic. It's from the original expedition."

"Wow!" said Carmen.

"So you can keep writing your own story."

"I love it," said Carmen. "I do."

Chapter Forty-Two

It was strange walking through a quiet Edinburgh, without cars on cobbles or alarms sounding.

Carmen's room, of course, was icy and she remembered, once again, that she wasn't waking up in her parents' cozy little house, or her sister's noisy place. Just her. That was all.

Well, she told herself, that wasn't too bad. She pulled on her dressing gown, added socks, and padded out of the room. In the conservatory, she let out a little gasp. There was a bright, perfect amaryllis, which had flowered in the night. Her very first flower. It was like a perfect Christmas gift; as if it had appeared by magic.

"Well, thank you, Santa," she said to herself.

She glanced at the numerous WhatsApp messages, and pictures of the children ripping into paper, timed 6 a.m., from Sofia, who said she couldn't be too late as she had decided the only way to cope with this was to get drunk and let their mom pick up the slack.

Carmen smiled. She had, in fact, got some treats to eat and drink for herself. But now that seemed a spoiled indulgence she didn't want. She felt restless, then she thought about it and re-membered that she still owed someone a good deed. And it was Christmas, so why not?

So she washed and dressed warmly, including a terrible Christ-mas sweater she had found in a charity shop and bought to cheer up other people, not her, because it was nylon and disgusting. Then she walked downstairs into the empty, bright blue, frosty

clarity of an Edinburgh Christmas morning, as bracing in itself as
a glass of champagne.

There was nobody about this early, not even dog walkers. The
world was hers. She came out and turned right and up the stairs,
and felt the world belonged to her.

THE QUAKER MEETING House filled early on Christmas morning, with bustling volunteers: It ran a hot breakfast, as well as a
Christmas lunch, for anyone who needed one, and Carmen was
happy to feel the warmth of the kitchen and the bustling noise of
everyone already working there, chopping, serving, or clearing up.
It seemed as good a place as any to finally fulfill her good turn.

"What can I do?" she asked cheerily. Ashima Jain, the beautiful
and extremely organized head of operations, directed her to the
coffee machine and told her to get pouring, which she did, direct-
ing a friendly smile toward the many men and women sitting in
the warmth of the meeting room, Christopher Pickle among them.

"They do a decent sausage roll here," he said, some crumbs
in his beard, his omnipresent bag of books by his side. "Not like
your place."

"I'm really glad to hear that," said Carmen, refilling his cup.

She glanced over: There was a commotion by the doorway.
Genevieve Burr had, it transpired, turned up with a film crew to
capture her doing a good deed at Christmastime. Oh God, thought
Carmen, as Genevieve, wearing an adorably tilted pink crown on
her lavish hair, spilled soup over the side of the bowls and giggled
apologetically as the cameras flashed. Christopher Pickle loudly
told her she was the best volunteer they'd ever had. Carmen
sighed. But two minutes later Genevieve was gone again.

Christopher turned back to Carmen accusingly. "Where's *your*
party hat?"

"I kind of feel I was already going all out with the Christmas
sweater," protested Carmen, and a gang of festively clad volunteers laughed and called her over. Unlike where Oke came from,

the Edinburgh Quakers were clearly perfectly okay with Christmas paraphernalia and the more she protested, the more people insisted she wore.

Which is how, when Oke walked in to start his shift—tall as a tree, green-eyed as ever, thin, but then it rather suited him; wearing as many layers of clothing as, presumably, he'd brought with him—Carmen was wearing not just the hideous polyester Christmas sweater, but also reindeer antlers that lit up, a party hat, and jingle-bell earrings, and someone had rouged her cheeks and put lots of freckles on her, elf-style, for good measure.

THEY LOOKED AT one another. Carmen let the coffee spill, until someone stopped her.

"You . . . you . . ."

Carmen couldn't speak. She shook her head. Which had the unfortunate effect of making her reindeer headdress, which was motion activated, start blasting out "Merry Christmas, Everyone."

"Oh, for God's sake," said Carmen, conscious that she looked insane. "I am getting *nowhere* trying to do good works."

Then her face fell as she wondered, how long had he been in Edinburgh?

"Oh my God. You're back and you never contacted me. You've been back for ages and you haven't told me. You didn't even . . ."

Oke looked confused.

"Sorry," she went on. "I didn't . . . I should have realized. Of course. You have a job here. Carry on. I'll work in the kitchen. I'll keep out of your way."

She turned to go, still unable to get rid of the awful tinny Christmas music playing in her ears.

"I've been back for one day. But, Carmen, you never contacted me after—"

"I called you three times and you never answered!"

"I lost my phone. But Mary said—"

"I don't care what you and Mary talk about. I hope you're happy together, I really do."

"But you didn't care when I was in the hospital?"

"*Hospital?*"

Now everyone who was there for their Christmas breakfast was taking a very keen interest in the goings-on.

Ashima bustled forward. "Why don't you two come and sit down in the staff room?" she said, adding, "This isn't *EastEnders*," but very quietly, underneath her breath, as she was a nice woman really.

CARMEN TORE OFF the antlers and the party hat and the sweater en route—she was suddenly very hot—and then turned around to look at Oke. He was as handsome as ever, but very thin, even by his standards.

"You were sick how?" she demanded. "You were sick and didn't tell me?"

"I got malaria," said Oke. "But Mary told you."

"*Mary?* The Instagram girl?" Carmen frowned. "Of course she didn't tell me. How could she tell me? I don't know her at all. Although it looked like you did."

"Well, I did. She was on the expedition," said Oke. Carmen pouted. "I asked her to tell you when I was sick. And she said she did."

"She didn't!" said Carmen in anguish. "She didn't! I check all my social media all the time; I am very uncool and a bit insecure!" She rushed to him. "Oh, my darling. Are you okay? Are you okay now?" Then she shook her head crossly. "But I never heard from you. Never once. I thought . . . I thought you were disgusted with me."

"But I never heard from *you*," said Oke. "You hated me. For not . . . for not . . ." He looked at her. "I regret that very much."

Carmen frowned. "Of course I called you! Oh God, it was awful. I poured my heart out. On the messages. God."

She looked at him. He shook his head. "What messages?"

"Play your phone's messages," said Carmen.

He did, on the cheap replacement phone he'd got in Brasilia.

"That's your Brazilian phone, you dope," said Carmen, her heart pounding. "Where's your UK one?"

"I haven't . . ."

Oke realized he hadn't changed the SIM yet; he'd been talking on his Brazilian number.

"I have been quite ill," he said. "I don't . . . I don't have my British number . . ."

"Well, dial in to your old number, pick up the messages," said Carmen.

He did so.

Carmen winced to hear her voice, after he'd scrolled through the other bits and bobs. The first two were awful, full of sadness and rage.

"Delete those," she said, and he did so. Then they got to the very last one, from only a month ago.

"I'm sorry . . ." came through, loud and clear. "I'm sorry. I miss you, Oke. I love you."

Oke blinked several times. Then he looked at her, his steady green-eyed gaze so exciting and calming to Carmen, both at the same time.

He took a step forward.

"I thought you didn't care for me."

"I thought you didn't care for me!" said Carmen. "That was the whole problem."

"I cared more . . . more than I could express," said Oke. "And also, I was an idiot. I think perhaps we can agree about that."

"You didn't see the wood for the trees," said Carmen, choking, but it wasn't the time.

Her heart was beating painfully fast. He took her hands in his.

"My love," he said slowly.

"Mine," said Carmen.

"Are you . . . um . . . keeping the freckles?"

"Do you like them?"

"I like everything about you."

And he kissed her, right there, hard, and the slightly open door reverberated to hefty cheers from everyone outside.

"I'M BRINGING SOMEONE extra to lunch," said Carmen down the phone to Sofia.

"Oh God," said Sofia. "Rudi just asked to bring Jackson and Minky and I've already said no to him, don't make me be even more of a Grinch."

Carmen laughed. "Oh no," she said, "I think you're going to like this one."

"Do you want to stay over?"

"No," said Carmen cheerily. "We've got our own place, thanks."

Chapter Forty-Three

Back in the silent attic room, at the end of a long, happy, noisy day, with more or less the correct amount of tears you get in any family with four children in it; now, in the quiet, the snow gently falling once more in front of the windows, the mood was solemn, though not remotely sad. Oke sat up on the bed, and Carmen was sitting on him, the candles lit, as very slowly, they made an intensely deep commitment to one another; vulnerable, open, and full-hearted. Neither of them was in the slightest bit cold.

Carmen sat on his lap and they looked into each other's eyes. "I felt so terrible that day," she said.

Oke's face was grave, and he pushed a lock of dark hair behind her ears. "I did not know how to say what I wanted to say."

He looked at her. He'd had a long time convalescing to think about this moment.

"All my life I have tried . . . to study, to learn, to do well. To stay calm. You came into my life, Carmen. You ripped all of that up. I did not deal with it well at all. I was a coward. I ran away."

"It was a very special tree," said Carmen.

"I told myself I was respecting you." Oke cleared his throat. "I think I was scared of you."

Carmen screwed up her face. "I'm not at all scary."

"Okay. Scared of what I felt."

"But, Oke," said Carmen, as softly as the snow falling, "I'm sorry I scared you. And I know it must have seemed dumb . . . I felt very bloody dumb, I can tell you. I still can't think about it without wanting to bang my head against the wall. But it's still me. That's me. A bit daft, a bit quick to anger . . . That's what I'm like. I'd scare you all the time."

Oke looked at her. "What about if something properly scary actually happened to me and I nearly died and I realized that I absolutely have to squeeze life with both hands?"

"You want to squeeze me with both hands?"

"Very much."

Carmen smiled then, showing her teeth; it made Oke immeasurably happy to see it.

"You're saying you only want to be with me because it's *marginally better than death*?"

"Better than death," said Oke. "Better than everything."

Carmen still eyed him carefully.

"But that day . . . I mean . . . Is there something weird about you and sex? Are you really hung up about it?"

Oke glanced down to where she was sitting in his lap, but Carmen was serious. He caressed her face, carefully, running his thumb over her lips, which made her shudder.

"Carmen," said Oke, "the reason I was so . . . careful about having sex with you is . . . is, I think you might be the last person I will ever have sex with."

Carmen gasped, a shiver running through her that had nothing to do with the temperature.

"Is that too much?" said Oke.

"I have a present for you," said Carmen.

"Is it you?" said Oke. "Can I unwrap you?"

Carmen reached down underneath her bed.

"Actually," she said, pulling it out, "it's a gigantic book about trees."

He laughed.

"I do not have a gift for you."

"No need," said Carmen. "You are a bit of me."

He pulled her closer.

"Is that enough?"

"No."

Closer still.

"What about now?"

She shook her head. "More."

He pulled her forward once more, and now they were chest-to-chest, face-to-face, as close as two people can be.

"Now?"

"More," said Carmen, and again, "more," until she had no breath left in her to say anything at all, as the moon rose over the Christmas bookshop and the grandfather clock struck midnight on a new day.

THE DOCKS AT Leith on a bitterly cold Boxing Day morning were an austere, chilly place. Unless, of course, you were with someone you were madly in love with and had spent the entire night with.

Under-slept and deeply, deeply happy, Carmen and Oke were helping Mr. McCredie, who had a trunk, not a suitcase. Allowed past the chain-link fence upon displaying ID, Carmen frowned, spotting a large group of men, many looking like they came from the east, some desultorily kicking a ball, others hanging around smoking or staring at their phones.

"Who are they?" she asked.

"Freighter crew," said the seaman who was leading them down to the beautiful polar exploration ship, the RRS *Sir David Attenborough*. It was absolutely gorgeous, and Mr. McCredie was wide-eyed with excitement; he looked like a little boy.

"They're not allowed to enter UK territory. Or any territory, really. They can't go beyond the fence."

Carmen looked at them, and then at Oke.

"Oh yes," he said. "It's the same in Brazil. It's the same the world over."

"But that's terrible," Carmen said.

"Aw, there's a mission padre who helps a little. Tries to get them souvenirs and things."

"Souvenirs?"

"Yes, for their kids—they can't get out to buy anything. But they only see their kids two months a year. And they like to send them things so the kids know where they've been."

Carmen turned around. "This is it!" she said.

"What?" said Oke.

"I owe the universe a good deed. And every time I try to do one, it keeps repaying me, so it doesn't really count. But this one will, because I don't want to do it *at all* and it means we'll have to wait down here in the cold for hours."

"Um, great?" said Oke.

Carmen made a phone call, then they settled Mr. McCredie in his surprisingly comfortable quarters, next to Dr. Francis, the polar physician, and what appeared to be 356 cans of beans. Mr. McCredie couldn't stop beaming.

"I can't . . . I hope you'll be okay."

"Don't worry," said Carmen. "We are going to shut up shop and go on a fancy holiday."

He looked puzzled.

"I'm kidding, I'm kidding. Oke is going back to his research at the university and he's going to live at the shop. It'll be fine. Everything will be fine. Better than fine."

Oke nodded his head. "We'll look after things, sir."

By the time they'd all hugged and kissed and said their good-byes, there was a large sports car situated on the other side of the chain-link fence.

Jackson scowled at Carmen. "You're really buying this?"

"For next to nothing," said Carmen. "Just to help you with your insurers."

He grunted. "It will. You have to let me do the invoices and the paperwork."

"Fine."

"So. What do you want with it all?" Jackson looked confused. In the back of the car were boxes and boxes of Nessies, Scottie dogs, British flags, and T-shirts, all the wrapping a tiny bit singed, and the odd water-damaged corner here and there, but otherwise absolutely fine.

"Bring it in," said Carmen, smiling, and approaching the large group of strange men. "Bring Christmas in. Bring everybody in."

Acknowledgments

Thanks: Jo Unwin, Lucy Malagoni, Rosanne Forte, Nisha Bailey, Kate Burton, Matilda Ayris, Cesar Castaneda Gamez, Laura Vile, Fergus Edmonson, Emily Cox, Joanna Kramer, Zoe Carroll, David Shelley, Charlie King, Deborah Schneider, Rachel Kahan, Sharyn Rosenblum, Jennifer Hart, Liate Stehlik, Gemma Shelley, Stephanie Melrose, Litmix, Mr. B, Fiona Brownlee, and all at Little, Brown and JULA. And a huge thank-you to the international publishing community, so many of whom I've been able to meet or revisit post-lockdown, and it is proving such a joy.

About the Author

JENNY COLGAN is the *New York Times* bestselling author of numerous novels, including *The Christmas Bookshop*, *The Bookshop on the Corner*, and *Little Beach Street Bakery*. Jenny, her husband, and their three children live in a genuine castle in Scotland.

READ MORE BY JENNY COLGAN

SCHOOL BY THE SEA SERIES